"A nameless investigator dogs New York streets made even meaner by a series of near-future calamities. [Larson's] dystopia is bound to win fans..."
—*Kirkus Reviews*

"*The Dewey Decimal System* is a winningly tight, concise and high-impact book, a violent, exhilarating odyssey that pitches its protagonist through a gratuitously detailed future New York." —*New York Press*

"*The Dewey Decimal System* is proof positive that the private detective will remain a serious and seriously enjoyable literary archetype."—*PopMatters*

"Larson's voice is note-perfect in this tour-de-force. When called for, his clipped, brisk prose expands to the lyrical, adeptly singing the praises of beautiful women, cockroaches, and rubble. Reading *The Dewey Decimal System* transports you to another world, and although that world is a grim one, you'll be sorry to leave it. Let's hope that this book isn't a one-off, that poor damaged Dewey will return to lead us through the ruins on another near-future adventure." —*Mystery Scene Magazine*

"*The Dewey Decimal System* is clever, inventive, lovingly satiric and easily one of the most notable debuts of the year." —*Bookgasm*

"Like *Motherless Brooklyn* dosed with Charlie Huston, Nathan Larson's delirious and haunting *The Dewey Decimal System* tips its hat, smartly, to everything from Philip K. Dick's dystopias to Chester Himes's grand guignol Harlem novels, while also managing to be utterly fresh, inventive, and affecting all on its own."
—Megan Abbott, Edgar-winning author of *The End of Everything*

"Nathan Larson's Dewey Decimal is a combination like no other—in a dystopian landscape, he's discursive, loves dissing fools, dissecting language and violence, and has a hell of a system. He's like Walter Mosley's sometime LA hit man Mouse, but with Chester Himes and Jerome Charyn threaded in. This novel is a love song to New York's streets and boroughs and people, even when they're decimated, and Larson's 'postracial' character, a mutt for all times, is someone I'd follow over and over again through whatever secret paths he finds in this world."
—Susan Straight, author of *A Million Nightingales*

NATHAN LARSON is an award-winning film music composer, having created the scores for over thirty movies, including *Boys Don't Cry*, *Margin Call*, and *The Skeleton Twins*. *The Dewey Decimal System* and *The Nervous System* are the highly acclaimed first two installments in his Dewey Decimal crime-fiction trilogy, and are followed by *The Immune System*. Larson lives in Harlem, New York City, with his wife and son.

THE
IMMUNE SYSTEM

A NOVEL BY
NATHAN LARSON

This is a work of fiction. All names, characters, places, and incidents are the product of the author's imagination. Any resemblance to real events or persons, living or dead, is entirely coincidental.

Published by Akashic Books
©2015 Nathan Larson

ISBN-13: 978 1-61775-339-8
Library of Congress Control Number: 2014955089

Akashic Books
Twitter: @AkashicBooks
Facebook: AkashicBooks
E-mail: info@akashicbooks.com
Website: www.akashicbooks.com

ot my right foot dug into the soldier's thick neck when I finally figure out what's chafing me.

Bells. That's what's wrong with this sonic picture.

Buried in the dense industrial drone of the Freedom Tower 3.0 re-rebuild, metallic and huge, cranes and bull-dozer treads, the flocks of choppers, the loudspeakers wailing Mandarin like a call to prayer . . . Within this cacophony I dig the bells, church bells, consonant clusters, occupying three distinct slots in the stereo field.

Somebody tolling them bells over at St. Paul's. Maybe St. Peter's. South too, probably at Trinity.

Soldier gargling, yank my full attention back to the throat I'm stepping on, the SEMPER FI tattoo and logo, attached to a compact middle-aged white man, here in this rinky-dink trailer/office on-site. Man gags and gulps.

That I can be distracted from this, the righteous killing of the cocksucker who snuffed my main man Dos Mac, this laboriously executed execution . . . that a bell can catch my attention is revealing. In that this here event is such a forgone thing, cause I killed this fuck countless times in my head over the last year.

Doing whitey now in a Chinese trailer. When a brother like me told the foreman to scram, best believe he scrum. Now witness Chinaman's hastily abandoned breakfast, some manner of alien donut, herky-jerky bits of office debris, a greasy calendar, Chinese characters reading MISS G-9 BEIJING, a faded nymphet showing us a naked shoulder, winking at the viewer from a lost era, wrapped in that ubiquitous red flag.

To say that such disorder disgusts me would be a gross understatement. Does, however, make me wanna speed this nasty business up. "Getting prepped to merge with the infinite, sarge? Just so you dig, this is really happening and it's happening right now." Say it through the surgical mask, only slightly winded from our brief scuffle. Doubt if I'll need chrome today but I hold my HK45 loose and easy in my reconstructed hand.

Prosthetic metacarpal. As bits of me break off, the government is there with a spare. The perks of the insider. In this case, I had high-fived a moving helicopter. Sure, I got stories.

Gloves on, natch.

White man grimaces, a tooth hanging from his lower lip by a thread of blood.

Balancing my full weight on the man's throat, whip my other brogue clean and hard into dude's kidney. Man expelling air like a burst basketball.

"Find it curious you've yet to ask me why this is going down. Reckon you already know then."

Salt-and-pepper hair shorn military close, character for the Chinese "Infinity" etched into the side of his head per Cyna-corp chic. That older tattoo on the forearm, with that eagle, globe, and anchor . . . not unlike my own tattoo, though blurred with age.

Vein in the man's forehead raised, engorged. Gargling suggests he might perhaps speak, I ease up the pressure on Sergeant Ferguson's airway.

Me saying: "Jimmy."

This not eliciting a response, I give him another foot to the gut. James heaves an empty, dry retch.

"Take it down memory lane, be sure you're crystal." Me saying: "Know me, bitch?"

Jimbo nuzzling his cheek against the rotten shitty wood of the trailer floor, nodding, nodding.

"So maybe you're doing that math. To assist. Hearken back, November last. Unarmed black man in Chinatown. Lots of computers, books. Took him out cold blood. You following, shitbird?"

His one visible eye swivels my way, attempting a connection I evade.

"That man was my brother. His name was Dos Mac."

Jim wagging his skull, yes massa, and I peep a sliver of something like hope in those Aryan scopes . . . yes sir. Perhaps he can logic his way out to fight another day.

Plenty nuff talking for me.

Step hard, breaking the cartilage of his trachea.

Grind northbound, shaking it off, already got my Purell™ out on automatic, eyes strafing the black glass of the Millennium Hotel, WTC 1 V3.0 to my back vibing wrong, vibing too tall, past a low wall of sandbags, armored cars, white shuttle buses sporting Skanska logos, dodging a manhole erupting terra-cotta steam, surrounded by a dozen drones in lemon hazmat gear . . .

Well, I ask you now, you think I cherish these sorry situations? This lopsided sadism? Think I get jiggy on the misfortune of my fellow travelers? Not so, y'all, not so.

Dip my hat at the Chinese boys flanking the gate, one of whom commences whistling a Christmas tune. See no evil, gents. I'll settle up with their boss later on, for the short-term rental. And associated cleanup costs.

But listen. Listen, friends. Fundamentally I am a man of peace, a retiring, scholarly gentleman. It's just that this brother also happens to be extensively and expensively schooled in kicking down doors and inflicting pain. So one does what one can, given one's CV. Especially round about these fucking times, where it's do or drown.

No shame in my game.

Full disclosure, to the degree possible with what I got in my skull: I used to be one of these private army heavies. Cyna-corp, though it went by a different name, was my team.

And I bailed. Broke rank. So you can imagine . . . makes it complicated cause said crew essentially runs the island.

Yeah, apparently I used to wear those colors. This period of my life is poorly lit, a casualty of the tinkering that went on in my skull at the hands of the doctors at the National Institutes of Health. Allegedly. So as far as Cyna-corp is concerned, I am still AWOL.

Worse still: I allowed the Cyna-corp founder and guiding spirit to be slaughtered right in front of me. Knifed to death by US Senator Clarence Howard, no less. Sad story, y'all. Another time.

Dig, pausing now at the corner of godforsaken Barclay and Church to pull down the mask and flame up a Chinese Lucky Strike. Helps with the Stench.

Swap out used plastic gloves for fresh, squinting skyward at the helicopters, always with the helicopters, as I apply the necessary Purell™ . . . suggestion of a light source through the heavy orange cloud cover would indicate approximately five in the p.m.

Trying to peep my driver. Need to get to Midtown. The senator has taken to leaving the office earlier and earlier.

This Ferguson thing, these were precious moments expended on personal business. More risk than I would generally allow for. But some matters cannot be left unattended. Jungle justice.

Suck three fast lungfuls, plop a blue pill on my tongue, and replace my mask; with the rapid deterioration of the air quality, that's about all my body can take. And with this I am one fine evening closer to death.

I call myself Dewey Decimal.

F rom here on out, it's gonna get grim, then grimmer, then it will all stop. And it's gonna marrow-level hurt every moment of the way down.

Devotion to the unimpeachable truth is paramount. Take for instance the recently deceased Sergeant Ferguson. *Painstaking* months went into determining I had the right guy. Many more hours comprising days of careful, cautious planning vis-à-vis his exit. Margin for error? Near nil—cause any other odds I could not afford nor abide. I go all out—or not at all.

Sure: truths, facts. Some facts are straightforward. Some are blurry, obfuscated. But certain facts hover there, buzzing, not to be ignored. Like these:

The urban splatter once known as greater New York City is mortally wounded, defaced, irreparable. Those with the means, be it private, state, or corporate backing, rebuild the environs according to their needs.

For the rest, we shuck and jive and parry and jab, and do what we can to stay upright—and we watch new Brutalist structures bloom out of the rubble of the dead landmarks.

Why we still press forward is a righteous head-scratcher. But press forward we do.

Blessed be the hopeful, because they are cursed, the most wretched.

Ho shit. How about sarge back there. Figured despite all evidence to the contrary, he still had half a shot. Thinking he could talk a man down. Not so, yo, not so. Not me, pal—I ain't the one.

Gritty. Fucking sand in my pant legs. Always with the sand. I go to shake it out and naturally, once again—nothing is in fact there. Coulda sworn. Phantom sand.

What I been doing? Same as ever: straight ballin'.

Allah be praised, or perhaps despite His best efforts, yes—I'm still on my hustle up in this tar pit. What's more, I got good and plenty of the little things that make this brother tick.

Still got that Purell™ in steady supply, keeping me squeaky body and spirit. Still got my pills, keeping my heart steady jacking. Matter of fact, I choke one back right now. Still got various chrome, allowing a man to rest easy.

And still got my System. By its rules I am guided and kept. We'll get to that in a moment—hang with me now, I need to know you're there.

Now I track a Chinese Humvee clone as it bounces up Church, wispy dudes in white chem-suits hanging simian off the back. I'm ignored and that's a positive plus. As the Hummie is enveloped by low yellow fog, I meditate on the System.

In the realm of the spiritual, you might view the System as a set of suggestions for negotiating movement, whether through one's thought processes, one's daily activities, or one's environment, all so as to maximize the harmonic.

Left turns STRICTLY prior to eleven a.m.

Frequent and vigorous cleansing with Purell™, essential to rational thought and movement.

On a scientific tip we can observe the System, like aspects of quantum physics, only after we become aware of its behavior. Weaving matter with dimensional units, time and physical space, creating a tight braid, a double helix within which is encoded the logic of all things, all structures, all other so-called systems, be they organic or . . . be they organic . . . be they . . .

Twitch. Lost that thread. Damn. My eyelid spasms. Touch the hard bump on the back of my neck. My platinum pearl. Could it be . . . what? Growing?

Whisper to it. Talk to the thing, my constant companion: "Gonna cut you, cupcake. Dig you out. Believe that."

Flex tough on the bastard, but never doubt the raw; I lose sleep over the sophisticated nanomechanics lodged in the base of my skull.

Reflexive pat on my vial of Purell™. True practice of the System necessarily involves rigorous application of Purell™ (or, I suppose, any equivalent alcohol gel hand sanitizer (AGHS)).*

Clean in flesh and thought, clean in bearing and *intent.* And as mentioned, the practice involves a complex of navigational rules regarding how one skates though one's day.

Left turn. Left turn. Left turn.

The benefits? Countless. And bitches? I'm worth it like Vidal Sassoon.

Was a time folks liked to clown a brother—attending to my mitts as I do every couple minutes, stepping backward in old-timey gear, hating on my exacting attention to detail, my commitment to the library and its Books. And I ask you today: where are said naysayers?

Dead and gone. Or at least gone, which is nigh as good as dead. So who's the clown now?

A surprisingly forceful and noxious wind gust from the ass of the island sideswipes me, rattles a stack of thin metal

---

* *Never, ever be punked: a functioning AGHS by any other name is Purell™, the OG, none other, now and forever. Be ye not deceived. If a so-called AGHS is even a single digit less than 62 percent solid alcohol, your body will in very short order become an overcrowded colony of microparasites and bacteria. Might as well be out snorting oven cleaner.*

girders, tagging unattended cranes and diggers as it rushes north, evil smelling and lukewarm. The din of construction roars on, suggesting life, but the visual tableau speaks of nothing but nothing.

Scope Church Street. Bleak as all get out. Thinking my driver has done gotten himself lost. Again. Him being an out-of-towner. Government kid up here from the District, itself sliding back into the swamp, as Ma Nature intended.

I do up the top button on my overcoat, freezing up in here despite the tepid poison air currents, touch my welding goggles, who would've reckoned this late chill, what with the ground superheated, the rivers creeping in, shoreline shifting by the hour . . . ?

Where's my motherfucking ride? Suddenly I feel very much exposed.

Nervy of me, having just dispatched a second-tier Cyna-corp officer. Nobody can know. The senator's office would toss me to the dogs. The Corp would clip my balls without a moment's hesitation, and gleefully so. Fuck knows they've been dying for a reasonable excuse to do just that, though my standing with the senator prevents this.

Yeah, starting to feel a touch lonesome.

And yet not alone. I see the soldier now, over yonder. Swaying solo, like myself, on the southeast corner of Barclay. Fellow been giving me the eye-fuck these last few minutes. Racial ID impossible at this range. Probably Chinese. Always a safe bet, especially downtown.

Taking my measure. Dude brings his assault rifle around, I note it's one of them M4 knockoffs—who says the Chinese can't make a extremely high-quality product when motivated?—this soldier adopting a hard stance, an approximation of menace. Could be misreading the sitch, wouldn't be the first time. Safety first. Street all but deserted save this character. Might as well be on the Pakistan/Afghan border, were it not for the construction.

Peeping your narrator, what does a man see? Dark-chocolate flesh pulled tight, shrouded in a trim suit, coat, and hat, Auschwitz skinny, surgical gloves, procedure mask, etc., anywhere from thirty-five to fifty, age being nearly impossible to determine as we careen toward the end of this fucked-up epoch, we're starved and insane, scrabbling at scorched earth, wrestling over tiny bones.

Look deeper and you'd see my moms in there, that Filipino tinge, but to most—black is black is black.

In this climate, human skin doesn't heal like it used to, so this split upper lip I rock is the result of damage inflicted years ago, a loop of reinjury, always moist with fresh red tissue.

This soldier—I'd tell you this individual there is admiring my tie, but I highly doubt he can see much detail beyond my flesh tone, and that's just the raw. Black known to blind even the most observant creature.

Hell. Thinking not for the first time about the wisdom of having a chauffeur at all if he can't set his watch . . . yet another concession I make to the senator, against my better judgment. Where is my fucking ride? Get primed to bounce on my own juice, reckon I hoof it or, with my bad leg giving me subtle grief, catch the next domestic military detail headed uptown.

Now shitbird figures he'll step to me. Shuffling across the street, theatrically brandishing his submachine gun.

Sigh.

Means I gotta start paying attention, thus fucking up my monologue. Can't believe I'm gonna have to expend energy on this sorry stray.

Not hearing shit at first over the machines, then: ". . . stanning." He's addressing me from midway across the boulevard, young, high-pitched Chinglish. "No stanning, you walk . . ."

For the sake of form I am lifting my hands, weary now, dangling my laminate, hearing myself switching to Mandarin, my cracked kisser croaking, "State Department, my brother. Thing to do is cool it down right about now."

Don't dig that his arms are trembling if only cause this can lead to accidents. Must be a fresh import. I lower my face mask, all kindza as-yet-unnamed pathogens no doubt bum-rushing my body, new shit without even a Latin moniker. I shiver, but I suck it up.

Brandish the plastic card, slow and deliberate. "See, pal. That's me right there in the picture . . ."

The gunman stumbles over his own kicks—what gives? Comes back at me in his native tongue. I'm hearing him. Yeah, that's right, I'm fluent in Mandarin. And nearly every other language under the sun. An enhancement, your tax dollars at work. Controlled, I have come to believe, by the implant in my neck.

". . . State Department, yes, okay," dude saying. "This area, People's Republic, so, ah, you have no . . ."

Open my yap to cut these tedious formalities short, and this is when the bells at St. Paul's sound again, disproportionately loud, and I'd be lying if I said I don't near soil myself. Cause it's been an age since we've heard anything like this, the sound resonating so very wrong in this blasted expanse.

Chinese youngblood three-sixties off kilter, nearly throwing himself over, and though my focus is on the church, I notice one leg is shorter than the other on this specimen.

A flood of empathy fills my chest, and I am annoyed at this knee-jerk weakness on my part.

Bell tolls four times followed by the impression of silence, even against the incessant industrial rumblings. And this:

There, near the church . . . through the haze I can make out a handful of human shapes, bearing . . . what? Flashlights? Flares? No. Candles. Actual candles. Battery-powered gear doesn't convincingly flicker and shimmy like that.

Pondering where the fuck a body would rustle up a for-real candle. The gimpy gunman is heading their way, yammering. Apparently I am forgotten, which suits me dandy, me thinking: *What's with the bells? Candles?*

Then it grabs me, and the scruff of my neck tickles as hairs stand on end.

February 14. Today. Two years gone. Second anniversary of the gutting of the city of my birth, this, the City of New York. The "Valentine's Occurrence."

First anniversary must've blown right past me. Forgive the oversight: a man has been crazy busy not getting dead.

Bells go off again. Soldier now engaging the gathering, count six individuals, this time I can hear him yodeling in pidgin English about trespassing and whatnot.

These are civilians. A rare sighting, this endangered species. Dogs are more common. But I'll be goddamned if they're not civilians. Fuck knows.

Clock my timepiece, which is solar powered, not the best choice in a world without sun, but it looks expensive and works if you squint. The thing giving me an anemic reading: 5:21 p.m.

Hearken back a couple years. 5:20. That very minute, coordinated demolition—not entirely successful but pretty fucking impressive nonetheless—of the Queensboro, Williamsburg, Manhattan, and Brooklyn bridges.

My gut rotates: maybe it's hunger. Maybe something else. Suddenly I wanna be over there lighting a candle myself, and I can't sanction any rough handling these civies will inevitably be subjected to. Where this spasm of do-right comes from, Jah only knows.

Draw my Heckler. Not wise on Chinese property but I do it.

It's just then the Escalade glides to a polite stop between the churchyard and me, the nonsound of a battery-powered engine, gangsta window tint, burgundy-wine shine even in this ocher haze. Government plates. My douche-chariot.

A final squint at the church, yet more armed Chinese military kids slinking into the yard from the east, the six scrawny individuals on their knees now, the soldiers barking, weapons out and held high.

And I'm loping across the boulevard, just on auto, my gun aloft, because we do not harm noncombatants. One of the codes by which I conduct this war.

My spirit guide intervenes, snatches my collar, saying simmer down. Check lest you wreck yourself. Vibrate for a moment there between engage and retreat . . . then spin and pull open the rear door on the Esco. Slide on in.

Dig those seats, gently worn leather, real leather.

No, Decimal. These civies, not your concern. Turf stuff, local doings. I drift above such things, operating as I do on the macro.

Thick divider separating me and the unseen driver, a white Secret Service agent named Chip. I am told Chip had his tongue removed. By whom is not clear, and this is the extent of what I know about the fellow.

Opaque glass comprises up the divider. My reflection. Masked cadaver returns my hazy gaze. My near-dead peepers begging the question: how much longer can *you* stay standing, Decimal?

Though I'd love nothing more than to just cozy up with some books, a scout like me is expected to debrief in person to my handlers. So it's:

"The Ark, Chip . . ." I rattle at the mic on the ceiling, throat thick and tight. Getting the cap off my pill bottle. The Cadillac pulls out, northbound. Drop a blue one down my maw and flip the cap on my bottle of Purell™.

We move forth. I do not look back. Shouldn't dwell, shouldn't speculate, but amongst that gaggle of Gypsies I swear I saw a child.

A child. Here in this hole.

Blinking rapidly on speed shutter, get those pesky grains of sand out my eyes. Only explanation for tearing up like this. Sand in the eyes.

Hands come away wet and clean—no sand. Again.

Them peepers, my peepers, in the glass—jerking my coattails, them saying: *Oh, you so hard, Decimal?*

Then what are you crying for?

S ome quick geography.

Manhattan Island has been carved into fillets, the borders of which are continually shifting but can loosely be delineated as:

Chinese control: Water Street all the way to West 3rd Street, and from the eastern edge of West Street to the western edge of the FDR Drive, and a patch of Midtown, roughly West 32nd and 31st streets from Madison west to 6th Avenue.

The Drives East and West, as well as the waterfront area including of course the ports and landings, have complex ownership, very difficult to keep track of. A constant source of static, the shit is headache-inducing so we'll leave it at that.

The Russians control the stretch of land from West 4th Street all the way up to 30th Street, and the whole shebang between the Drives.

The Coalition runs the grid stretching from 33rd Street (with the inclusion of the derelict Madison Square Garden), technically up to the northernmost tip of the island at Inwood Hill Park over to 9th Avenue . . . but in reality, they're not active above 96th Street except for some token patrolling of the major throughways (116th, 125th, 135th, 145th, and so on). Also the small patch downtown from Worth to Ann Street, from Broadway to Gold, encompassing the old City Hall. And, of course—Wall Street, from Broadway to the river.

And then there's little old me.

My little postage stamp, my little pied-à-terre. Running things between West 40th to West 42nd south to north, and the Avenue of the Americas and 5th Avenue west to east. This area, obviously, encloses the Main Branch of the New York Public Library—my crib—and the stretch of concrete formerly known as Bryant Park, which I got paved over six months back cause everybody seemed to get the feeling like they could burn their garbage in my backyard, and in this I include Russians, Chinese, and Coalition alike. The arrogance of that.

The boroughs? Left in darkness to the various tribes, right along the lines which they had always been partitioned: Brooklyn to the Jews, Dominicans, Polish, and the blacks—the interior. The receding waterline, formerly Red Hook, Coney, Brighton, etc.—to the Russians.

Staten Island has been entirely evacuated, as every possible inch of land surface now serves as a dump, a metastasization of Fresh Kills.

Queens is a medieval fiefdom under strict Chinese supervision. That's all the information I have on Queens.

The Bronx, that blotch on the map which birthed me, now serves strictly as worker housing, again split neatly into quadrants representing the four major groups: the Chinese (under whose wing fall the Koreans, the Southeast Asians), the Russians (Ukrainians, white Eastern Europeans), the Dominicans (who would rather keep to themselves . . . this including all brown-skinned Latino groups, as well as black Americans), and the Coalition, who to their credit make no real distinction based on ethnicity, although naturally: the lighter your skin, the better off you're gonna be.

There is no conceivable need to go to these godforsaken places.

I look west, through the darkened glass on the Escalade, out across the Hudson.

What goes down in Jersey? That's anybody's guess. I've been there twice in my life, as far as I know: once as a young man to an away basketball game in Camden, and once to the airport. That's it. Its dismal shoreline, never a pretty picture, is now barely visible through the soup.

What goes down in Jersey? Who cares? Who knows? And we are no poorer for that fact. Are we?

Stressful fucking metal locker rockets me to the top of the shop, ears and pills popping, me white-knuckling it all the way. Shaky at the observation deck I'm issued a gas mask, which I automatic wipe-down with some Purell™, this documented by several cameras and the deeply bored gaze of palace guards.

Contemplate the air even at this elevation. Typhi of all motherfucking types.

Cyna-corp, Cyna-corp, everywhere. My Cyna-corp radar is pinning, legion in their wet suits, that logo, once clearly a stylized *C*, looking more and more like two Nike swooshes to me.

Me thinking, *I just killed one of you all, and it was too easy. Like Sunday morning.* Tough not to get smug when—let's just be all the way real—you're one of the smartest cats on the island.

I'm waved out on the west-facing terrace. Amble onto the concrete esplanade in the way that a gimp in a gas mask can, movement an effort in the heavy winds all the way up here.

And yonder, the big man hatless, no silly-ass gas mask for the boss, his substantial back to me here, camel-hair floor-length coat, fur-lined collar. Through the thick atmosphere I can make out his gators, the sine waves of his conk. Big man, surveying his fiefdom through a pair of dainty silver binoculars that recall a Dillinger.

Senator Clarence Howard. Big man presenting a classical silhouette, suggesting a gargoyle on one of those European

Gothic cathedrals I never did get to see except in coffee table books—yes, a gargoyle, were it not for his fundamental good looks.

"The scholar." Doesn't turn, doesn't need to. Basso profundo, as always.

Don't respond cause a chopper comes in close enough to drown out any sass I might conjure up. Dip for a smoke, not out of need, more cause a cigarette irks the boss and tones down the sand.

Lift the gas mask (airborne E. coli) and slide the Lucky between my torn lips.

Senator Howard bobs his big old noggin like he's contemplating some profound shit. Fussing with his flag pin. Fingernails against silk, I involuntarily shudder. Though I can't hear it, I imagine the sound. Wears them nails long, like a woman.

This hulk of meat, like all of us, has shucked some pounds. Still a linebacker, but his suit jacket billows a touch, vibes at least one or two sizes up.

Ghetto bird banking away now—me saying, "We straight with Shanghai, downtown, site 1A. Vibe conveyed. No more Russian metals for those boys anytime soon. Got 'em buying American like proper citizens."

Man tilts his head, briefly. Intent on something or other in his opera glasses.

That's as much as we discuss these matters, my little assignments. Which suits me down to the cold hard ground.

I hang back, no great master of heights. The senator gestures east, extending an expensively gloved finger, tapping the Plexiglas twice, and holds the binoculars out.

"Bear witness, Librarian. Come forward, son, and bear witness."

Think about it for a moment, huh—

This after all being the man who stuck a rapier into my girlfriend while her hands were restrained, who left her to bleed out on the Brooklyn Bridge. Though our relationship over time has matured beyond these unsavory things, it's situations like this when I gotta take such history into account, regarding the senator.

What's more: could he conceivably know about the sergeant? Impossible. That's a body that will never be recovered. Way I left it, Ferguson was to be interred like King Tut in the concrete foundation of Tower Five 3.0.

From the observation deck, I'm gauging the height of the glass, the curvature up top. I'm gonna have to bet it'd be tough to hoist even a 115-pound bag of bile like your narrator over that there barricade, so I drop the dice and lean forward.

I and I and the big bad senator, nigh on cheek to cheek. Irksome how he wiggles the binoculars, which I accept, thankful for my gloves, me not knowing what to look at.

Strafe eviscerated Manhattan, vista of black broken up by splotches of overly lit patches of construction, cranes, toy vehicles, buildings partially powered, buildings fully powered and improbably unchanged, more frequent groupings of towers standing dark and dead as the moon, windowless obelisks. Looking north like this, naturally, I'm pretty much only taking in Coalition territory.

Pull back the fancy binocs, reckon silly is the move, me saying faux-misty, "Time was, shit. Eight million stories in the naked city. Now it's more like three or four. Ya heard?"

Senator furrows his brow at this trifle, squeezes the bridge of his nose. Jabs a finger into the thick plastic of the protective barrier. "Son, use the eyes God gave you. Just west of the reservoir. In the park. South of that. Round about 66th Street on the east side too. Up north, west side, closer to the top if you can see that far."

I reapply the 'nocs, and despite the dense "cloud" cover I'm able to spy what the man's on about. This thanks in part to a grouping of choppers, making lazy circles, searchlights creating a PowerPoint-type tableau.

"Those are some pretty big motherfucking tents. Gotta be a lot of them out there."

Senator Howard winces or shivers or whatever, fluffs up his lips like he's trying to inhale his mustache. "This language. You are one rough diamond, son."

"Thought y'all cleared it, the whole park. Walled it off good."

Senator lifts a heavy shoulder, pokes the glass again. "The hand of man is a fallible thing, scholar. All glory to the one God. Talking about too large an area."

Can't see anything beyond the southernmost section of Central Park but I get the drift. Say as I hand the glasses back, "So we're thinking, who are they?"

Senator does the lip-inhale thing again, manipulating his tiepin. Basso profundo: "What did they call him then, Librarian, that did lead his children into the wild?"

Here we fucking go. The senator and his Jesus nonsense.

"Well, boss, heathen that I am, I wouldn't dare guess, now would I."

"Praise his Holy Name. We can speak of the one man Moses . . ." Howard extends his arms, a passing chopper illuminating his just-this-side-of-crazy eyes. "*And the children of Israel said unto them, 'Would that we had died at the hand of the Lord in Egypt, for ye have brought us forth into this wilderness, to kill this whole assembly with hunger.'* Book of Exodus 16:3."

Regarding me now like this is some kind of clarification. I give a grunt. Feeling a little woozy, if I'm honest. Might be the altitude.

Senator rumbling on, "Which is to say, Librarian, this very insubstantial thorn in the capital's side. Well, now. We could be shod of it in a jiffy, God willing. Yes indeed. Cast them out in a matter of hours."

"No doubt."

"Indeed. So not unlike the Israelites, it's probable that these folk are wondering how they got themselves into such a fine pickle."

"Sure enough."

"And good odds are it wasn't the light of the Lord led them hence; odds are it was some fool dime-store Marcus Garvey thinking he could make some kind of political point. A false idol. Such futility."

I'm tapping out another Lucky, and in doing so note my claw trembling. Bad omen there. An aura, and what's coming ain't a migraine. Though I get those too, and fierce. The tremors kicking in. Me trying to stay good, saying, "So cut 'em down. Smoke 'em out. You got machines. Why do you feel the need to relate all this to a lil' boy like me?"

Though I know the answer. As cautious as he is with me, he doesn't trust Cyna-corp either. It's a tricky one for the boss, who offers the diminished skyline a tight grin.

"I'm going to issue you a shortwave. As you leave. I truly dislike the sense that I cannot contact you as needed."

Shrug. Sure.

The senator continues, "These are complicated times, Decimal. Matthew said: *And then many will fall away and betray one another, hate one another.* We have to be alert."

"Never sleeping, sir, I feel that." Thinking, *Hmm.*

Vibrates like trouble within the Coalition, the shadow government to which the senator kneels. A grouping of wealthy crackers mostly, some Arabs, politicians, developers, high-level white-collar criminals all. They run everything north of our current position, and are a relatively new crew. But represent those who have always controlled the world.

The senator nods. "I am not a cruel man, Decimal. And though I would never pause to serve as vessel of the Lord's might, I've no desire to see needless violence done to the Creator's flock. Wayward though they may be."

As my peripheral vision dims, here it comes, I marvel yet again at this sanctimonious motherfucker's ability to spit vast amounts of verbal cotton candy, and his seeming inability to get to the point. Light that cigarette with effort. My flipper is flapping like I'm trying to hail a cab, but the senator takes no notice, him saying, ". . . person of the people like yourself. They see a uniform coming, we spook 'em. Can't have our boys just come barreling in. Counterproductive. So a gentleman such as you, of the common class, a soft touch, a casual approach . . ."

Another helicopter sweeps into the sound field and takes over, me desperately trying to get that cigarette between my lips . . . somewhere the senator droning on, ". . . identify the head of the serpent. Or heads. And then, with God's guidance, simply *remove* them . . ."

And *bam*, I find myself not exactly recalling the topic of conversation. It happens. Call it a Freddo.

Through the hazy lens of the Near Freeze, I recognize this man, this is one Senator Howard. I assume I've been here awhile, my cigarette nearly down to the nub.

I am impossibly high above street level.

Howard mimes covering his ears at someone behind me. I don't turn around, near-panic, willing my brain not to seize up completely cause I don't want to suffer a Full Freeze in front of the senator. He'd use that soft spot, oh, trust a man.

Howard shifts back to me, showing me those Great Whites.

As my vision wobbles, color begins to slough off—but that's okay as it's dark enough out not to matter hugely. My Lucky begins to singe the rubber of my gloves, while the big man speaks once more in the distance . . . that's me thinking: *Ah*. Whatever the fuck we're rapping about, here's the rub.

Always delivered with a predator's smile.

T hen there's the dream, as familiar as sleep itself, almost comforting in its dependability.

American housing project in winter. My perspective is from the parking lot, which itself is sparsely occupied.

Sweep through a sad play area. Toddler-size Rocawear sneaker, always one shoe, these urban mysteries. Chicken bones, discarded malt liquor bottles, crushed packs of Salems.

Proceed.

This is not a new dream. But—of late a new detail pokes out. I may not be alone here. I may have at least two companions.

I can sense this at the door, which is caught by a gloved hand that does not appear to be mine. In the stainless steel elevator, I can detect more than one presence, breathing while I do, slightly winded as if I'm coming out of the cold.

Exit the elevator into the hallway. Key in hand.

Check my pistol, disengage the safety. Listen at the door.

Enter when ready. After all: I'm merely coming home.

O TIS, reads the brass plate on the floor of this tiny room with a latticed gate, a masked Cyna-corp sentry and myself in seeming free-fall, plummeting toward Hades, my neurons shooting dry loads, seized up in a Full Freeze. Though the worst has passed, I am near helpless, and weighed heavy with fear.

Not exactly positive through which structure I am traveling and what the purpose of this journey is, numbers lighting up but not making sense, *1150, 1125* . . . furthermore an antique, why not something a stitch more modern . . .

Vomit a little into my mouth. Don't do elevators well and I am not ashamed to be that guy. The state my diet's in, ain't nothing but pill-dust and bile, burning my throat as I choke my gorge back.

Try and fail to speak. Wanna be let the fuck off this Model-T cocksucker.

Soldier peeps me askance, him saying, "You better not be throwing up in here. You sick?"

He's got a black scuba face mask on but I'm betting this is a yahoo white guy. Most of them are. Nodding, nodding, yes, very sick, so much things to say, gullet otherwise engaged.

"Better not be puking. I'm serious. I'll *fuck you up*, Special Deputy Agent Whatever, don't care who you're tight with. No puking, these are new boots. Break your fucking face, not a problem."

Air-tickle with my fake hand in an effort to hush this

dude. I can dig it and can get behind concern for new threads and spunky shoes.

But what brings a man here? What misfortune deposits me, in this moment, wedged in a vintage elevator with a rent-a-cop? Think, Decimal . . . there are the bells . . . and I throttle a white man . . . then I get in a car and go somewhere else. A conversation with a large man who might be my father—if I didn't know my daddy to be a criminal deadbeat out of Trinidad, who for all I know has died a vagrant's death in a San Fernando gutter. Hopefully he suffered.

This tidbit, and the bells . . . *whoosh*, and the lift comes to a halt, emitting a weak old-timey *ding*, my only known friend dragging the gate back fast, I stumble-skate out onto wet-looking marble, a crowded atrium, my heels going *click-clack*, spin to the left, clock a huge bas-relief plate on the wall depicting that familiar phallus, the words: *EMPIRE STATE*.

It all comes back, excruciatingly swift, a deluge of words and images, Allah only knows I hate this sick-making sensation—all too familiar to me now—like a deep suck of weaponized crack cocaine, the fear that my cerebral cortex just might become overwhelmed with this reintroduction of everything beyond the events of the last few minutes.

In time, I will hemorrhage, my skull brimming with blood, with too much fucking information. That's a bet.

The Ark. Or so the Empire State Building has been rechristened. The Death Star, the Tower of Power, deco control center for the Coalition, new New York. And, if the powers-that-preside will have it, the cradle of the new New World.

Bounce, Decimal.

Lower my shoulder against the watery babble, the tangle of security types, a rainbow of uniforms, among them NYPD, baby-blue UN helmets, MPs, digital camo—a paramilitary melting pot, the concept of which is heartwarming, is it not, yo?

"Fuck out my way." Mumble just generally, nobody paying mind, otherwise engaged . . . sand on my tongue. I spit straight down, aiming discreetly for my own brogue. So many bodies, me thinking, *hep B, hep C, TB* . . .

Through the full-body scanner on my exit, unsteady with my laminate high, the metal in my body enough to trip the alarm, pausing only to collect my weapons from Checkpoint Charlie and receive a pocket-watch-sized radio per the senator's instructions.

Hopscotch out onto the scarred 5th Avenue, angry with various construction and combat vehicles, luxury and cattle-car transport, civilian and official, idling or parked three deep. Uniformed chauffeurs bear plaques with Cyrillic and Arabic lettering.

Sand in my craw. Awful sensation. Yet: hock one on the pavement, and barring the general unhealthy hue of my spit, I can see no trace of anything sandlike.

Worrisome, as this spook-sand thing is a new development. Gonna wanna clear the dome.

Best bet—fuck a ride. Opt to leg it home, direct myself uptown. Get to bopping, worrying at my Purell™.

Past a clutch of soldiers and building security are the civilians, their dwindling ranks, the amputees, the luckless, haunting the periphery, good as dead, hoping for . . . ? They call to me, snatch at my coat as I lean north. Gently now, I brush this debris aside, cause a man has problems of his fucking own and only so much love to give. Need some me-time behind doors. Can't really get that clean-and-sparkly feeling down on the street, out in this bacterial chowder.

A block beyond the clamor, past the sparse shanty, the lean-tos . . . sure, it gets quiet in a jiffy, once you get outside the orbit of the Ark. Lay a gloved hand on the back of my neck. Touch the thing, bas-relief. Pop a pill, choke it back, replace that mask. Thinking System.

Contemplate my new assignment. Which was . . .

Gimme a fucking minute. I take a broad psychic swipe at the cobwebs in my cranium. And come away with: *Unsanctioned congregations of unknowns in the park. The gig—a simple walk-through, an easy look-see, give the trespassers a stern once-over finger-wag.*

But before I am forced to tackle this one, there remains plenty of time to get some work done back home. Back at the library. My true work. So much to be done.

Twitch, tilt my mug back toward the mother ship, toward the heavens, obscured as they are by drifts of methane and cancer and Christ knows what else, snorting burnt plastic and garbage, above me a battered crane, the structure swaying subtly, no, no, no, and beyond that the helicopters. Always with the helicopters.

Gimping up 5th Avenue, the first fat droplets of poison rain smack the pavement. Gathering my coat around my frame, me and my shadow, headlights on the burgundy metallic Escalade flipping on, the car a discreet half-block to my back.

Truth is, I don't know who I work for. In theory I am on the State Department "payroll," though "money" has been usurped by goods, daily necessities, and guaranteed safe passage.

I engage in cleanup for the Christ-crazy blowhard Senator Clarence Howard. But behind his considerable girth I dig the movement of a far larger creature—massive, complex, and by no means godly—and it is this entity that I serve.

It has a name: the Coalition.

And precisely why a brother like myself finds himself in the theoretical employ of the likes of snaky Senator Clarence Howard, and by extension the Coalition . . . well.

Stop on by. There you are, striding between that famous pair of lions, up the steps and through the revolving doors, avoiding the pools of water that collect on the indented, unlit marble stairwell that carries you to the third floor, at points having to feel your way past the murk. A couple of lefts through huge, silent halls, lit sporadically by helicopter spotlights.

And yonder, you'll find me, killer of men, happily ensconced in the middle of the cavernous Rose Reading Room here in the Main Branch NYPL, my home, my castle, my charge.

I shuck my jacket, roll up the sleeves, and hit the books. Working on a realignment. Having scrubbed my flesh raw, I set about the work, surrounded by hedgerows of books, all sensible, short stacks. No more five-meter towers leaning hither and thither. No more chaos and mess. A new order prevails.

How a lost child of the South Bronx, a damaged veteran of ops black and white, finds himself the custodian of a national landmark like the Main Branch is a lengthy story indeed. The books. That's how they keep me.

See: a significant segment of the New York Public Library's priceless collection was (shall we say) compromised beyond repair. Up in smoke. An act of God. Force majeure.

Okay, not exactly. Specifics: some nutjob took a flamethrower to the stacks. Best forgotten. Above all else, we move forward around this bitch, and don't get weepy about what's done.

So, Senator Howard re-upped the book supply, supplementing the damaged or destroyed volumes with irreplaceable material siphoned off from the Library of Congress. And the material keeps on coming. And I keep taking it. Like the blue pills, the pistachio nuts, and Purell™. The stuff of Life. Senator Howard provides. So you might say I am in his thrall.

There are . . . episodes, occurring with greater and greater frequency. Events I want to keep to myself. The Semi-Freddos. The Full Freeze. The minor fugue state. Time grows vague, insubstantial, slippery. Wake up in various places, with little clue as to how I got there or what may have been my errand.

Come to on the damp marble stairs. Under a table in a vast hall of dead computer monitors. In the Map Room, my dome on a book about mollusks, or Dutch colonialism. In the tiled bathroom, choked sink overflowing with rusty river water. In nothing but my briefs, upon a pile of microfiche. I might be losing minutes, or days. It doesn't particularly matter, in the sense that I set my own hours, but it makes System protocol difficult to stick to. And it makes me look bad. Touchable.

I ain't never lied. I know what it all means. I'm sloughing this life. On the slow fade. A partially asymptomatic carrier of, perhaps, everything.

As noted, I have the sense these episodes might compromise my standing with my benefactor—and with those who would wish to take me out. Therefore, I do my utmost to prolong the inevitable and make like I'm operating at 150 percent. You'd think the cameras would pick these anomalies up, but so far, nobody has commented—so I just keep it tight-grill—they must reckon I'm a napper. Or a narcoleptic. That is if anybody's out there, and that's a big if.

All this work. I shake my dome at the stacks. The books. My loves. Touch a blue leather spine.

I should be thinking about a successor. Mind, my conditions for coming into my jobby-job for the senator were extensive. Nothing extravagant, and nothing they couldn't accommodate, but they were for sure deal-breakers from my perspective. Conditions include:

Under no circumstances will I be subordinate to any individual or group, specifically my former employers Cyna-corp and the United States government or any of its various tendrils, particularly the Senate, the legislative branch in general, or any branch of US military. Okay, we might run jobs in tandem, and sure, there will be some interaction, some overlap. But my contract is directly with the senator himself, the very man, having no intermediaries, and absolutely no bullshit.

As for my duties, they remain largely unarticulated. Think this is for the sake of deniability as much as anything else, and I'm comfortable rolling like that.

This was how we kicked it back in ops: you got thrown a mission, and you went and did the motherfucker. Full stop. Some entity catches you ass-out? That was your problem and your problem alone. So the way to glide was this: give 'em exactly nil and not an ounce more. Blank those silly bitches, sit tight, savvy a soft spot, kick, cut, or eat your way out. Long as it takes. Baby, I like it like that.

Did it in Pakistan. Did it in Somalia, Damascus, Tripoli. Did it in Frankfurt, did it in Fallujah. So too did the shit in Bethesda, Maryland. Did it in ghost towns, no-name twilight locales not on any GPS.

Wasn't nobody coming to spring you either. Nobody to holler for. Strictly off-grid. A fellow's gotta be highly motivated. Self-starter. Saying how we *did* this fucking thing. That's the job.

So. Isn't outside of my paradigm, this valley of the shadow. Comfortable here. Good place for a brother who hates the sun, hates its cruelty, hates exposure.

Clarence Howard. US senator, man of God, sociopath, realist. If the single remaining source of power left in the city lay in the control of its reconstruction, then Howard and his cronies and the larger Coalition were there first—looking to consolidate and take full possession of the whole motherfucking shebang. You had to concede points for balls, for grand thinking, for epic visualization.

This meant a gradual annexation of the various construction firms, generally defined as they were along racial and cultural lines. Dominant were the Chinese, Russian, and domestic criminals. And then there were those outfits defined not by the composition of their crew, but by the money behind them: the Saudis, the Israelis. Former eurozone members in there too, but these were so intermixed with the aforementioned groups they hardly counted.

Until recently, this was all a hell of a mess. So the bosses figured: why not pool their resources . . . and lo, the Coalition.

So what's my day look like? Well, float it my way, senator: The contractor who gets uppity. Expansionist. Looking to strike out on his own, or get with the competition. Or one of our own contractors gets to misbehaving, making sloppy with the kickback math. Toss it here. Lippy, itchy folk wanna buck the status quo. Would-be soloists, prospectors, and high fliers.

The senator voices a name. Just the name is all I need. Sometimes this name is guttural and spiky, sometimes it's a sing-songy tongue-twister, and sometimes it's monosyllabic plain-Jane homegrown as a side of high-sodium grits. The name I'm given is immaterial. Me take a stroll, have a word, set a shitbird back on the path of the good and the mild. And should they wanna try and play me, should they not want to step back in line . . . Well.

I tsk. See this? Bit of gunk on the book here, some shit like fish sauce in the whorls on the leather. Extract a disinfectant wipe and carefully dab at the offending particle. Cause people, I run a *clean* library.

My original purpose here in this spot, that of reorganizing the entire catalog according to the Dewey decimal system of my youth, has been expanded to actually and thoroughly *cleaning* each and every volume, freeing the texts of (in some cases) more than a century's worth of accumulated grime, not just what can be detected by the eye, but the settlements of microorganisms, the infestation of weevils and worms and wood mites.

To release the Word from such squalor, and to return order and dignity to this wounded house; this is my single goal. I do it with the mindfulness and respect one would bring to restoring the world's greatest works of art, and with the patience, care, and discipline the paleontologist applies to the excavation of a prehistoric chicken bone.

That I not die is a necessary aspect of this single goal. I go, and so goes all of this. Y'all could consider keeping myself alive a kind of secondary goal, cause I take the shit as seriously as I do my primary goal.

Where am I at with the books? Hit a very productive period with 030, as reference texts are pretty easy to log, and taking liberties with the original system, perhaps a little display of artistic license or rebellion on my part, I cruised right on over the periodicals with speed, blazed religious texts of all kinds, gave parapsychology the bum-rush, mowed down general statistics, made quick work of ethics and Eastern philosophy . . . and after nigh on two years gone, still moving at a steady clip—behold, I run up on section 330, behind me the recently reorganized residents of political science.

Progress, y'all. Scraped and bruised, this is still America, after all, and we do nothing if not shred ass. Theoretically.

Dig that the appointed hour is drawing near. I place *Modern Trends in Labor Economics* tenderly and with ceremony on the appropriate stack, the first entry in 330. As I apply the Purell™, my peepers flip up to the cameras . . . old habits . . . and there they are, discreet in the corners and (I have learned) the massive custom hanging lights. There are a minimum of eighteen throughout the length of the Reading Room alone, that I am aware of.

Old habits. Used to dog a man that his every twitch is duly recorded for posterity. Now I could give a frozen fuck. Most of the shit is gotta be me sleeping. Rest of it is me sifting books. Whose gonna wanna scope that? Plus, yo, what am I gonna do that I haven't already done? And anyway— what are they gonna do about it? Ten to one, half these cameras are fritzing anyways.

Wind and water lash at the huge multipaned windows, running the length of the building—a bass hit of thunder jerking me out my stupor. With suddenness I retch on the sand blocking my windpipe, and with equal speed the sensation is gone.

Check the watch. Time. Suit up for the money gig, Decimal. On some monitor somewhere, my scene looks a little something like this:

Colored man swaps out his dusty shirt for a clean one,

and a fresh suit. Tight: British cut, hemmed just at the ankles, no fold. Coming correct in the details. Spends a moment shaking everything out. Selects a hat, carefully, from
an eye-level built-in bookshelf on the northeast side of the
room. A choice of six hats, exactly, each a very slight variation on the same tune. Places said hat on a nearby table as
this is the last element to slot into place. Colored man swallows blue pill. Knocks it back with a dram of warm spring
water.

Popping the fake panel that covers my cubbyhole, I withdraw today's guns: the HK I stashed earlier, and a new-ish
Beretta 8000, chambered for a .357 cartridge. Grab an extra
clip for each cause you'd be a fool not to smoke 'em if you
got 'em.

In addition: handcuffs, switch watches, slapping on
something cheap and digital with a precision timer.

What else? Penlight. A big knife. Nasty diver's blade gets
strapped into place near my ankle. Oh yeah: the senator's
walkie.

I think of the subbasement beneath me, the unknowable
catacombs, moldering paper, packed-dirt walls.

The twin Louis Vuitton steamers overflowing with high-
grade explosives, from which I earlier grabbed a morsel of
C-4, mounted in a shockproof Silly Putty egg.

Upstairs, dressed proper now, nice suit and tie, coming
out of my crouch, my robot knee emits a explosive pop. But
pop is not the word. Hold up a sec, make sure it's all still
connected. Gingerly move my toes. Check. Proceed.

Coming apart as I am. Despite the fancy weaponry and
my skills in the ring, I'm a hastily scribbled fusion of Scare-
crow and Tin Man, exhibiting both characters' physiological
shortcomings. No amount of dope threads can alter this fact.

In short order, everything's gonna crack, collapse, and I will expire here, of thirst perhaps, throatful of ghost sand, as the digital cameras roll. Simply not wake up. That moment is hurtling toward me. The lump at the base of my brain tells me this is so, and I have no cause to doubt it.

But in the meantime, what's a man to do but keep popping?

Yeah. Brainless, heartless, hollow metal and straw. And I already dig the wizard is just a trembling white man behind a green sateen drape.

My Emerald City, fragile cubic zirconia, looking tough from a distance, but so easily broken. Easily broken. Not easily killed.

Coming up on midnight. Retrieve my dual shoulder holster from a nearby sconce and slide into it, that leather worn almost to translucence. Feels right to tool up the two guns, feels natural. I love my books—but the Buddha knows I love me a pair of burners, and a tight outfit by Paul Smith outta the UK.

One might wonder why I forgo the Kevlar vest that has two times saved my pissant life. The answer should be clear: vanity. Vesting up makes a tailored outfit vibe lumpy, deformed—and I'm much too old to go out looking any less than success.

Get my look right and tight. This, as much as anything, is System-correct. In this way the dice is thrown.

My implant shifts, settles in. Shiver.

Apply Purell™. This done, I pat the hat down on my nappy head, in mourning already for the water damage my threads will sustain.

Snatch up my woolen overcoat, and scoot.

* * *

Escalade dodges and dips as if over choppy water as we head alongside the park via 5th Avenue, nearing the northeast corner at 105th Street. Still well south of the South Bronx, but I feel the ghost-energy of the streets of my youth. Wonder what remains in the hinterlands.

Furthest north I've been in months, and there's natural sense in that. This is the land of the lost. The Coalition-controlled Great Rebuild terminates round about 96th Street, as nothing of value lies uptown. Some might tell you this has always been so.

Slide out the Escalade into a medium-hard rain, grimace, flipping the collar on my wet-dog overcoat. Note the phalanx of Cyna-corp positioned near the long-suffering Vanderbilt Gate, which has lost none of its grandeur despite the barbed wire—in fact, it looms all the more forbidding.

Beyond this, the Jungle.

Hard looks from the guardsmen, though surely they were apprised of my arrival. Or not.

Tap the driver's window, which whispers open. I get an impressionistic look at Chip, only my third or forth in the whole of our collaboration. Smallish white dude, blue government suit, those overlay computer glasses all these cats wear, displaying constant shit like inaccurate weather forecasts.

I lather up the Purell™ and pop a pill, saying: "Chip, my son. Keep the motor running, willya?"

Chip emits some sort of grunt which I find hard to interpret.

With a slightly tweaked gut I rotate toward the gate, withdrawing my badge, lowering my face mask, and attempt to contort my mug into an authoritative yet friendly shape. Official business or not, these Cyna-corp motherfuckers hate me.

✻ ✻ ✻

Short splashy descent into the bush and it's a whole new scene. My penlight is dead, fuck it. I steer left toward the Conservatory Garden, blinking, limp down the main path, illuminated by the occasional chopper and the spot from the NYPD tower. City employees were doubtless hipped to my activity here and told to hang back.

Irregular shadows, uncomfortably organic, impossible to decode. Not a cityscape, and therefore outside of my comfort region.

The brogues are louder than I would have liked on the chipped stone tile, though the rain obscures most sound. I rest a finger lightly on my Sig Sauer. Dressed all wrong, but this is more or less my only outfit. In most situations it's a good one.

Sand in my ear, which I'm attempting to ignore.

Plants dead and dying, those hardy enough to live off this air growing unchecked. What terrain I can make out is monochromatic brown. My heart is jacked, techno BPM.

A set of holes, blackened areas in one indicating recent controlled fires, the presence of charred wood, perhaps bone . . . the next thick with algae.

The primary path is blocked off by a dam of garbage and branches, and I am forced into a narrow corridor which could have been described at one time as an arbor. Fuck if I want to crawl in there, but I've got no options.

Exhale and shuffle forward. A snarled, low-hanging canopy of crab apples creates a claustrophobia-inducing tunnel, and I am forced to slightly duck my head. Once I'm inside, the rain batters away at the dead wood and leaves above. Lions and tigers and bears. Despite the "natural" setting, I've rarely felt more constricted in this city. Seems counterintuitive that vegetation would flourish so, given the poison air and water. This thought in itself is disturbing.

The Stench is unspeakable, sweet and rotten. Dead fruits recall shrunken heads. I gotta confess my nerves are a mite strained. Can't make out anything between the trees as they have fused together to create a solid mass.

At once—the deceased Hakim Stanley is here with me.

I can detect his movements over the tattoo of the rain, folding himself out of the tree cover overhead and onto the pathway. Naturally: the young brother is always there, in the dark, in every patch of darkness, waiting, a hole in his head, in boots and digi camo for all time. He is at my heels now, his breath on my neck, the metal within.

Resisting the urge to either turn or break into a run, I attain the ass end of the tunnel, scuttling away from the dank tube, not turning lest my sense of Hakim be confirmed. Couldn't handle that at the moment.

Frozen now, breathing, listening, here at another juncture; the road to the left would seemingly loop back and lead me from whence I came. Take this moment to swap out my gloves, shake out some Purell™. Grit under the tongue. I hock it up and spit into darkness.

Check my clothes one more time, and check 'em good . . . dirt-carrying spores get into a sliver cut, next thing a sucker knows he's bent over backward, some *Exorcist* shit. Lockjaw. Not a desirable way to go out.

The path to the right, toward the Harlem Meer, is where I must go. Snaking a soft right behind some tall brush, I gingerly creep a couple meters, rounding the corner . . . and where I should have a view of the Conservatory Garden I glimpse a skyless mass. It takes more than a moment to sort out what I'm looking at.

A vast canvas tent, stained and discolored by filthy air and water, a structure of the type used for larger outdoor gatherings, weddings. A heavy plastic flap is tied open, and within I can detect electric light, and movement.

Hold it here. Scope the trees, which are poor cover, skeletal and thinned out. Peepers peeled for lurkers, gatekeepers. Seeing nothing, I get clean with some Purell™, pop a pill, and lurch forth.

Prep for enclosed space. Mask tight. Gloves secured. Thinking: *Bacterial meningitis*. Step into the massive ad hoc pavilion. Orderly rows of cots, in surprising number. Children, elderly, the works, laid out amidst the cut-back shrubbery. The rain patter and the spaciousness of it all lends a fantastic calm to the air.

Realize I'm not breathing. It's a fucking extraordinary sight, and I'm blindsided by a complex mash-up of emotions . . . It occurs to me that it's been a long stretch since I've seen a group of human beings in such close quarters who weren't a faceless construction gang, or a military formation of some kind. Move my hand off my gun like I've been stung, with an intense impression that I am by my presence endangering everyone.

Off my game to the degree that I don't see the kid until he's up in my grill, hissing, "Hey. Hey. That's far enough."

Dominican kid, early twenties, me saying, "Take it easy, son. I got—"

"Keep it down, wake everybody up." He looks around wildly. "Our legal people . . . got papers . . ."

I lower my voice. "Take. It. Easy. Just came to chat with your boss, that's all."

"At two o'clock in the morning?"

Crack a grin, take the boy's ear, and rasp, "Son, don't

you know the whole motherfucking world ended back when you were learning to crawl? Ain't no office hours anymore. Now take me to your fucking leader."

Middle-aged white lady in multiple layers of thrift-store gear, gray hair up in a tight bun, old-fashioned horn-rimmed glasses held together with tape. She squats near a statue, formerly a fountain, a trio of dancing women in bronze, holding a flashlight by which to read, though she's got a decent fire going.

A cot lies nearby, occupied by a pubescent kid. I can see the face on it, a dark-skinned female whose radiance is clear even in sleep, mouth agape, an explosion of curls. I hate to disrupt this peaceful tableau but I'm a busy dude.

"Evening, ma'am," I stage-whisper.

Lady flips the flashlight in my face, turns it off hastily. "Oh, excuse me, did Makasi let . . . Yes, can I help you?"

"My name's Dewey Decimal. Might we have a word?"

She regards me for two or three breaths. "As in the Dewey Decimal classification system?"

"Precisely, yes."

Taps her Patricia Cornwell novel against her knee. Wanna grab the book, tag it, clean it, file it. The librarian in me.

"Who did you say you were with?" the lady inquires.

Clear my throat. "Here on my own. Not 'with' anybody tonight."

Her peepers: there's a quick strobe of exchanged electricity, zing. I shudder—she's a witch.

I know from witches. I know all about witches. Fucking Dominicans I came up with . . . chicken coops in unused lots

. . . the Botanica near Grand Concourse and 183rd, by the ninety-nine-cent store . . .

Begin to back away just on reflex.

Woman has her headlights on me tight, and they appear brighter than they should in this light. They are the eyes of a much younger woman.

"Pssts," she says dismissively, waving her book. "It's just science." Witch rifling through my mind.

"What's that?" I say, hoping my fear isn't completely apparent, knowing she can read me anyway.

"Quantum physics, all that. Are you going to be all right?" An open smile.

I nod, and so does she. Looks to the sleeping kids. Then she stands, brushing herself off. Frowns at the little girl.

"Let's step outside so as not to disturb the children."

"Wet out there, ma'am," I hear myself saying, indicating my soaked coat. Truth is more like I don't dig those haunted woods. If I'm real: not thrilled to be alone with a witch scanning my brain.

She tugs her dark-green Parks Department jacket tight around her torso, saying friendly like we're just popping out for a coffee, "I think I'll be fine. Made it this far."

"Tetanus," says the white lady as I'm handing her a Lucky. We're parked under a dead tree about twenty feet from the bivouac.

"How's that?" Next I go for the Purell™, hearing shit like *tetanus*, slap it on proper. Any mention of . . .

White lady watches me working without comment, says: "My granddaughter. You saw her. She's very sick."

"Yeah? That's rough." I'm seized by the sudden urge to be out of there. Me yakking, "Nowhere to go out of the elements? Is that it? Cause . . ." Lady just shaking her head with a spooky smile. Shift it, say, "What's your bag, ma'am? You some kind of, what? Anarchist? Environmentalist?"

Lady gives a short barky laugh, then: "Marcia. Marcia Stanislavski. I taught kindergarten through sixth grade, over at PS 20."

I cluck my tongue. "Couldn't have been much easier than all this survivalist stuff, damn. That was in Flushing, right?"

She gives a small nod, smiles politely. I shuck the bunk small talk, saying, "Fuck do you people want, really?"

"You think this is political. Why should we want anything?"

"Everybody wants something, teach. Way of the world, I don't need to tell you that."

She takes a sharp drag. "All right then. We want to live."

"Shit, I want to live too. However, I opt to do this in spots where I ain't committing criminal trespass—"

Lady holds up a hand, damaged, fingers sealed together, via extreme heat would be my guess. That's something we share, I suppose, crippled appendages.

"I wasn't quite through, sir. Yes, we want to live, but more than this: we want our children to live. And not as slaves."

Shift my weight. Gauge my position. Grit on my tongue. Movement nearby, aspiring for stealth. I let it be for the moment—

Stay gold, Decimal. You're a boss.

Say, "Y'all gotta get up and go 'live' somewhere else is the thing. Otherwise, don't see anybody stopping you folks living, ma."

"Oh no?" She gestures due east with her claw, which I can't help but notice has an undamaged, well-chewed fingernail protruding from its tip. "What do you see there?"

I drop my cigarette, not digging her tone, which has veered preachy . . . Sigh, regard a tangle of cranes, girders going up, one site among many, perhaps fifteen blocks south. Chewing on sand. "This some kinda political—"

"No politics, I already said that. I'm asking you to simply look around."

"Above my pay grade, ma."

"I ask for your impressions, that's all."

I exhale again. Dig on the broken cityscape, indulge the woman. "All right, ma'am, I'll play for a minute. I would describe that as one big-ass construction site, provided you're not trying to drop a metaphor of some kind on me."

She looks west. "And over there."

I don't even need to look cause there's only two things to see—nothing, or: "Yet another big-ass construction site. So what's the nut here, ma'am, or are we just taking a tour of our past and future skyline?"

"I want to know what they're *actually* making."

Recall asking myself the same question several lifetimes ago, gaping up at the Empire State. "More big-ass buildings to replace the old big-ass buildings . . . Okay, I see where you're going with this."

"Do you?"

"Can you drop the Socratic shit? It's irritating, you know what I'm saying?"

"Apologies." She looks sideways and motions with her head. Behind the trees . . . ?

"Hey, hey, hey. Na. Your people try anything now and I'll shoot everybody I see dead, understand?"

She moves her mouth, tightens her lips. "We have no weapons."

"Well I do, ma'am, and I want everybody to back off."

Feeling queasy, casting my marbles hither and thither.

"It's just us."

I listen, breathing. Regaining a dominant stance, though I'm holding my stomach.

"Just us," she repeats.

"Fair warning," I say, "okay?"

She nods.

"Okay, let's think this through. You want to talk about what's going on? Wax philosophical?"

Lady shrugs. I can't see her as well as I'd like so I attempt to steer her into a patch of light. Saying, "I dig you. You're pointing out the obvious here. Right, so they're rebuilding all this mess to suit a certain segment of society's needs. Restructuring everything to suit different agendas. Common factor being wealth." Finding it harder and harder to come off cold about the realness I'm putting voice to. Start to really feel it, cause I've always felt it. "Housing the money, protecting the money." And I'm angry, unexpectedly angry. Slightly horrified to hear myself jabbering: "Nobody's building you or me a place to call home, that's for damn sure. What they're setting up . . . You think I don't know how this game ends, lady? You think I don't know where the fucking chips fall here?"

I angle slightly away, face hot. Said more than called for there. And I did not feel in complete control. I allowed myself to be drawn out. Damnit, I'm stronger than that. My stomach . . .

Woman nods. Pupils coal black like mine, like my daddy's, with that unnervingly inner light. Moves closer, saying gently, "So I suppose it's up to each of us to decide where we come down on this issue."

Can't be playing this game. Trifling. Lady running some

voodoo on me. Gonna have to refocus on what I've been tasked with.

"Listen here, sister teacher. Consider this an extremely generous courtesy visit. But an official visit nonetheless." I badge her, she squints to read it.

"State Department, is it now?"

"'S'right. Now you all, all of you, are in violation of at least four emergency mandates, including trespassing, illegal congregation, occupation of government property, endangerment of minors—"

Her monster paw is abruptly aloft, drifting my direction. Lizard brain reacts first and I smack her mitt out of the air.

"Don't you fucking touch my suit. You do not fucking touch my suit."

Overdone a bit on my part. Lady cradles her hand. Hit her harder than intended, but this witchy bat is tough, and doesn't emit a whimper.

"Now I've been a gentlemen. We've conversated, I've heard your hippie rap and now you hear mine." I say it calm and tight.

She confirms she's heard me by nodding.

Back up a step or two. Breathe, Decimal. Schoolmammy's a ninety-five-pound slip of a thing. She's been touched, got powers, so what.

Rustles flanking me indicate the definite presence of others. I go ahead and pull out my Beretta, letting it hang and be seen, figuring I've nearly done what I can here.

"Please," she says, "that's not necessary."

This I ignore. Hawk up something meaty, spit it into the brush. "Here's the upshot, Miss Lady. Noting you're pretty well dug in, noting what you folks are up to, I'm going to report back to my superiors that y'all are harmless. Can't guarantee they'll listen to me. Ya heard?"

Schoolteacher nods. I raise my voice so that everything in the vicinity can partake.

"But. It's important that you understand this condition. IF you and your people have NOT vacated the park within seventy-two hours—I'm coming back with some of my less sympathetic coworkers, and they're gonna burn this tree house down, not giving a fuck who's in it."

"Oh my," says the lady, not sounding too concerned.

Feel like I'm not making quite the impression I'm aiming for, but I press on: "And with these motherfuckers? It's gonna be Vietnam ugly from the jump. Trust when I say they love this kind of shit, and these motherfuckers are bored and mean. Now, I want you to tell me you fully appreciate what I've just said."

The lady has moved into the shadows, and this makes me edgy.

"But you can help us, Mr. Decimal."

"Did you or did you not just hear me tell you . . ." Goddamn my gut . . .

"Yes, yes," she says. "But we've got nowhere else to go. You can help us. We need supplies."

Heavy breathing to prevent any vomiting. "The fuck makes you think I'm helping anybody? What you know about me? I'm evicting all you all is what I'm doing."

I can't see her in the gloom but it sounds like she's smiling as she says, "Bleach. Just plain old household bleach, for drinking water. And the DPT vaccine. If you're truly with the Department of State, I'm certain you can secure these small things."

"Miss Marcia," I respond, my broken robot hand starting to vibrate now, "what on fucking earth have I done to suggest I would help you in any way shape or form—"

"Your heart is on your sleeve."

"*Excuse* me?" I'm trembling. It's not unpleasant.

"I'm a pretty good judge of character. I've seen a lot of kids grow up. And I get the feeling you've got a soul in there somewhere. Behind that mask, perhaps."

I recoil, because I don't like how this is unfolding. As in—now I'm not wholly sure she said that last bit out loud. My peripheral vision begins to darken like the end of a silent film.

Backing up. The woman is a witch, projecting witchy X-rays, scanning a brother with ill magic.

No, I don't like it.

Don't like people poking around in my psyche, foraging for data, intuiting shit about my nature. Wanna come with something clever but I'm stalling out.

I'm a killer. I got no country save Hades. Don't speak of the *soul* with me.

Can't recall what I say or do at this point, but Miss Marcia dissolves.

Bam: I'm crashing though the sticky underbrush, dirty water in my eyes—

Wham: in vehicle southbound—

Slam: somehow back at the library, scrabbling at the massive stacks . . . but even this image evaporates as a full Freddo bodychecks me.

Again there's the dream, as common a thing as I know, and every element, every aspect, every movement, is cut deep into my muscle memory.

South Bronx housing project in winter. My perspective is, as always, from the parking lot, which is sparsely occupied. The details change but their nature is the same . . . a Department of Housing vehicle, a stripped cop car, a Honda held together with duct tape, a spanking-new Audi . . . but these are not important.

Ghost playground. Upended Dora the Explorer tricycle, unnaturally colorful against the grays and whites, the ash and the frost, steering chassis removed. Popeyes bags, a Papa John's pizza box, a couple loose Twizzlers. These objects.

I'm right about my companions. They're burly dudes, each one of them outweighing me by a bunch. I can see their breath. Again: here, at the door, caught by a gloved hand that does not appear to be mine. In the metal, piss-infused elevator, we are a tight fit, the three of us. We are uncomfortably close together, and it occurs to me I do not want to be near these men.

Exit the elevator into the hallway. Key in hand.

Something new here, because I falter and stop. There has been a failure. There has been a failure on my part. I have welched on some kind of deal. That's why we're here.

I'm asked if there's a problem.

Yes, there's a tremendous problem. Its size and depth are beyond me. Its scope is such that the problem itself is impossible to grasp, because just when you think you've seen the end of it, there's more.

I proceed, reasoning there must be something we can do to help correct the problem. What we do now, and what we will do in the apartment.

Check my pistol and disengage the safety. Listen at the door.

There are a woman and child inside, though I imagine they're holding their breath, the woman's finger to her lips, praying that we'll continue down the hall.

But no. My key is in the lock. Our entrance is unrushed. Cause after all: it's my place.

C ome to on the street in an entirely different part of town, hours and hours later, waves of familiar yet unpleasantly exotic smells washing over me. Somebody saying, "Fuck off me, get the fuck off me . . ."

Occurs that I'm the speaker, and I clap my yap. My suit's a damn mess, overcoat heavy with wet, mud-streaked. Spitting sand and rainwater . . . think: *Gastroenteritis, gram-negative pneumonia* . . .

Panicky pat-down, still got my guns, my hat . . . fuck fuck fuck, the C-4, with great caution I smooth my pockets until I bump up against the egg, thankfully intact. My Purell™, my pills. This is all far better news than I deserve.

Try to pinpoint myself on my internal grid, and I do it on smell alone: Chinatown, Chinatown proper.

Rain has tapered into a needle-fine drizzle. My shoes scrape at the film of grime on the concrete as I attempt to stand, actually gasping at the hurt that whips through my chicken-bone body.

Find myself down a short staircase leading to a basement-level store of some kind, and despite my disorientation, my mouth and nose are filled with a cocktail of smells and textures that are specific to one area in such intensity.

In Chinatown's very colon, at 5:53 a.m. by my watch. This is where the death-dealing chickens and livestock reside, vessels for unnamed viruses . . . like myself, potential asymptomatic carriers of anything.

Chinatown: it's only really here, in this section of the

island triptych, that one can nearly see all the shapes and colors of what once was. Entire blocks remain virtually untouched, which makes the speed at which the rest of the city was deleted all the more sinister. Fuck, how did that happen? Within the space of a single year, it's all changed.

But the organic matter. The filth. It's a horror show. I would never knowingly be here . . . but then I see it. Dead across the street, I dig it all now: 154 Hester Street, the Oversea China Mission building.

My brother Dos Mac's work/live laboratory, and the site of his murder.

Innately I reckon it's good and proper that I'm here, despite the risks . . . I'm in freaking Chinatown, for fuck's sake, unsanctioned. Should a randy patrol happen by I could be shot on sight.

And damn if these freezes are getting progressively more disturbing.

Pull some Purell™, choke back a pill, aim to piece it together . . . Come on, Decimal. Back it on up. Focus. Rewind.

Me shaken by my bump-up with the hippie school-teacher/sorceress, shaky in my ride with Chip at the helm, woozy and wobbly, watching a benighted 5th Avenue rip past, *feeling* the good logic of the grid, *feeling* my head begin to track once more . . . the attendant relief.

System—I have Chip making all proper left turns, not that there are many to be made.

Jump cut. As we get south of the park I am at about 80 percent normal function.

Jump cut. Incongruously, an old pop song playing the car, or perhaps only internally, I mumble along unsure about the lyrics:

> *Yellow cab gypsy cab dollar cab holla back*
> *For foreigners it ain't fair, act like they forgot to add*
> *Eight million stories out there, and they're naked,*
> *Cities is a pity, half of y'all won't make it . . .*

Chip deposits me at the library per my instructions, 3:50 a.m. . . . Manically, I vault out the vehicle, in the grips of the euphoria that can follow a true Freeze . . . wildly saluting the white boy, me grinning wide, so goddamn happy to be back, do my traditional System-mandated caress of the northern-most lion's ass, jauntily mount the steps as my head gets to the chorus: "*Concrete jungle, where dreams are made, oh . . .*"

* * *

Forty-five seconds later that's me stumbling south down 6th Avenue, the Freeze rushing back in, wide sheets of rain wafting off the boulevard, throttling my hands with that good Purell™, even this cold comfort, my long jacket saturated, throat tight, sand on my tongue, heart choked with dread.

I'd had my bad flipper on the door to the library when I saw my home for what it was: an obscenely outsize tomb, a gargantuan crypt worthy of the pyramids, vessel for the long-dead and dying.

With nauseating clarity, I envisioned myself, already so like a corpse, laid out on my bedroll in the Rose Reading Room, black garbage bags full of paper, pages torn from my beloved books, prepped for incineration.

And lo, I beheld the devils, the wraiths, the phantoms, men, women, and children, perched in the great chandeliers, salivating, primed to pounce and strip me of my papery flesh.

It was this last vision that stopped me cold, and in doing so saved my sorry, careless ass . . . because through the glass of the double doors, I dig two pinpoints of red light, blinking in tandem.

Didn't clock the shots, but as I dropped sideways, bullets whizzed and popped behind me, ricocheting off the marble archway . . . me falling painfully on my shoulder, thinking, *Fool, get up and go go go.*

Interloper in my home. Intent on gunning me down. A cheap, shitty ambush. Highly fucking uncool, y'all.

I'm deeply indignant, and then I'm cheek-beating like a little bitch, as my synapses unspool afresh.

Moving south on foot, and from there it's a slow steady fade to black.

. . . AND NOW IN CHINATOWN, 5:54 A.M.

Two hours? Maybe two lost hours, leading me here now, to Chinatown, with its distinct brand of rot.

Mount the stairs onto Hester, back in the moment, poking at my implant.

So. Some unconscious part of me reckoned I'd deliver word of Sergeant Ferguson's dispatch in the flesh, to the man who the late sergeant did in. As if any aspect of Dos Mac were still present here in this hole.

Well, why not? I'm this far south as it is.

A passing trip of beat-looking comfort girls in school uniforms, giving me the stink eye, huddled together under a broken umbrella.

Hellllll no. I learned a year back that to fuck with the Koreans is to court mad pain, especially the females. Trust me on this.

Strictly left turns before eleven a.m. Crab it on over to number 154 . . . the metal door is intact, I give it an elbow and unsurprisingly it pops open simple as that. I look at the old-tech CCTV pointed at my dome. Unsubstantiated sense that I'm being observed, causing me to glance around like an amateur. Seem to be fucked up a lot of late. The whine of a massive drill starts up somewhere to the east.

Elbow my way inside, working from memory here, running my arm along the wall (left) in search of the mains. I'm betting on power cause the Chinese have their own grid down here, best in the city, beating out the Coalition's patchy setup, if you ask me . . . What they have down here runs off that much-contested behemoth they plopped down near the Manhattan Bridge at Pike Slip. Main thrust of protestation was and is the juice would be Chinese alone, no share-sies. In the end indigenous New York couldn't say shit about the issue, so up it went.

And here. I throw the switch, *pop*, banks of overhead lights come to life, sure enough.

Turn and scope it. Not that I expected anything more, but my gut dips a touch when actually faced with my man Dos's former digs, or rather the absence. Between Cyna-corp cleanup crews, the Chinese military itself, and the expected looters, the bones have been picked Cascade clean. In essence I'm looking at what could be any other disused warehouse.

All that remains is a pair of antique computer monitors in a couple states of busted, shoved into a corner. Even the heavy furniture I recall is history.

Think: black mold. *Stachybotrys chartarum*. Might at first just feel a little run down. Then your peepers get itchy. Then, as your lungs fill up with blood and fluid . . . from there—well, you get the general flavor.

Also reckon: *Damn, Dos, I could really talk to you, son.*

"Ferguson's on ice, Dos," I say out loud, into nothing. "Went out hurting too."

There's the hum of the fluorescent overheads. Feeling foolish I spoke aloud. Na. Fuck this mopey noise. The Reaper preys on the slow, the fearful. Picks 'em off leisurely.

Kill the electrics, stepping back out into the street, sideways, left, left, left. Step straight into six space-ninjas, their fossil Humvee purring at the curb. No way to ID them, as they're fully geared up. I groan.

"Come on, y'all. I got nothing for you. Let's just forgo this, save everybody some drama."

The largest of the group is up on me in a heartbeat. "Hey, faggot. Forgot your ass-plug at your boyfriend's place? Thinking about the way it was, bring some flowers by, reminisce?" Voice-scrambler so it comes out sounding vocoded, but by the man's size and shape I can pretty safely ID him, the man I know as Scratch. Their organization seems more and more chaotic but as far as I can ascertain this dude is one of the shot-callers in the Cyna-corp hierarchy.

"Na," I say, "somebody done told you wrong, Scratch."

"How you figure that?" asks the helmet.

"Heard your mom was back in business down here servicing Chinamen, figured I'd get my dick sucked, relax . . . you know how I do, scout."

Somebody hits me, hard, across the kneecap. One of those sharp-looking extendable truncheons. These cats still have the choice gear, for real.

The bad knee, no question these motherfuckers know my architecture. My leg gives and I hit the cold pavement.

"Know what I think?" says dude through that Cylon bug head.

Don't say shit, but homie kicks me in the teeth anyway with those weighted boots. Feel a couple loose ones in front give, and I know he didn't put much into that kick either.

"I think you're that nigger returning to the scene of the crime. Huh? Your boy is pushing up faggot roses, and that's 100 percent on you, you copy?"

"Hard copy," I manage through my teeth.

Dude two takes his whip to my crotch, which I was half-expecting and manage to deflect slightly, but even so, the thin oxygen is sucked out of my lungs, and I retch.

Man saying to his comrade, "Hey, Ace, I got a feeling. Mind you, it's just one of *those* feelings."

"Like a hunch, something like that," says Ace, straight man, his junk all cyborged out too.

"Yeah. Hey, what gives with Jimmy Ferguson? Sarge doesn't wanna answer his 'com, and that ain't like him."

"No, that's the kinda deal makes you concerned," says Ace.

"Fucking A. Then finding this sack of shit here. Gets you thinking. Right?"

"Sure, sure. Makes you wonder," echoes Ace, followed by some R2-D2 bleeps.

Main man returns his attention to me. I'm trying to determine if my jaw is broken.

"But hell, I don't wanna go talking aspersions."

I can't help it. "Casting."

"The fuck you say?"

"*Casting* aspersions, you fucking caveman. Can't *talk* an aspersion, ya heard?"

The dude is quiet for a moment. Digital clicks and pops from within his helmet. Then he kicks me again, harder this time.

I twist my head so he catches my cheekbone, which for positive breaks like a twig. The sound is shockingly loud, at least to me.

"One of these days you're gonna have to teach me to read, Professor Faggot. Feel like it's really held me back, not knowing how to read."

"Yeah, I imagine that's a handicap in your racket . . ." I slur. I'm courting further damage, but these gents are done.

"Have a nice fucking day, Decimal."

The guys clamber in and the Hummer drifts off. A small

crowd of Chinese drones had gathered and now wanders off, chattering and chittering.

Blood and sand in my mouth, I don't even bother to get up. Flat on my back watching the sun wrestle with the atmosphere, attempting in vain to make itself known, as another beautiful morning graces the island of Manhattan.

The rain picks up, slightly. I'm alone here.

Me thinking: *Bleach. A box of that DPT vaccine. How hard would that be to get my hands on?* Me thinking: *Fuck it. I'm gonna help those people. Save a beautiful little girl.*

Leave, at least, one small sliver of light to mark my haunted fall through the black bloody fucking hole that is this life.

Local hero at thirteen, that was me. Yeah, I wasn't always trash, y'all . . . For a shimmering, transient moment the city raised a collective glass to my tiny black ass.

Some confusing, nuanced shit for a ghetto star child, however well read, however street-hardened. I wasn't given space to wrestle down the complexities of what had actually put me in that position, and I certainly couldn't have been prepared for the postscript.

At the Main Branch, in the Rose Reading Room, it's all there in the microfiche. Crank through the headlines. The dailies ran with all the minutia of the story for at least two months solid:

New York Daily News, June 12, 19__
BRONX BABY-NABBER GRABBED

South Bronx: Yesterday, the NYPD took one Leroy Dubois, a Bronx native, into custody, and formally charged the 46-year-old public housing superintendent with three counts of first degree murder, 17 counts of aggravated sexual assault, and a host of additional charges. Mr. Dubois is being held at an undisclosed maximum-security facility pending trial. Bail has been denied.

Leroy Dubois is thought to be the individual behind the heinous crimes attributed to the locally coined moniker "The Boogie Oogie Man," and is believed to have been responsible for the disappearances, rapes, and epidemic of murders of many 11-16-year-old boys since the grisly killing of 13-year-old Deshawn Wilkins in May of 19__.

In a news conference yesterday, NYPD Captain Nick Deluccia said, "This is a monster whose many evil crimes will very likely keep coming to the surface as time goes on. There's no telling how much terror he brought to the neighborhood in which he operated, and it seems as if the more we learn, the bigger this story is. This guy has probably been active for 10 or 15 years, and it's thanks to some great police work and, crucially, the cooperation of the public, that we've got this killer off the streets."

Singled out as being pivotal to cracking the case is an anonymous 12-year-old male who provided key information that led to Dubois's apprehension. The boy is also believed to be one of Dubois's intended victims who managed to make a dramatic escape and lead the police directly to him.

"The entire City of New York and particularly the residents of the South Bronx owe this brave young man a debt of gratitude," Captain Deluccia said yesterday in the press conference from One Police Plaza. "He has shown tremendous strength of character for an individual of any age, and it's especially impressive in such a young kid. He's truly a hometown hero, and we applaud him."

A private ceremony is being held today where the 12-year-old (whose identity is being protected due to his age and pending testimony) will receive the Citizens Service Medal from the mayor. He will be the youngest recipient of this honor in the award's history.

"If there were more youngsters out there like this individual coming forward with information," a spokesperson for the mayor's office said, "we'd be living in a far safer city for everybody."

Captain Nick pulled me out of the ghetto gangs. And into a new uniform . . .

T wisting the flag pin in his tie, Senator Clarence Howard repeats: "Said, son. Last time. What happened to your face?"

And even a huge individual such as this is dwarfed by the massive pair of flags, yet more fucking flags, that flank the floor-to-ceiling window of his office, creating a pretty frame for the unscathed Chrysler Building uptown, hazy and lit up like midnight, even at two p.m.

"Told you, big boss. Slipped on the stairs, boom-bam. Looks worse than it is, ya heard." I ain't a rat. After-school beefs I can handle on my own time.

Clarence is clearly pissed, and neither does he buy what I'm selling . . . but he's tired and more than this, the big boy is trying to stay Christian.

I change the subject. "How's the lady senator?" I grin, knowing we don't discuss Kathleen Koch. "Still up at that facility? Recuperating okay?"

Howard flips it back like he didn't hear me mention his catatonic wife, herself once a firebrand archconservative senator. Till she ran into me. Howard will not touch this one, cause her unraveling was as much his responsibility as mine. So he rumbles on, and even as the man himself is shrinking bodily, his boomy preacher's lungs seem all the more energized.

"Because if I get wind of any . . . *tensions* between members of my security brotherhood, it . . . concerns. We should live as brothers! *He who does not love his brother, whom he has seen, cannot love God, who he has not seen.* That's John 4:20. You should have stayed in the hospital with that face, son."

He is not wrong. Hairline cheekbone fracture, a fair amount of tooth loss. But this is me saying, "Fuck that. I'll lean on the spirit, look to prayer. Praise his motherfucking *name.*"

Love to goose his big ass. But the senator is not a man for banter. He's a man for monologue. He regards me for a spell, seems to let my nonsense drift, and carries on, talking loud like he's addressing a sizable congregation, or a chamber of politicians.

"AND the good LORD saw fit to put bounty in the earth for man to harvest. Fit to fuel his engines, build the machines that would raise great monuments to glorify Him . . ."

It might be the painkillers but I have not got a fucking clue what the big man is on about. Got my mind on things microbiological . . . also contemplating this trouble with Scratch.

He knows, Scratch. He's that funny kinda dumb-smart you find so frequently in the military. Animal instincts are right on, could live in style for years in the desert—but the dude wouldn't make it five minutes at a cocktail party.

Baby steps.

Dragging my dopey attention back to the senator. He's always been loco, but my sense is the man's starting to lose the plot in a fundamental way. I wade through more of this verbal fog.

". . . and lest we forget the selfishness of those who stray from His grace, folk who once did set the foundation for the Tower of Babel, well, sir, we see what that got them. Ruins, Decimal. Total collapse. You *cannot build* on the shifting sand of disbelief."

Does a horizontal hand-jive, those big paws wiping at his desk's aura in what I assume to be an imitation of shifting sand. His gaudy Masonic ring blinks at me, momentarily catching the light.

I Purell™ up. Touch my eye cautiously, wondering if it might be compromised too, what with the cheekbone. Can't stand it any longer, and my face hurts like a bitch, so I try to get things moving.

"Let's . . . let's get to it, yeah? Assume you gotta be talking about the squatter situation. Listen now, sir, with respect to that there—"

"Point being: the very earth beneath our feet belongs to the Lord and the Lord alone. So those who wield the sword of righteous belief have the moral obligation to see to it that the Lord's things are put to godly use. To whit—"

"Na, I get it, boss. It's all prime real estate, ain't nothing free, no free rent."

Howard frowns. "You misunderstand me, son."

"I don't think so," I say, "and I can get biblical too, like this one here: *Blessed is he who is generous to the poor.*"

"And again from the Book of John, praise the living Word. Today is John's, honor him." He pats himself down, pulls out a Montblanc with the great US seal, mumbles to himself as he jots a note, "Today we must closely study the Book of John . . . all of the apostles, for that matter." I know I'm fuzzy, but is the man wrong about John? Fuck it. Wait till he returns his attention to me. "You were saying so eloquently, son."

"Uh-huh. And what I'm trying to communicate is these people got nothing. It's kids up there, the elderly. The vibration is not political. It's about some noncombatants trying to flop is all."

"I don't understand what you're recommending, son."

"*Blessed are the merciful, for they shall receive mercy.* See, I own a Bible or two myself. What I'm saying is live and let fucking live, boss. Let 'em live."

Clarence is showing me his noble profile, brow furrowed.

"I will . . ." he begins slowly. "I will make note of your observations here and take them onboard with respect to any decisions, going forward."

"Fuck does that even mean? This ain't a press conference, Howard, that's some misdirect, that's a non-fucking-answer."

He swings his mustache back to me. "Mind your wicked tongue, son. Peter and his apostle did say: *We must obey God before the counsel of men.* I serve only God. And his nation, the United States of America. And His allies. So it's to God I ultimately defer, not the testimony of man."

"Yes, Lawrd," I reply, countrified. Pushing my luck. Truly I dislike this Bible noise, it's never more than a cheap smokescreen for a sinister fucking agenda.

The senator shows his capped incisors. "Mock all you want, soldier. Mock like Lot's wife."

"No mockery over here, Senator," I say, fingering a cigarette. "Just praying to pretty lil' baby Jesus we gonna wrap up this mano-a-mano so I can get something popping today. Salvage a scrap or two."

More ivory teeth.

Shake out a pill, pop that.

"Decimal," says the senator, regarding me sadly. "Son. These pills . . ."

"Keep me upright."

"Yes, as you choose to believe. Your illness, son. I'm saying you can leave it in God's arms. Just hand it over to Jesus, He'll carry you—"

"To hell that much quicker, no thank you, I'll stick with the drugs. Jesus done nothing for me yet. Got things to do."

I put the smoke in my mouth. Knowing Howard hates it.

Him saying, "Yes, yes. Ever the dedicated working man. Always good for a cynical quip, ain't that right? You got all the answers to any matter of the earthly or spiritual, don't you?"

I lift a shoulder, light up. Long drag. Longer exhale in the senator's direction.

"You the boss, hoss. I'm just what you need me to be."

Give him a lungful. Those fabulous teeth disappear.

"Only you," says the senator, "could get away with blaspheming and blowing foul tobacco in my chambers. This once. Because you've been doing a fine job, a fine job. But mind yourself. And remember your position, young man."

The orbs behind those heavy lids track over to the silent Cyna-corp storm trooper parked near the door.

Oh no, we're never alone in a room, me and Clarence, who is far too clever for that. Though I checked my gun at security on the first floor, as protocol dictates, he's well aware what I'm capable of.

That's why I'm his main gravedigger.

Feeling surly, but memories of past punitive beat-downs lock me back in step. "Yes sir. We were discussing . . . ?"

Howard slaps the table. My stomach jumps but I keep my hands steady and my smoke aloft.

"Have mercy. It is what it is, Decimal. See now. Without a fiscal base. It all comes to a quick stop. Everything. I mean ev-ry-thing." He taps out the syllables softly on his desk. "You understand that, don't you, Decimal?"

Rotate the cigarette, lift a shoulder. Say: "Sure, the cash gotta flow."

Howard shakes his head. "Street talk. You're an erudite man, Decimal. Rough around the edges, to be sure."

"Well, hell. I run a library, you absorb this and that. Osmosis."

"See? Vocabulary. An *educated* brother. Why not make use of proper grammar."

"Player, please. Forever shall I remain ghetto to the marrow. I'm a vet and a criminal doing what I gotta to stay good this side of the rainbow. I know my own self, Howard, let's put away the butter and please get to the meat."

The senator frowns, looks insulted, lower lip protruding. Opts not to pursue it. Says, "Our Saudi Arabian partners have come to me with a mighty task." His mustache is bouncing up and down. He looks agitated.

"I'm listening." I tilt my head and blow a mouthful of smoke at the congressional seal in the ceiling. The Saudis. They're done. Everybody hates 'em. Ousted from their own country, adrift, ass-out without a camel.

Howard clears his throat, pats down his tie for the umpteenth time. What gives? Never seen the man the least bit put out.

"We are faced with division. *For the son treats the father with contempt, the daughter rises up against her mother.* Folks are breaking rank, Decimal, do you hear me?"

"Uh-huh."

"What we need now is those allies that remain . . . we need them healthy and happy. Can you dig that, my son?"

"I can dig it. We still talking about the Saudis? Cause I don't need to be the one to say those people are bad fucking news."

Slapping this away, the man saying, "Listen here. The United States of America takes its allegiances seriously. We do not abandon friends in their hour of need. And the royal bloodline . . . that is, the Saudi royals . . . the bloodline is thinning."

Me thinking: *The Saudis?* Major Coalition players, course they are. But fuck 'em, let that evil-ass "bloodline" die out then. It'd be a kinder world. "After what went down in Riyadh, how can these motherfuckers . . . ?" But I've answered my own question. "Course. They still got their money, even if they don't got a kingdom. So it don't matter."

Howard is quiet, caressing his tie.

Me continuing, "Last I heard? Pashas all on their crazy pimp boats, floating around with no destination . . . and nobody, no port anywhere, will have them. Like when we tried to ditch our garbage . . . who wound up taking it? Wasn't it Haiti? As if they had a choice. And look at Haiti. *Only* our garbage remains, no doubt."

The senator takes another moment. Fingers his tie yet again, sighs. "True, yes, the Saudis are between locales. A temporary situation."

I snort. The senator smacks his big hand on his desk and despite myself, I jump.

"Enough. You must realize, son," he says, face set, eyes hard, "as financial partners, we have nobody even in the same league as the Saudis. They are, despite their focus on False Prophets, very much our brothers in all things."

"Yes sir, I understand, if they pulled all their loot . . . that'd be game over, now wouldn't it?"

Howard grimaces. Flexes his hand in front of him.

Feeling his unease, making me want badly to cleanse. Glance around for somewhere to kill my smoke. Nothing appropriate presents itself, his desk is bare and clearly unused. Save a box of Slim Jims, which I apparently scope hard, as the senator is now saying, "Help yourself, Decimal. Sustenance . . ."

I smirk but grab a couple, shove them in my pocket. Rip one open and bite off a bit with my back teeth. Gonna have to get some dentures. Fuck that, I'll get a grill. Solid fucking gold.

"Point being," the senator goes on, "they truly need our help here, and it's a must that we do all we can."

"I heard. I heard. What's the crisis, they got their big-ass boats and no doubt more supplies than all the rest of us combined. What's the drama?"

Senator tilts his head. There's something complex, perhaps delicate, he's trying to frame. "A prince and a princess are on their way to our shores."

"Sounds magical."

"They need protection, Decimal. There are many who would see harm come to them. Defectors. Traitors by the dozen. Oh, they're out there. On these shores and everywhere. Within these very walls."

I nod, chewing. "No doubt."

"And what's more, the House of Saud, their numbers, their great House, their numbers are diminished."

"As you mentioned."

"A brother and a sister."

"Uh-huh."

"But still . . . the line must be unbroken."

I stop chewing.

Howard looking at his hands. "*And the Lord said, be fruitful and multiply. Repopulate the Earth.*"

I wait for the rest of it. Really listening now.

n the dead arbor of the Conservatory Garden, outside the tent, I'm there with the shoulder bag and flight cases as the older medicine woman approaches me.

Fear not this old-world magic. The System surrounds me.

Lady appears even older in the daytime, but then who doesn't? Sleeping rough. She wears her multiple layers, on top a Brooklyn Nets T-shirt and her Parks Department windbreaker. Hair up in that practical bun.

"Well, it's the landlord. Mr. Decimal System. Did you bring your things, come to join us? Or did you come to put us on official notice?" She gets a solid gander at me, my crushed face. "Good Lord, what on earth happened to you?"

Set the bag down.

"Your teeth—"

"Miss Marcia. So you got these two cases of standard bleach. Sealed up tight, that's just how I got 'em, so you'll have to take my word for it on those. Should tell you, I don't know nothing about how that method works, I boil my stuff. As for this here." Unzip the bag, flip the top. "Preloaded single-dose one-shots."

Marcia is dumbstruck. I'm rolling up my sleeve.

"I don't know quite what to say."

"Pick a card." Indicating the syringes.

Marcia hesitates, plucks one. I take it from her.

"For your peace of mind." Spike myself in the crook

of the elbow, depress the little plunger. Mind you: they're *sealed*. So it's all good. Were they not sealed . . .

"Oh, well, my . . . well, that's not needed."

I fold up the arm. "Would've been one of the oldest tricks in the American playbook, Miss Marcia. You know your history, teach. Be smart."

"I don't follow you."

"Government medicine? Think Tuskegee. Or those TB blankets Custer gave old Sitting Bull's people."

"I'm not positive that was Sitting Bull—"

"Wounded Knee, whatever. You see what I'm saying."

She shakes her head. "Yes, of course. I'm afraid I'm at a bit of a loss, this is just so very . . . kind."

Clearing my throat, I roll down my sleeve and button up. "Yeah, well. Use in good health, heard. How's your girl doing?"

"Poorly. She'll certainly be better now. I don't know if she could have made it another seventy-two hours, to be honest. Mr. Decimal . . ."

"You'll be hearing from me, Miss Marcia. Don't sugar me. And don't kid yourself like this is a regular thing. Quid pro motherfucking quo, ya heard?"

"Understood. I wish we had greater means to thank you, Mr. Decimal."

"Don't worry yourself about that, no doubt I'll be looking in on you soon enough."

"Mr. Decimal, we were about to eat, if you'd care to . . ."

But I'm already heading away. Duck into the Tunnel of Terror to check on Hakim Stanley and his bullet hole.

Swerve past the sentries at the Vanderbilt Gate without incident and I'm down the block, mopping my mitts free of jungle dust with that good Purell™.

Chinese truck loitering in front of the old high school on Madison and 106th. Driver chewing on a toothpick, raises his eyebrows as I lurch at him.

"Deal, my brother," I say in Mandarin, "so here it is." Drop a plastic CVS bag in his lap, which rattles like a rainstick. "You got your Percocet, your Oxycodone, Valium, Demerol, Viagra, penicillin . . . just a grab bag, I got whatever was handy." They like their Viagra, these Chinese, what with all their comfort girls.

Hope I didn't do more than concuss the hospital pharmacist. For real, though, they should have better security, way too sloppy for a military facility.

Dude nods.

"All right." I toss a Vicodin down my beak, just cause why the fuck not. The world's already ended. Plus, my face hurts like a bitch. Dry swallow. "You gentlemen headed back downtown?" I ask. "Mind if I grab a ride?"

Chinese man indicates the back with a toss of his head. As I'm swinging up and in, something else occurs.

"Y'all know a dentist still up and running?"

―――――――――

Former HSBC bank lobby on 40th Street, windows intact. Chinese dropped me off a block south and I slid on up there with panache. Got a fair view of the library looking north.

Thanks be to Jah: despite the loss of my overcoat I am still in possession of two pistols, the diver's knife strapped to my knee, two bottles of Purell™ (bit worrisome there—cause that's low), my pills, one of which I pop now.

As well I possess the three Slim Jims, and it occurs I haven't eaten anything save the fourth Slimmy in two days. This is not unusual. I pull back the plastic and gnaw at the thing, but between the sand and the item's extreme staleness, once I'm able to get a fragment down I immediately vomit it back up. Expecting to see the sand though none appears present.

Mop at my mouth with a glossy brochure for 0% mortgages. Gumming it. My mouth straight fucked. So much for that, the whole eating thing. Upside being: elimination of possible food-borne bacteria. Salmonella and the like.

Down East Broadway in a decrepit dental clinic, I got fit for a set of front teeth. Thug fashion dot-com. Doctor explained he could make a cast but I'd have to see a Jew goldsmith up 47th to get the shit done proper.

Oh yeah, they're still there. Somebody's gotta service the Russians, who still can't shake their thing for bling. Swung by and got something cast on the spot.

Press the set of teeth into place now. There's a lot of

blood but I manage to get 'em in there good, take a couple experimental air-bites. Slick.

Now far more urgently: what motherfuckers want Dewey Decimal dead? Who wanna violate my block?

Cyna-corp bitches top this list, that's for positive. But are they that clumsy? Tempted to say yes . . . boys coming with the frequent beat-down, such as the unfortunate run-in yesterday in Chinatown . . . but a straight-up assassination? I'm Howard's boy, for better or worse, and that's no small thing. Big man is quite aware of the tensions between myself and my former classmates, and a gangland-style rub-out wouldn't sit nice. Despite their autonomy, he's still top dog on the island, and in order to operate you need his good love.

The Chinese? Unless I gravely misread those people, we have a pretty comfortable understanding. They'd be tossing aside a valuable relationship, and those cool cats are pragmatic to a fault.

Koreans? Those people don't stick their nizzles out unless really provoked. And I reckon we're straight, regarding the static of last year. I did all I could, and I figure they know that.

Russians? Ukrainians? Despite our past issues, I bet I'm pretty square with that mob as well. Plus, their effectiveness is on the wane, and they've been getting steadily shouldered out by our Asiatic brothers. Just sheer numbers doing the work.

Dewey Decimal. Like usual. Keep banging—down by law, and yet still tethered to the man. It's a fuck of a spot.

Scoping the entryway, can't see much directly since my view is blocked by columns, but I spot no vehicles on the street, save the hollowed-out FreshDirect truck that's been there since the Valentine's Occurrence.

Peep deeper . . . say what now? Somebody's landed a chopper on the roof, or more correctly the entryway over-hang, which is flat enough to accommodate this.

Still, it seems a pretty fucking unlikely spot, and I've certainly never seen anything perched up there before.

Can't make out much of shit except for the bird is matte-black, probably not military . . . could be Cyna-corp, sure, but then again, it could be almost anybody.

Toss a brick in this town and you'll hit a chopper, no doubt . . . but to park one on top of my crib? Be a tough bit of pilotry. And it just vibes weird.

Only reason for it I can figure is the obvious: in order to gain access through the roof. Which, once up there, could be very easily done.

Shoulda sealed that shit from the jump. Shoulda woulda coulda. But then again, the roof is a handy spot from which to throw a body off should the need arise, so I never gave securing the doors much consideration.

Sigh. We live and learn, y'all.

What if they're fucking with the books? That's my main thing. They'd best not be fucking with the books. So much yet to be done . . .

Que sera. I'll get in there and clean things up. In the meantime, best to keep my head down and get on with im-mediate business.

Now this Saudi bit of cray-cray on my docket. My inbox sits heavy with that illness. What's cracking: I have been tasked with providing security for two surviving members of the House of Saud, who are apparently being brought in by sea.

Fraternal twins. Brother-and-sister team like. Presum-ably with the intention of taking up residence with the rest of their ilk here at the Ark.

And then there's the part about a fertility clinic.

The senator could barely cough this bit out, as if too distasteful, even for such a bent motherfucker.

Two by two, that's how it worked, right? The Ark. Biblical shit.

Breeding. That was it. *Inter*breeding. Spitting out sheiks with two heads and whatnot, under natural circumstances.

Howard had further details, though again, it pained him greatly and required many scriptural tangents with which I would never bore a true friend.

Apparently, a military/medical/industrial-complex-financed doctor has sussed a method of harvesting an embryo, and combing out any genetic imperfections brought on by an unholy thing like interbreeding. No earthly idea as to what purpose this rather foul science serves, but I reckon here's a situation in which you might apply it, if you were twisted enough.

The term *comb*, when applied to a discussion of human biology . . . somehow makes a man squirm, i.e., mother/son, father/daughter/brother/sister . . . healthy baby.

Some shit ain't right by any kinda measure.

Howard had more to say. It was crucial to good relations that the US of A demonstrate its continued can-do solvency, its continued superior know-how, by offering this humble service to the sheiks. Apparently, nobody else has the formula for a clean interbreed . . . and what's more, nobody will host the Saudis. So there's that.

Dig it: this Saudi dimension is a real conundrum, as far as I'm concerned, strictly on a personal tip. Cause damn if I didn't spend half of my adult life getting shot at, blown up, cut, beat, and tortured by elements entirely or partially funded or otherwise encouraged by that particular royal family.

So what's the percentage in seeing them carry on into the New Era?

The senator is crafty above all things and of course he knows this well. Speculation: there's an angle here I'm not feeling beyond pleasing one's creditors.

But what do I know: I'm just the help.

Fuck me, the mind gets going on that one. I'm figuring the story is too sick to not be real.

Tonight. Saudis coming in under cover of darkness. I'm to be at the waterfront approx three a.m. to intercept the royals. Me running point . . . and Cyna-corp representing too, with their boys for cover. Oh joy.

Why me?

It's not a solid call. Straight sloppy. The senator has gotta know I'm slipping quick. First impression: setup. Though I don't know why—or who exactly is getting set up. I'm hardly worth the effort in the larger world of the Coalition.

Much mess to sink a foot into. But I gotta be me.

In order to intercept the Saudi twins, I had quickly formulated, and pitched, a simple plan. Seemed to pass muster and, as I understood it, is in the implementation process. Hackneyed and ad hoc as the shit is. Another case for the setup vibe.

Strip. Hooker bath, Purell™ head to toe.

Set my watch. Roll up my suit jacket, bunk down as best I can, taking care to move clear of the small patch of my own puke. Place the C-4 a safe distance away lest any of my parasomatic tendencies should manifest.

Requested Chip bring me a blanket, freezing as fuck in here. Doesn't look like he'll be coming back though.

Rain kicks up again, sudden and violent, then quieting, a lullaby drone against the glass.

Gingerly lift out my mouthpiece. Wrap up a bit of gauze, slip it under my upper lip. Reckon that'll absorb the slow bleed, and it's comfortable to sleep with . . .

Don't even take off my shoes and I'm out like a child, under a bank of blank ATMs.

The follow-up story regarding myself, the Boogie Oogie Man, went unreported and was perhaps less feel-good. The beat-down I suffered at the hands of fellow Young Skulls, of which I was a junior member, the day the story hit the newsstands. Simply for having gone to the cops at all. Never mind the fact that I didn't actually go to the cops: I was taken in for attempted assault on a couple of Glory Stompers, with possession of a switchblade and a couple of blunts.

Nick Deluccia, then a police detective angling for captain, later the founder of the outfit that evolved into Cyna-corp . . . Nick pretty much squeezed the skinny out of me, regarding the Bronx Child Raper.

Being a brilliant and ruthlessly ambitious cop with a near psychic understanding of an individual's soft spots, he smelled that Dubois fuck on me and latched on like a tick till I spilled. Plied me with candy and snacks.

Quit the precinct shitting-in-my-Jordaches scared, had to beg the uniforms not to give me a ride home in a squad car, which would have spelled instant fucking death. If not from a local gang, my father would I'm sure have been happy to rock honors. Dad had been sporadically trying to kill me since I popped out the womb.

Yo, I had no qualms about giving up the sicko who fucked and killed a couple of my buddies, it wasn't that. It was, and is, inner-city law number one: Don't be a rat. Don't be a fucking snitch. No matter what.

Snitch is a permanent designation, that's a bad-news tattoo can't no man remove. That's for life. There are very few crimes more egregious. Child-raping being the only one that comes to mind. Sort of a catch-22, huh?

So a young buck needed protection. I found that in the form of the

Police Athletic League, started to spend more time in Harlem where those kids would hoop. And once Deluccia made captain, I was, via his sponsorship, brought into the Police Cadet Corps.

From there it was a just a simple hop-skip over to the military, to which I was apparently well suited (and via Nick, well-connected for a ghetto boy). Spent so much time in the desert that I became known as a bit of an aficionado, and the filthier arm of the NSA reached out and touched me. Lost contact with Deluccia for a while, heard he had moved into private security after a famously disastrous drug bust left a bunch of bystanders dead more or less forced him out of public office. It was just prior to Gulf War 3.0 that he contacted me and offered me a position in his start-up company, Cyna-corp. Private military-contracting stuff. Seemed simple enough and paid vastly more than the conventional civilian military, why say no to that?

From there I jumped from locale to locale, the view getting progressively dimmer, until the morning of February 15, when I woke up in the New York Public Library, with no name, a strict System, brand-new job. And a fresh canvas. Upon which I swore I would never splatter blood.

Cop to it. This was a promise I broke within ten days.

Pier 54 juts unenthusiastically out of Manhattan into the sickly Hudson, steady rain slapping the nondescript brown runway, hardly able to draw the eye, once overgrown with greenery until the air killed nearly all but the hardiest of plant life.

If you've noticed this place at all, you've observed a decommissioned strip at the juncture of Little West 12th Street and 11th Avenue, approximately.

Perhaps you've wondered when the city intended to either incorporate it into the sprawl that the Highline had become, or simply tear it down—and then likely you went on about your business.

But this spot has roots. Deep history. And at the moment it's lit up like a movie set, with plenty nuff hustle and bustle.

With the desolation that was once the moneyed Meatpacking District to my back, I flip up a collar and try to square my shoulders against the chill and the wet. I consider the sad stretch of land. Ask myself, rhetorically, *Am I the last motherfucker standing who knows all this historical bullshit?*

The powerful lights of a medium-sized ocean liner are visible downriver, sparkling drowsily through the haze, swarmed by skittish choppers and what appear to be naval and UN frigates, as well as the overflowing garbage barges.

Note, as the System would have it, I make left turns until eleven a.m. The System doesn't give a shit if you've slept or not. The System is old-fashioned when it comes to the clock: after midnight it's a new day, folks, and prior to eleven a.m.—left turns.

Scope my watch: 3:52 in the a.m. Me thinking, *Damn.* Chewing my cud, knowing that gristle I'm gargling is a product of my misfiring brain machine, and wondering if that makes any difference, cause motherfucker if it doesn't feel like I deep-throated a sandcastle.

What was I saying, y'all? Oh yeah—mad history. Trivia is a fine distraction, and getting back to it—no less a celebrity sea vessel than the *Titanic* herself moored here in this very place once upon a time, Pier 54 serving as the dock of choice for the White Star and many other storied Atlantic lines. Later on, the *Queen Mary.* And prior, probably a slave ship or two.

My DNA smells that tar, the human shit (so much, so many bugs spread through fecal/urine contamination), the saltwater. It's encoded—if you can't smell this, you're not breathing air. Like I said: deep, dark history.

But I was just . . .

Even in this chilly drizzle, a droplet of what is unmistakably sweat slides across my eyeball. Fuck. I paw at it . . . talking about . . . oh yes, talking about historical shit, historical boats. Not so sure anymore what I was . . . maybe the *Titanic* survivors they brought to this joint, just the survivors. Somehow less sexy. Anyhow. Events of significance, now lost in the ether. Rally, Decimal. Brain flirting with a Semi-Freddo. Cannot afford a vulnerable facade. Gotta flex and floss.

Assess the mess. It's quite an assembly hereabouts, the number of boots on the ground indicating serious static anticipated. I am tempted for a moment to simply turn around and break the fuck out of here, but I hold steady.

Fucking Howard. Again my gut cries nasty stitch-up. I shouldn't be running the Special Olympics fifty-yard dash, let alone an op of this apparent magnitude.

Megawatt industrial lamps have been set up, giving the scene a weirdly overlit juju. At a glance it's between thirty and forty men, multiple armored vehicles, JLTVs, open jeeps, even a Stryker . . . and more weaponry than an old-fashioned gun show . . . antiaircraft cannons, shoulder-mounted surface-to-air doodads, snipers up on the elevated track that used to be the Highline.

Should make me jumpy, but I chalk this display up to appearances rather than anything else. Like a North Korean Sunday parade.

Yeah. Ass-deep in Cyna-corp. That's what puts me on edge, not the show of force as such. The insectile bodysuits, nearly everybody tricked out in those spooky masks. Everything about these folks says money, and preemptive aggression.

A faceless sentry scans my State Department laminate.

Cyna-corp and I. Me and Cyna-corp. Officially, we have no beef. Unofficially? I am considered a hostile, a traitor. Having, from their perspective, been one of their own who betrayed them two or three times minimum. If they knew the half of it.

Judging from my dustup yesterday morning, they just might.

My head is no less fucked up than it was five hours ago. Point of fact, my lips are even more swollen, engorged, like I've had some cheap work done. My cheekbone aches profoundly. Not exactly shining out over here.

Returning my badge, the soldier throws a half-assed salute, and even this manages to radiate contempt. I squint at that familiar logo, the double C swoop above his breast.

My gaze strafes the vicinity. I steady a tremulous hand with the other, focus on my breath. Another aspect of the scene bothers me. No other agency is represented, save the useless UN weekenders, themselves cowering in their ridiculous blue and white golf carts.

A young MP, upon clocking me, is suddenly mesmerized by his fingernails.

Three burgundy Escalades sit curbside, hanging back, waiting on my signal. Okay, there's that at least. I finger the walkie-talkie in my jacket pocket.

So here am I, Howard's main boy, disgraced deserter, a touch shaky, balls high in a box of snakes. Fucking Clarence.

Control what I can, that's my word. Think System. Purell™ up, pop a blue one. Run my tongue over my new front teeth . . . Watch the back. Stay hard. Be a boss. Allegiances shifty. Picking at whatever paltry garbage remains, and it's an ever-diminishing pile . . .

I won't lie, y'all. Color me intimidated. Color me pissed the fuck off to have had this sitch misrepresented to me. Again consider beating cheeks.

I half turn (left) to confirm that my personal ride hasn't slunk away—enjoy a split second of relief in spotting the vehicle again.

This, as something hard and cold is jammed into my kidneys.

"Morning, fuckwad." It's a voice I am not likely to forget, that degree of gravel, rock salt on sandpaper. "What's up with the face? Problems at home?"

A masked man looms, tall and bemuscled beyond your average grunt. Fuck me if this isn't the third time this bitch has crept on me unawares. I'd fear I'm softening but I know Scratch to be supernaturally smooth.

Play it mellow: "What's good, Scratchy. Hot to see you again so soon. Mind getting your cock off the suit?" My eyes drop to the matte-black machine pistol shoved into my thorax.

Scratch gives it another five seconds. Hear him breathing through that filter.

"Got no idea how close you are. You smell the grave, fucknut?"

I pause, make like I'm considering that, say, "Na, don't smell nothing save your nasty crack. 'S'probably your upper lip. Take that gun away, now, play nice. Made your point, I won't step to you, Scratch. You're a for-rizzle top, you're a big man."

He then jams the gun even deeper before withdrawing it. Inwardly I wince but don't allow this to inform my expression, which I hope communicates boredom and superior strength, despite the obvious fact that dude could crush me in a jiffy should he be so inclined. Bitch is big.

Scratchy snorts like he's about to spit. Says, "So. Calling shots on this one, soldier? That's the sit rep? Huh? Seems like you don't care who you're working for as long as that money's green. A real patriot."

"Shit. Starting to figure me out, Scratch. You continue to impress, son, going places for sure. Plus, you'd know all about that mercenary mind-set, right? You wrote the handbook on that steez."

A molded rubber finger flicks my SD laminate. Strokes it, wipes away the brownish water, saying: "Look at you, with your fake gold teeth, hiding behind this dusty Federale stuff. Huh? You're batting for the wrong fucking team. Not much left of that office, huh? Buncha ghosts floating around moaning about the way we were. No real power there. No way. Not no more." He drops the lammie and pokes his in-dex finger into my neck, hard. "Not that we'd have you back, you piece-of-shit turncoat. Rat-ass motherfucker."

Deflect his hand. I step sideways (left), put him between myself and the bulk of the soldiers. Best they can do now is shoot me in the back, I reckon, thinking about those snipers.

"You talking like I'm a joiner, man, but I never did no work for nobody but myself, Scratch, and I am doing just fine. But dig, the concern is appreciated. Your crew on the other hand?" I tsk tsk, a damn shame. "A dying breed. Shit's natural selection, ya heard? Plus: we're supposed to be on the same side."

"Fuck you."

I carry on: "You wanna talk about Washington got no more mojo? Well, y'all clowns are on motherfucking life sup-port, DNR style. Just ain't competitive no more. Losing all your best gigs to the new kids . . . Yo, I understand, Scratch, you get tired, man . . . These Chinese, son, they got mad en-ergy . . . and they just keeping coming . . ."

Scratch gets yet further in my muzzle, snarly. "The way I see it, you're already dead. Huh? We got a running bet back at HQ over when you're going to figure it out—sneak away and dig yourself a hole, stop wasting good citizens' time."

The barrel of his old-school MAC-11 returns to my mid-section. It's '90s ghetto kit, a drive-by prop. Known to jam or misfire.

Reflexively, I slide a hand into my jacket, touch the butt of the Sig .357, and this action excites Scratch enormously.

"You gonna draw on me, sergeant major? You gonna draw on me now, right here?" he rasps, voice cracking like a teenager, pushing his jaw further into my personal space. "Just give me a reason to air you out and I can die a happy man. Do yourself a favor, buddy. Huh? Spare yourself some misery. Go ahead and draw on me."

Fluttering my eyelids against the precip, I show the man what remains of my yellowed chompers, or the absence thereof.

By now I'm pretty sure he's acting on his own. Getting emotional like that. So I relax a touch. "Scratch, where is the *love* tonight? I'm stung, fam. We go back, I thought we was tight. Trying to say this thing we got is over?"

The bigger man isn't giving a centimeter, him hissing, "The moment you stop looking over your shoulder, I'm gonna be there, Decimal. It'll be my personal . . ."

He keeps spieling in this vein. Thing about it is: I believe him. Which is an issue.

Disconcerting talking to somebody when you can't see lips move. Much less having never seen his face.

Yeah. Old Scratch has grown into a thorn I ignore at my peril.

There's that particular cocktail of mixed emotions when you know the man you're looking at is gonna have to die. Add a couple degrees of bitter when it's you who's gonna have to do the duty. Y'all know what I'm spraying. God bless you if you don't.

Yes sir. A mash-up of adrenaline-fueled impatience, let's just do this fucking thing, and the depressing inevitability of it all.

Look south. The cruise ship is nearing, everybody getting a better look at the monstrosity.

Christ on a crepe. That's no commercial pleasure cruiser. I hear walkie-talkie chatter amongst the security. Folks checking their weapons or just plain gawking. Try to discreetly shake the sand out of my sleeve . . .

By the lights of its escorts I can make out the vessel's name: *PRINCE ABDULAZIZ*. I'm looking at a privately owned boat, a yacht if something of this mass can be termed such, and it's an obscenity. Turning now, apparently with huge effort, into the docking area. Though little can be heard over the roar of multiple engines and the churning of displaced sludge and water, I can see the reception committee stirring, exchanging glances.

Very few have witnessed anything like this, even those having done time in the UAE or some such place, and that's most of us on this dock. Moodily, I pop yet another pill.

Scratch still talking low, saying, ". . . in your sleep, junkie, any fucking night of the week, Decimal. You might as well—"

Cut him off: "Damn, Scratch, you still here? Okay, let's wrap up this convo, my man. No need to butter me further, star, I'm all yours. Plenty of time to kick me on my way back down." Wink at his mask.

Man snorts again. "You'll get yours, Decimal. I'm not worried." Thus sayeth Scratch, his attention diverted to the appalling *Prince Abdulaziz* now as well. He taps his helmet. "Not worried at all." Then, "Copy that," he says into an unseen microphone.

Pat the man, gentle on his beefy shoulder. GI fucking Joe. "Sure you're right, son. On the flip then."

Step left around Scratchy, him back on the job too, jabbering staccato into the built-in 'com on his headpiece . . . Set to limping toward the docking area, I raise my laminate. Slip on the soaked leather soles of my wingtips, regain and push forward into the bright staging area.

Trying to clear my tract, what for the fucking sand . . .

"State Department! To me, folks, I'm on point!" I call, and the boys fade back.

The choppers flanking the outsize boat bank away, take up hover positions. The smaller gunboats peel off as well.

The *Abdulaziz* looms, nautical Arabic bling writ supersized, its searchlights making the scene vibe Hollywood on Oscar night. I'm looking everywhere, rain obscuring certain details, thinking these Saudi people must have their own security here . . . Saudi Mabahith or whatever . . . but I'm unable to make a determination. Take a moment to apply Purell™. When did I have my last pill? Fuck it, safety first—I down another.

So yeah: fuck it. Guess I'm just gonna wing this suicide gig, which is how I tend to roll anyhow. Cause most of the time the only way out of shit is to go straight through it.

A mobile stairwell with *DELTA* emblazoned on the side is shoved toward the edge of the dock as the ship draws forward like a glacier. I figure what the hell, spin left, clamber up the stairs, Astroturf carpet waterlogged. Turn (left) to face the troops. At random I signal a pair of soldiers closest to my position.

"Listen up! You two up here with me, let's go! Everybody else, back up and keep your eyes open!"

The men hesitate. One turns slightly in the direction of Scratchy, standing on top of an armored car, arms folded. The situation wobbles.

"Motherfuckers!" I holler, my throat fatigued with all the sand. "Whatever personal issues you may have with my ass, fact is I am running point on this operation on behalf of the State Department and the United States Senate body, et cetera. Whose desire is y'all motherfuckers follow my orders, ya heard me now?"

Still, one or three ass-clowns look to Scratchy. Unbelievable. Other heads turning, domino style. Losing ground.

Scratch gives an exaggerated bow in my direction, extending his hands as if in supplication. Asshole taking his time with it. Energy shifts back toward my end of the court.

The boys jog up the steps as the behemoth scrapes the rubber siding on the dock, water churning, splashing up the edges of the pier. River's a fuck of a lot higher than it used to be since Greenland slid completely off the map. Though folks like the senator and his catatonic wife will tell you it's just been an unusually precipitous winter. Still these fucks cling to that tired rap, as if it freaking matters anymore.

Man below pushing the stairs flush with the area where the gangplank would normally extend, and squinting through the nasty wet I get my first look at a quartet of Saudis onboard. Red berets and digital camo. A short, puffy guy, maybe midfifties, standing slighting in front, sporting a highly structured goatee and red brassard around his arm, this is clearly the ranking officer. All cradle assault rifles.

Back it up. Just not getting the logic of putting Dewey Decimal in charge of this here op, you'd expect at the very least some kinda . . . diplomatic welcome, this being a state visit kind of deal, after all . . . What's clear is I'm here for a reason and am likely to get fucked. I am very aware of my pawn status as I raise my hands in . . . what? Do I salute? Who are these guys?

Just cause I speak the language don't mean I can rock the protocol, especially with royalty. Trying to summon up my most sincere look of pleasure, and attempting to not imagine the sheer tonnage of foreign bacteria swarming off the boat, nibbling eagerly at my immune system . . .

Over the grinding boat motors I greet them in standard Arabic, put a foot on the boat. "*Ahlan wa sahlan*, welcome to New York City, gentlemen! We have—"

Whoopsie daisy. Scuffle as two soldiers quick-step around the goatee, seize both my arms, and attempt to force me to the ground, me saying, "Whoa now, hold up, hold up . . ."

Cyna-corp guys overdo it as usual, commence hollering and raising their guns sideways like they do, me trying to dial it back, "Stand the fuck down! Stand down, gentlemen!"

The Saudis are wrestling with me, we're skating all over the slick deck, but I lock my knee and am somehow able to remain standing, steering things leftwise. Keeping it in Arabic, saying into my armpit, "Gentlemen. I am State Department, proxy for US Senator Howard. Any misunderstanding—"

"Tell your men to put away their weapons," says the goatee. Quiet, calm like that.

Me saying, "All right. All right. Let's everybody relax." The Cyna-corp boys stay aggro and I do a little lopsided dance, attempting to simultaneously shuck the Saudis and get a hand on each of my guys, repeating in English, "Relax, you fucks."

"Okay," says the goatee mildly, barely moving his mouth. His people withdraw.

I'm catching my breath. "Sir, we're not—"

"They will need to disarm," he interrupts, indicating the boys.

I just figured out what the issue is with his mug: the man is wrinkle free, his flesh like an infant, vibing major Botox. His affect is waxy and flat, sizing me up, my suit, the rubber gloves . . .

"I'm sorry, we can't do that just yet." Present my laminate. "As I was saying . . ."

"Where is the senator? Where is our escort?"

See what I'm talking about? This looks more and more

like a straight setup. Mental note to have a word with Howard, should I scrape out of this one. Say, "Getting off on the wrong foot here, gentlemen. I represent the senator's office, and in this capacity—"

"To send a *civilian*. Can you imagine?" Goatee sighs, looking at my front teeth. "And a Negro as well. So very . . ." Words fail him. Man wags his head.

I grimace and try to let that jive float. "Yes sir, all apologies. If it improves your dim view of the scene I am not a civilian. And the transportation is arranged, as specified . . ." I lean back, lids fluttering against the spray, hold up two fingers in the direction of the street. All Escalades start rolling forward.

Goatee surveys the vehicles, regards the mob on the dock, mouth slightly open, brow spookily still. He has a gigantic mole on his cheekbone from which thick hairs protrude. Wiping his unlined forehead with a handkerchief, he glances up at the choppers, seems to be mouthing something. Then faces me head-on, forced to angle his face up to compensate for the perhaps nine-inch height differential. Gazing long and deep into my eyes for what seems like a fucking age. I'm freezing, drenched, and feeling the aftereffects of my wrestling match. But for all this I'm still braced for any fucking thing. Fully expecting a bullet to the dome, good night and goodbye. Why not?

"Okay," he says finally. "Stand aside."

appens fast as fuck, and per the plan.

Doorway pops open and out come two figures, wrapped cap to toe in black and white burqas, respectively. A Saudi soldier produces a huge umbrella with a Hermès logo, hustles them down the stairs and into one of the Escalades.

Within seconds, an identical pair materializes, black and white outfits, indistinguishable from the first. They too are shielded against the elements with a designer parasol, this one by Moschino, and guided off the vessel and into the second Escalade.

My ride pulls forward, boy Chip at the helm. Gives a little nod.

Yet a third pair of Saudis appear, presumably one male and one female, but who can say for sure, tricked out in that contrasting white and black.

"Fi amanullah," says the goatee to me flatly. His insincerity is palpable.

No time to indulge a hater. I'd be paralyzed should I try to address 'em all.

Lacking a fancy umbrella, I simply grab the two hooded royals, rotate left, and guide them down the steps but quick, the three of us followed by a perspiring Saudi security officer, doing the tango with a vast Chanel umbrella.

"Your Highnesses," I say to the shrouds, and get nothing back. The one in white, presumably male, flinches as rain hits his head garb.

The officer is unable to get that umbrella open before I'm

bundling the three of them into the back of the vehicle. Can already tell this guy will be a problem, he radiates a worryingly hapless vibe, and what makes me think this might be purposeful on somebody's part?

Pirouette left and commence sliding in the passenger seat, pulling out the walkie-talkie. Freeze as I clock:

A bizarre sight now—a for-real civilian in for-real civilian duds, bareheaded and bald, a park squatter no doubt, one of Miss Marcia's, a female (I think), unfurling a handmade sign, *THOSE WHO CANNOT REMEMBER THE PAST R DOOMED TO*—I know the passage, Santayana from his *Reason in Common Sense*, oft misquoted, and Scratch is approaching her, vibing bad bad bad, I've got the door open and am halfway out into the rain yelling, "No, no, no!" unheard over the choppers and vehicles peeling out . . .

Scratch has his Kel-Tec P-11 up, popping the female in the back of the neck, and she slaps wet concrete quick like a bag of rocks.

Scratch just dug his own plot. You don't do noncombatants, that's just the golden rule. Dude just jumped the line VIP style, made the tippity top of my shit hit list. But not today, cause I'm working, even as things get swervy, feeling ill . . .

"Go! We must go!" the sweaty Saudi soldier is yapping at me and I realize he's been doing so for some time. I shut out what I've just seen re: Scratch, file it for future processing, Scratch and a growing number of soldiers strolling casually toward a group of maybe eight unmasked civilians across 11th Avenue, bailing on their posts, what the fuck, paramilitary breaking into a light jog as the civies start to turn one by one, make a break for it . . .

"Hold your positions! That's an order!" My voice thrashed, I say fuck it. Slide back in the Caddy.

"Diversion." The Saudi is beside himself, straining his neck to peer backward at the ship, where his boss is looking toward the site of the shooting. The cloaked pair sit stock-still. "Oh, this is what they do. For the love of God, let's move."

Snap to, Decimal. Reflections come later. I depress the talk button on my walkie, light-headed, go on autopilot, hearing myself say: "All right, y'all, roll out in order, stick to your route and don't go crazy with the wet roads."

One after another, the vehicles continue reversing out of the dock area, tires squealing.

I watch cars one and two take off in opposite directions— they've got their routing and we've got our System-friendly run.

Chip hits it, left up 10th Avenue, a sickening left around a traffic circle, left again south down 11th, losing traction slightly . . .

"Fucking slow down," I tell the man at the wheel. My lips are numb. Still on autopilot.

As we rip past Gansevoort I try to get a look at the doomed civies (what the fuck are they *doing?*), but we're moving too fast . . .

Hairpin left onto Horatio, driver showing no sign of having heard me, and I decide that's totally fine. Bounce the short blocks to Greenwich Street/9th Avenue, cut left, and shoot north.

At 35th Street we take the left, one block and another left onto Dyer, another block and we careen onto 34th Street, eastbound.

Three vehicles. The designated safe house a former NYPD precinct down on Varick. Only myself, the senator, and Chip know this. Fair enough, so far, so good.

NATHAN LARSON ✳ 105

As plans go, I'd give this one a C+. Not bad. Not great. But it's an oldie and I reckon it's worked more than it's failed, so why not give it a whirl. Something quaint about this approach.

Three cars, three targets. It's barrio classico. We called it the Monty Hall, a.k.a. the street version/tourist trap known as "Three-Card Monte." In the Philippines they call it "Meatball." Or my personal favorite—"Find the Lady." Seems like you've got a good shot at hitting the prize, am I right? Doesn't seem so tough. One in three odds, right?

Wrong, fuck-o.

Bam, past the shell of Madison Square Garden, open-air deflated like a soufflé, steam rising out the gaping hole in the roof.

The setup here is fundamental. I'm assuming that hostile entities are monitoring all this with the intention of disrupting events. Including any shortwave radios. Working under this presumption, we have established a shill, a Saudi agent who will be on the horn calling out misinformation. He's been at work, supposedly, since yesterday evening, tossing out tasty morsels to attract the rodentia.

This accomplished, we have the shill "flip one card," and let whoever's listening know which vehicle does *not* contain the royals.

Bump over 5th Avenue, traffic lights blinking yellow, yellow, yellow . . . you still see a working light from time to time. Hard rain slaps the windshield.

Let's say you're the mark, and you buy it. Eliminate that vehicle as a possible target for whatever it is you've got in mind. You're going to reckon you've got a 50/50 chance you're gonna to pick the correct vehicle out of the remaining two.

But bitches—this is not mathematically correct. In fact,

you have a 66.6 percent chance (two out of three) that your next selection will be the *wrong* vehicle.*

It's human nature to fall for this one. It's a short con with a lot of solid psychology at play. The brain and the heart want to believe we have not been nudged into a tighter spot, want to believe the odds remain the same once one unit is removed as a possibility. Interestingly, sociopaths and individuals whose "conscious" centers are somehow compromised tend to not be suckered by "Find the Lady." Which must mean there's hope for this black soul, cause in my youth I lost mad loot to some of those hustlers up on 149th Street.

You've got to believe in the basic goodness of humanity to get duped by this here scam.

Quite a digression. And all of course for naught should the mark just opt to . . .

This idea sounding shittier by the minute. Clearly I am not myself.

The Saudi-in-back's radio squawks, I can't quite make it out, but it's clearly somebody in distress, a couple of numbers repeated franticly in Arabic . . . I gotta wonder what channel he's on, cause I'm not receiving on my walkie. An uneasy sensation.

"God protect us. The first car has been destroyed by an explosive."

As I was saying, you always have the option of just flipping all three cards. Or in this case . . .

See, I wouldn't put me in charge of some way-heavy shit like this. I model my grand plan on a tourist scam? This is a setup.

---

* Don't just take my word as bond: for more on this controversial theorem I refer you to DD classification code 519 (the "probability" subheading of 510 "mathematics") . . . and for the layperson I recommend Jason Rosenhouse's excellent The Monty Hill Problem (Oxford University Press, 2009).

Me saying, "Fuck. Hit it, hit . . ."

Making some on-the-spot adjustments to my shitty "plan" in light of this new development. Stitch-up detector at max. Nobody should have sanctioned this. I was in an altered state when I made the proposal. It's madness.

Swerving crazily to dodge a massive crater in the middle of Madison Avenue, two wheels up and off for a heartbeat, then on all fours again, regaining 34th Street . . .

"Left, left, stay left, man . . ." not wanting to buck the System, not ever and especially not now, under these circumstances. "If you gotta duck something, stay left."

Chip throws a look at me. He was of course aware of my preferences in terms of System-adherent travel, but in this situation he's reckoning yours truly is certifiable. He's not wrong.

Dig: didn't actually believe somebody would try and hit us, hence my Tonka toy plan. Again: why was it allowed to be implemented? Was this whole thing really my idea?

I spin and once again attempt to address the figures in the back flanking the panicking Saudi. I can't read them at all . . . in Arabic, "Your Highnesses, I want to assure you, God willing, I will deliver you safely to—" Then I see us so close to Park Avenue, and I do a quick calculation to stay System-correct, realize I have to steer Chip, me talking fast, "Gonna have to take the left onto Park, another left at 35th, and back around headed south . . . then at 33rd we turn into the underpass, ya heard?"

Fly into the turn at Park, the armed man in back reckons he can bypass me and appeal directly to the driver . . . chin-wagging in snotty-assed English: "It's very many laws of traffic, must we obey all this?"

Then great misfortune befalls the man, as his radio

crackles again, in Arabic I hear very clearly, ". . . *about three minutes, then take out both of them.*"

The royals bug out, jabbering and spitting.

Turn and regard the security dude, sitting between the two chattering mummies. Shit scared. Doing his best, I suppose, and it's never been good enough.

"Take out both of them?" I repeat, in Arabic.

The guy opens and closes his mouth, his face filling with blood. Either he's here to kill Chip and me, or to kill his own royals. Either way he's shit out of luck.

Reach up and turn on the interior light so we can all see each other better. One of the burqas is squawking a prayer of some sort.

"So shocking that an ugly American can speak your language, *habib*?" Lift the HK, direct it between his eyebrows. Say in Arabic, "There are higher laws than traffic laws. How about the laws of Allah?" Drag out the words, make a presto-genie-in-a-bottle flourish. Smile, wide, saying, "*Takbir*, put down your gun."

He capitulates immediately, like a punk, letting the cumbersome rifle fall to the floor . . .

The royals simmer down, still twittering. I try to vibe reassuring.

"What's your name, friend?" I say, congenial, focused now on the soldier.

"Faisal," says the man, peepers brimming.

Folks chewing on this breaking development as we three-sixty back onto Park southbound, another hairpin curve and we go careening into the Murray Hill Tunnel in the center of the avenue that ferries traffic underground, then up, above and around Grand Central . . . We scrape the concrete embankment but remain otherwise unharmed.

My man Chip recovers the road, accelerates down the incline and into the black of the partially flooded tunnel. Moving through two to four inches of water.

"Stop midway through the tunnel, Officer Chip."

We pick up speed. What the fuck is this? Stomach shifts.

"You heard? Pull over."

See him by the interior lighting, his jaw set, focus on keeping the vehicle moving as quickly as possible through this amount of water, no easy thing. Operating on higher orders. Still accelerating.

Sigh.

I withdraw my Beretta with my left hand, crossing my arms so I'm covering both the Saudi soldier and Chip, aware that by pointing a weapon at a Secret Serviceman I am now crossing over into unknown, yet sadly familiar, territory.

Chip begins grinding his teeth. It's the correct sound for this tableau.

"Stop the car, son. Do it."

We're not slowing down. The dip upward that will bring us above ground onto the Grand Central Viaduct proper (flying blind on that one, and hoping it's still intact, I'm really hoping this) is maybe four hundred feet out.

No choice but to go def con. Another sigh.

Boom, squeeze one off across Chip, over the steering wheel, the report stupid loud in the cabin of the Escalade. Female shriek from the back, short and sharp. Bullet making a nice clean penny-sized exit hole in his side window.

Good man, Chip, he doesn't exactly lose control of the vehicle, but we duck and weave. His yap hangs open, say ahh. I place the barrel lightly on his cheek, and he recoils a hair, disturbing a light dusting of dandruff on the shoulder of his blue poly blazer.

"Pull. Over. Now."

He finally digs the wisdom of doing so. Still, not an easy maneuver, fast as we're moving through this wet tunnel. Chip pumps the brakes as one should, still with that mouth ahhh, we're turning slightly as we skid across the creek, thankfully less water here at the head of the steep incline, coming to a reasonably controlled halt against the concrete wall, the front of the Escalade crumpling with a sensational slow-motion crunch and a white shower of sparks.

We're all thrown forward, I go to stabilize myself on the dash, Officer Faisal taking this moment to attempt some heroics, carpe diem, the man grasping the barrel of my HK, eyes flashing wild and hot. Damnit. Me saying, "Yo Faisal, my man. Cool out, that's just a bad idea."

Trying to reason with the guy, he's gotta know he has no control over this situation, jerking the pistol around like a tiny dog with a big bone. Another female shriek, the two hooded Saudis attempting to get as far away from Faisal as possible, tough in the confines of the backseat.

Chip wades into the action, getting his hand on the pistol too, though it's not clear what his intentions are. Me saying, "*Et tu*, Chip? Come on, y'all. This gonna affect everybody, so just . . ."

The Saudi gets his ring finger inside the trigger guard, wearing a determined grimace, I'm alarmed that dude may honestly be attempting to get himself killed, me trying to engage the safety with my thumb, my index finger trapped . . . but it's too late—as he gets another digit in the guard the hammer drops, *boom* goes the pistol, and Faisal leans back in the seat, hands folded neatly across his gut.

He's still got that cracked grin slapped across his mug, pair of burqas (burqi?) in the back both howling now, one frantically pawing at the lock on the door. An astonishing amount of blood is surging out of Faisal's midsection. Always more blood than you'd think.

Me thinking, *Fuck*. "Chip, we got any towels?"

Chip wags his head no, no, a fine cloud of skin cells coming off his scalp . . . I note he is clutching his leg.

"No towels?"

He leans forward, apparently wracked with pain. A knife handle protruding from his leg.

"Man, what happened there?"

Chip grimaces.

I flash on it. "What, you gonna stab me, son? Don't look like that panned out. I thought we were compadres, Chip. Saddens me. Reckon you hit an artery too." Consider grabbing his blazer, but instead I'm cursing and pulling off my jacket (my nice suit jacket, mind you. My *really* nice jacket.). I ball that fly stuff up, lean over the seat, and press it into the Saudi's stomach. "Hold that there, really fucking put pressure on it."

Faisal just takes the coat, lifts it parallel to his face, and looks at it, blood heaving out of his tummy. Okay, it's his life to lose, people, did I not try to do the right thing?

Turn to Chip once more and the jackass has a red cylinder in one hand, futzing with it . . . I recognize it as a thermite grenade and snatch it easily from his loose grasp.

"What is wrong with you fucking people?" I say this to the universe, really. Truly dismayed. I thought I had some kinda crew, but na.

Gotta get us out of this vehicle presto pronto. Holster my Beretta, pocket the grenade, and disengage all the door lockswith a heavy clunk, saying, "Everybody out."

Don't need much prompting. The duo of burqas go tumbling into a calf-high lake of rainwater and Christ knows what else. One is still sobbing, the female, and sinks to her knees. The other moves to attend to her, speaking fast and quiet in Arabic.

Well this is just fucking lovely. Vintage Decimal, setting alight both ends of the dynamite at once, cartoon Wile E. Coyote style. Either way—me and everybody else get burned. And inevitably I fuck up yet another buttery suit. Funny the stuff you think in moments of crisis.

Quick. Gonna have to corral the Saudis, a glance back at Faisal tells me the boy is nearly bled out. Gut shots are rough, pretty much sure to drain a man. Shucks, that's a real shame—but player had to go and be a funny guy, didn't he?

The female is having some kind of anxiety attack, and the male jaws rapidly at her. I address them both as I pull down my mask, lift my goggles, Purell™ out . . . fuck, standing water. Malaria . . . shake it off, me rapping to the twins, "Wouldn't y'all be more comfortable if you got those hoods off?"

Them cowering, female mewling . . . Me reckoning they can suit themselves. Come on, Decimal, speed it up.

"Listen, Your Highnesses—cool if I call y'all *Your Highnesses?*"

The pair appears to be bobbing their heads, yes, good.

"Getting on the same page. Reckon we all saw that, right? With your escort. That was raw and unfortunate and all, but it was some *accidental* shit. Dude more or less shot himself, can we agree on that?"

More skull-wagging.

"No international incident–level stuff, pretty clearly just some bad luck, people not thinking a situation through . . . Am I telling it like it was?"

Continuing to bob their heads, the two fall into perfect

NATHAN LARSON ✳ 113

sync, which looks a little silly. Holding out my hands, I pull on some fresh gloves. "Your Highnesses, I'm gonna ask you to hang tight while I get a handle on the lay of the land up in here . . ."

Okay, they're not going anywhere. Splish splash. Que pasa? I wheel (left), and it looks like Chip is out of the car and making a break for it.

Apparently he has quite severely damaged his right leg, which prevents him from really getting anywhere, struggling with that thing flaccid and heavy . . . it's a pathetic sight, the guy in far worse shape than me—and despite my limp I easily run his ass down before he even gets close to the incline leading out of the underpass.

Got the recently fired HK floppy in my fake hand, I just show it to him, grab him by the collar, spin (left), and drag him back to the fucked-up Escalade like a puppy. Slam him on the collapsed hood. Windshield wipers still swinging uselessly, side to side.

What to do with Chip, who is looking shaky but relatively together, save the skewered leg? Sets his hands on the back of his head, turning onto his cheek, breathing through his mouth. Boy seems to be expecting some handcuffs, so I oblige. Snap one end on his right wrist, pull him gently back into the cabin, and attempt to secure the other ring around the steering wheel.

When the boy realizes where I'm taking him, he digs in his heels to prevent me from doing this. That he wants away from the truck—this alone tells me mucho. Red lights ahoy.

Hurry it up. Pop a pill, bust out more Purell™. Lowering my mask, I lean on the motherfucker, saying, "You really thinking you gonna *stab* me? What's the story with you, son?"

Chip looking the other way, unresponsive.

Sigh. I proceed. I can't really hate on young Chip, I know I should but I always thought he was okay and the boy is clearly just trying to carry out a set of orders like the rest of us. "So, Chip, man of few words, I'll make it simple. Yo, jiggle your head yay or nay. Dig?"

Curt nod from the Secret Serviceman, no nonsense. He won't make eye contact. I wrench his wrist backward and get it clipped to the wheel. Kid makes a noise.

"Chip, look at me."

He does it. Can't be more than midtwenties, pimply mug. Shame about his skin. He's hyperventilating.

"Breathe easy, man. Just kick back, once we figure this out it's gonna all be good, I promise you that."

He seems to release his jaw muscles a bit.

"You got family? You got people?"

Chip searches my face for a moment, then nods, hesitant-like, as if it's a trick question. I readjust my goggles, cough. Tough to get oxygen.

"Wanna see them again?"

Nod.

"There a bomb on this car?"

Chip swallows, blinks. Reckon that's a yes.

"What makes it go boom, son?"

He's resolutely attempting to bring his training to bear. I can actually see him make the decision to not answer me. Mind you: he's a hard case, any motherfucker who gets a big sensitive muscle cut out of their mouths for God and country and holds it together, call him righteous hard. Or a head case.

Or a fanatic, which makes him more or less the same as the cat who got Chip's tongue.

I look to the Saudis, wiggle my flipper, shooing them.

"Y'all do me a favor and start walking back the other direction. Get away from the car, heard me? Bomb in the car."

They're scrambling through water, robes heavy and soaked at the hem. Return to Chip, continue, speaking low and quick, "Me, I don't care one way or the other, heard? What I don't appreciate is folks trying to clown me, cause it's insulting. What's the trigger on this bitch, Chip?"

Nothing from Chip, his mouth a tight slit.

"I know you ain't holding the button, cause you've got that live-long-and-prosper vibe, you're a dog fighter and fuck if you'd go down with the ship. I feel you, Chip. Let me kick it to you from another angle. You work for the senator?"

Chip auto-wags his noggin, yes sir. Hurry up, Decimal.

"This the senator's gig then?"

Chip thinks about this tricky one, gives me a no sir. Hurry up.

"How'd you know about the bomb, son?"

Extending his jaw. Grinding his teeth.

But I think I've put it together. GPS remote monitoring, some such elementary tech. I think about the surface-to-air hoo-has the Cyna-corp kids had sitting around back at the pier. Lord, I'm a jackass. Blame myself.

Chip's a rock. Fuck this. Straighten up, replacing my mask.

"That's all right, Chip. Remember, kid: walk toward the light . . ."

I turn on him (left), leaving him hanging from the twisted steering wheel, commence stepping. Got the Purell™ out again and I'm giving myself a good going over, get about fifty feet and the boy takes up a horrible calflike keening. Mind you, dude is short a tongue so it's a uniquely unpleasant sound.

Turn back to the boy. He's digging one-handed inside his sportcoat.

Sigh. I lift the Sig.

"Okay, star," I say, "let's not push it, I'm letting you drift as it is, cause I'm soft touch."

Chip continues fumbling around, withdraws what looks like a leather wallet. I cock my pistol, really not wanting to have to cap this child.

"You know what? You hang on to that there thingy. Think it through, dog."

Fuck if young'un doesn't chuck the wallet toward me, I'm thinking some kind of explosive, it arcs through the shitty air, I'm gearing up to shoot him but he saves me the effort . . . Cause before I can say, *Who's your daddy?* Chip has his own .38 revolver out and in his mouth, barrel to the soft palate. Chip groaning, making gargly sounds.

My mouth opens too, me saying, "No, man, Chip, come on—"

The leather object lands with a plop in the shallow lake, about the same time Chip pulls the trigger on himself, *bang*, gray and red pulp Pollocking the interior of the driver's door of the Escalade. Goes broken-puppet slack into the water.

Me thinking, *Goddamn it. Motherfucking shame.*

What gives with everybody popping themselves? Starting to vibe like a bad trend.

Relative silence, save the rain, which continues to slap at this wounded city. Then about one hundred feet back the female Saudi re-ups her shrieking.

Limp toward Chip, who minus the back of his skull is deader than fuck and hardly warrants a peep-see. Dig the brackish, evil water covering my wingers. A slow-moving stream, thicker than it should be. Pull on a fresh glove, checking my natural instinct to puke, and dip my hand into the tunnel creek approximately where he tossed his wallet.

Fish it out, hold it at arm's length. Gagging. Get a handle on it, Decimal. Brown leather passport-sized thing. I flip it open. US Secret Service badge. With a photo of me, and the name: *Chip White*.

Hairs go erect on the back of my neck. I don't get it . . . This an elaborate gag? Is it my my birthday?

No time at the moment . . . gotta stay grinding.

Move. Turn and gimp toward the Saudis, ditching the soiled glove and spraying the badge off. Water-borne disease. Pathogenic parasitical protozoa, dysentery, intestinal worms.

Fuck it. I pocket the mystery shield, thinking, *Gotta stay below street level*, talking fast: "Your Highnesses, my deepest apologies. Please allow me to escort you to an alternative exit."

A subway station at 38th and Park? Bitches, why not crack a book and get down with your history.

Okay, never a subway station exactly. Originally built for horse-carts back in 1870, well before Grand Central was even conceived, with a transition to electric streetcars in the last few years of the nineteenth century. The tunnels which house this ghost station were once open-air tracks for the very first railroad system in New York City.

Stay lively, y'all. As this land is razed and transformed, these tidbits get more and more important.

In 1850 the rails were roofed over from 39th Street to 34th, creating the surface that later became the Park Avenue Tunnel. Upon the underground station's construction two fine granite stairwells were installed, on the east and west sides. One of which I am now descending with two Saudi Arabian royals. This is where I find myself.

It took some doing, but I managed to dig a crowbar out of the Escalade, as well as a couple of electronic road flares.

Thought about it. Grabbed the dead soldier's radio too. My overcoat fucked up, drenched in blood. Freezing without it, but what's a brother to do? This being where you wind up, trying to play the gentleman.

The egress which housed the doorway leading to the stairwell, roughly at 41st Street, had probably not been opened in several years. Application of will and elbow grease popped that thing in under five minutes, open says me.

NATHAN LARSON ✳ 119

Just another forgotten door in New York City, unloved and unsecured.

Couple of sheets hang back, shapeless and sad looking.

"If you please," I say, switching out of English mode, indicating the open doorway. "Take this light here. Please. Move onto the stairwell with caution, then stop and wait for my signal, I'm behind you." Hustle them into the black, they disappear fast.

I see the LED flare come on, like a rotating red police light. Disorienting but better than nothing. Move. Working on getting my own flare going when the Saudi's radio comes alive in my pocket, making me jump. In common Arabic . . . though not a native speaker: *"Lost signal at this position. No response from subject. Entering at 33rd and Park, over."*

So. Get both guns up and push myself into the doorjamb. Face south and breeeeathe, silky. Think System. Been keeping clean, taking my pills and my lefts. Dark in here, feeling relatively confident I'll remain unseen.

Echoey in this funnel, sound slapping around and hard to pinpoint, but over the downpour I think I hear vehicles coming to a stop near the south entrance, my line of sight compromised on account of the slope leading into the underpass. That's all right. I'm a patient kind of guy. For the time being I ignore the hockey puck of sand in my mouth.

The dead Saudi's radio crackles, and I set my gun down to cautiously shut the thing off . . . not before I make out two numbers, again with the language-school Arabic: *"Ten-three, out."*

Ten-three? That's what . . . that's old-school American cop or trucker slang for "switch channels." Am I to believe this is a universal military code, in use throughout the world?

Highly improbable, y'all. Little clues, little seeds, shards of a broken test tube.

It's an easy misdirect to throw suspicion to the Arabs, especially amongst us dumb-dumb Americans. Shit is too easy. It's like the black thing—even some of the smartest motherfuckers can get thrown off track by a little color. They smell a turban and reckon they got it all sussed. Bearing this in mind, moving forward.

When the folks with guns come, they come slow.

Counting one, two, three, and a forth against the eastern wall, and a trio of shooters pressed to the opposite side. My tummy wiggles and jiggles as I squint, clock via the early-morning daylight at least four drenched but distinct uniforms: the powder-blue helmet of the UN Peacekeeper, an NYPD outfit, standard grunt wear that could be either US, Chinese, or Saudi Arabian, for all I know . . . and natch, that now nearly ubiquitous Cyna-corp amphibious ninja chic, probably the only motherfuckers who aren't suffering from getting rained on. It's like they threw together the most random sampling of gear to fuck with a brother. Needless to say, all these folks are strapping big heat, gat-tastic.

And needless to say: I do not know what in the good name of Allah is going down here.

And that's as much as I can scope before a powerful searchlight swipes the tunnel, forcing me to pirouette (left) back into the alcove.

It's a self-conciously mixed grab bag. An all-too-motley crew. Smells bad, bad, bad. Think on it: *Who comes yonder? Vertically integrated death squad or harmonious international rescue unit?*

Their lamp alights on the big Escalade. Chip dangling there.

Anticipatory cleansing, I holster the HK and get my Purell™ on. Low speech from the posse a block or two south, well into the cistern now, the water amplifying all sonic events. English is being spoken, though I can scarcely make it out. Reporting the discovery of the vehicle I would reckon. Naturally, it would be unwise to engage this potluck. Not until I can glean their intentions. Should they be hostile, the only smart move would be to lam it with the royal twins till I can suss an angle.

Replace my gloves, don't remember if I've thrown back a pill lately . . . Fuck it, I spit to clear that imaginary sand, and swallow another Beauty Blue just to be sure. Holster my pistolas, and again grab ahold of the electric flare, getting primed to scramola. I'm woefully outgunned. Trick is to know when to hold 'em, and know when to fold 'em.

The portal leading below is open a good three feet. Don't want the search party to spot this door, or at least don't wanna hasten that discovery, but they're preoccupied with the wrecked Esco as it is. The men having a quiet conversation.

Searchlight makes a slow frisk of the vehicle, landing once again on Chip's soggy corpse. Wipers still going *swish swish*.

Assume some sort of decision is made cause bada-bada, extra loud in this reflective tube, Chip starts to shimmy and twitch, machine-gun fire perforating what remains of the young man, making him jump and jive. It's certainly an indignity, but one has to assume Chip is beyond such things. In a happier place, which would be anywhere or nowhere at all.

Gunfire halts, the crew giving things a beat to see what shakes out.

Think I know as much as I need to know at this point. Were these folks here on humanitarian recon, I highly doubt they'd be apt to shoot up a potentially wounded and salvageable individual so thoroughly. So with that, and because

I feel myself falling into a bit of a Freeze (who are these people? What are we all doing?), I duck out, through the neglected exit. Or entrance, depending on your perspective.

Thinking I'm smooth like that, I exhale and unclench my ass cheeks. Brain function inching back toward "normal." Put my back against the door and attempt to ease it shut—causing a tremendous scrape against the stone as the warped metal resists my shoulder. Fuck.

It's an attention grabber. The searchlight swings our direction, followed by a gunshot volley. Constellation of bullet holes appear in the rusty iron just above my head, I go facedown, pressing myself as flat as possible against cold granite, as the door is systematically shredded.

Feature lead flakes in my mouth, in my nostrils . . . Yet more keening from the hooded ones, swaying paralyzed on the first landing, that hypnotic red light spiraling a tight circle.

"Move! Watch your fucking step but we need to be quick," me saying, hastily adding, "God willing, Your Highnesses." Hauling my bones up.

They get the gist and get to traipsing, treacherous on the dead walkway, into the guts of the island. Go, Decimal.

I'm bopping lopsided right behind them, cursing myself for not seeing this job for the suicidal undertaking it was. The whole bag is a sham and the only thing to do now is not catch a slug in the neck. Must think pretty highly of myself if I didn't—

One of the potato sacks stumbles, nearly taking a nosedive. Steadies, then: muffled: "Fucking hell. Forget it." She says it in British-tinged English, for it's def the female. Funny cause I had thought it was the other way around . . . thought she was the male of the two.

Girl hikes up her full-body skirt, revealing her calves, encased in high-cut pricey-looking jeans (Swedish?), fancy ankle bracelet bling, and Miu Miu six-inch heels. Yeah, I ID them no sweat. If you've got brand radar, you can't turn that noise off.

Not ideal footwear for spelunking. Not ideal for upright walking either, for that matter, but I'm certainly one to allow fashion to trump safety . . . witness my lack of a Kevvie vest, today of all days.

Me moving to assist . . . her shrill-yet-oddly-resonant sibling speaks, aghast in alto flutey Arabic. "Haifa!" she hisses through her veil. "Cover yourself, sister, even here modesty is your most valuable . . ."

Hold up: the heart of another woman beats beneath that cloth for sure. Two women?

Man, if this op isn't a big old-fashioned fuck-up. Got two bitc . . . two ladies here. Now, as screwed as this job is, this here gender-fucking aspect of the whole deal is not on this brother. At least that can be said. I thought we were getting a gal and a guy straight-show. I'm a bit hazy on the details, but wasn't that the whole goddamn point?

"Hey, I was expecting a brother-and-sister act here—"

"Can't bloody *see*. No, fuck all this bloody crap!"

She could easily be from North London with that accent, slight Jafaican in there . . . unexpected from a Saudi Arabian princess.

This one known as Haifa is attempting to wrestle out of her robes, I manage to catch her around the waist as she nearly pitches forward into darkness. Met by the type of costly musculature one can only obtain through the likes of a strict Pilates regimen.

"Easy," I tell her as she surges forward. "Stop freaking

moving if you're gonna try to get this mess off you . . ."

Help her grapple with the robe and get it over her head—revealing an explosion of hair, designer faux-military jacket. By the circling red cop light I dig candids of big clear eyes, dark as her hair, framed by thick Cleopatra makeup, dramatic and stark, and a rope of scar tissue above her right brow.

She's a whiz-bang knockout, by any standard.

"Thank you," she says, quiet, in and out of the dark, the rotating light. Mid to late twenties.

Goodness me. Goodness my.

"Princess," I say, "it's a pleasure."

She shoots me a look, says in that incongruous accent, "And who the bloody fuck are you?"

Hey, Decimal. Sure, she's sweet to peep, but first order of business is not getting dead, which means slip, slide, and shake the goons upstairs.

"Haifa," repeats the other girl, a throaty purr, "at least consider a luxury hijab."

"Don't let's fucking start, darling," replies Haifa, her cat's eyes still considering me.

"They can be very stylish, as you know."

"Ladies," I interject, trying to keep things jumping forth.

"I don't want to go snapping my bloody neck, do I?" Haifa spits, stepping toward the other woman . . . her sister?

I just don't dig it. Help me out. "Ladies."

And in Arabic, "Not a blessed word to me in four years and this is nearly the first thing out of your mouth? You're a shallow one, aren't you? God is great. That you've any family remaining who will speak to you at all—"

Drop my light, couldn't get it working, and taking them both by the waist I'm rushing the pair down the stairwell, trying to mind where we're stepping, say, "Ladies, plenty of time to get back on the same page later, for now let's focus on walking, okay? *Carefully*."

"I can see perfectly fine," the fully covered gal says, nearly losing her footing.

Haifa halts, swivels on me. "Oi. I didn't get an answer outta you, did I? Give me your name, sir, your agency. I *demand* a bloody fucking explanation. I'll have your head on a bloody platter, and I do mean that literally."

Throw an eyeball north, up above us now comes the searchlight as our friends grapple with this situation. Go. Steer the women. "Let's walk and talk, shall we? All will be clear . . ."

Heels clattering on the granite, luckily the boys upstairs seem to be consulting each other. By the cherry light I praise Jehovah that we've almost hit the old platform, *bam*, we do it—the searchlight traces the identical stairwell along the far wall, jerks back in our direction.

Happily, whoever is holding the searchlight is a dumbass and by the time they're running it across the landing, aha, we're already off it, sloshing into the narrow northbound tunnel through a good six inches of yet more bilious stream.

Anaerobic bacteria. Dengue. Though that's the tropics. But these days . . .

Haifa gags. The other girl holds steady but presses the material of her headpiece into her mouth. We're deep now, and the Stench is indescribably putrid, especially in an enclosed space like this . . . and this is not even sewage, this is just a collection of rainwater and possibly reservoir runoff.

I hate to admit that I'm pretty much used to it. Chewing on that sand, pulling in air through my nose.

"Uh, this is—"

"Breathe through the mouth."

"Why should we be running at all? By what logic are we down in the bloody sewer with you? How do we know you're not meant to hurt us?"

The sister gets caught in her gear and almost topples, Haifa grabs her elbow and rights her.

"You reckon I'm enjoying this? You did notice we're all being shot at, no?"

Catch a bit of uneven ground, whoops, manage to land in a plank position. The ladies don't pause. That's good. Push myself up and out of the shitty water, press forward.

"This is hell. We're in fucking hell," yammers Haifa as I catch up to her, those jeans . . .

I grimace. "You got no idea, Your Highness. No idea."

"Oi. Don't address me like that. I left all that nonsense behind."

"Is it so . . . is it so shameful?" mutters the sister, moving with difficulty.

"We make choices, darling. You make yours, I make mine." Haifa is pulling ahead, clearly the superior athlete here.

Let all this smack drift. Hopefully we'll live to get to know each other, but for now I gotta keep these girls motivated.

"On the positive side, Your Highnesses," I say in English, feeling like some positivity would be welcome here, "ya won't see any rats. Rest easy that the rats and whatnot up and died about a year back. All of them."

"Oi. Bad. Subject. Stop," breathes Haifa.

"They got huge, off-the-chain huge, everybody was all, *Damn those are some big-ass rats!* And then either they couldn't live in this poison water . . . or something higher up on the food chain got to 'em—"

"Sir," interrupts Haifa, "if you don't mind, you're just making it bloody worse."

I realize, sure, I'm not exactly painting the prettiest picture. Digging there is no bright side to any of this, not if you look long enough. "Just trying to orient you is all," I say, lame as fuck.

Haifa staggers a couple steps, then carries on, one leg longer than the other.

"Break a heel?" says me. Rhetorically.

No verbal response to this, but she boogies on one foot for a moment and gets the other shoe off, tosses it aside like it's no thing at all. Flashes me the shit-eye. I dig that.

Yet more good news is that we're on an incline, so the water begins to taper a bit as we get farther along. By my estimation we're coming up on the tangle of tunnels intersecting at Grand Central . . . the tunnels expand, a little less tight, higher arches. Older ruins.

Presuming we're still heading north, we come upon an east-west conduit, maybe the 7 train. . . but I don't see a third rail. Possible we've come upon the long-decommissioned Steinway Tunnels, which I would find more exciting if I didn't have other shit constipating my inbox . . .

Eastbound. Barring any obstructions, that jammie will take us straight home, to the library. Please, by all that is holy . . . I want to be home.

This has undoubtedly occurred to our pursuers. This destination.

Quick, Decimal, think it through: obviously we're not going to the police precinct on Varick, per the official plan. Not till I know what's what.

Can't go direct to the senator cause fuck knows who's fucking who here.

Can't turn around cause behind us lies probable death.

The revolving cop light screwing with my vision. Come to a sliding stop. Freeze town. Droplet of sweat runs down my cheek like a tear, despite the fact that I'm frozen solid and only vaguely aware of my feet.

"Oi. Mister . . . you look," the princess is saying, at a remove.

She's beautiful. Love that scar. Huge effort to keep that face in focus, but I'm floating . . .

"Don't you bloody fucking dare pass out on us. Don't you dare . . ."

But even as she says this the ladies take a step back, sensing a strange departure in me. I spin with the LED, blinking in tandem with the signal, hand to my internal companion riding the back of my neck. Tunnels and tracks in four directions and me, feeling that aura, the onset of a Semi-Freeze. Please, Jesus, not now. Not here.

"What's the fuck's that?" inhales Haifa. "Oh my God, what the fuck *is* that?" Calling me back.

Though the present is receding, though my surroundings grow more and more unfamiliar and alien, I listen, hard. First I only hear my blood. Then the filthy water coming off the ceiling, moving across the walls. Go to speak, choke on my gab. Cause that's when I hear the dogs too.

If you are from the ghetto, your relationship with the canine is generally pretty straightforward, like your relationship with a weapon of any kind, i.e., if you're on the business end of one, you take it serious. You back the fuck off. Or you kill it straight away.

Likewise, if you're the one holding the chain, you're feeling pretty good about yourself. Big scary motherfuckers step out the way and do so quietly. A dog is a walking, shitting security system, a self-defense mechanism, bred to be lethal. And if it ain't pulling its weight, why would you waste your good cheese on the motherfucker?

This impression was further reinforced by the NYPD's dog squad, which employed their animals in much the same way. Anybody who's spent an evening in, say, the basement of the Brooklyn Detention Center on Atlantic Avenue can attest to this. And certainly we put what we learned at home to work for us overseas . . . I would indicate the so-called human rights violations that occurred at spots like Abu Ghraib and countless other locales. Standard procedure.

Funny how quick a frothing German shepherd will change your attitude, especially if you're bare-assed, chained to fence with a truncheon all up in your rectal cavity.

But hey, yo, not that I condone such techniques, having been on both ends of that nightstick. As it were.

Never been ashamed about where I'm from. So I am simply providing you with my ghetto perspective. Fuck y'all.

Point being: I don't like an unfamiliar dog, and what's more, I'll stab or shoot Fido till Fido is good and dead, and sort out the wheretofores afterward. All of which is to say, the sound of a large number of dogs is extremely unwelcome in the best of times. The only dogs left on the island are still around because they've been trained to carry out a specific task: guarding construction equipment, keeping workers in check, etc.

Apparently, Saudi Arabian royalty share this vibe with me, cause Princess Haifa is all saucer-eyed terror. Her sister doesn't seem thrilled either, but really, who the fuck can tell under that sheet?

Standing ankle deep in viscous liquid, the world tar-black save that seizure-inducing police light, shit is already looking unmanageably grim, so I don't really have a better solution to a kerfuffle such as this.

The plan would have to be: sprint the opposite direction from whence the dogs approach. Problem being, down in these tunnels I'm directionally challenged and by the sound of it the animals could be coming from at least three points on the compass.

Which only leaves us with north as an option, in the much more recently constructed East Side Access LIRR tunnel that shoots uptown and ultimately hangs a right, under the river and into Queens.

Jam a quick brain scan of that routing . . . issue being the East Side Access is so new, came so soon prior to the Valentine, never did get a chance to physically study the final product . . . Course I know the blueprints, and if I'm not wrong there's a couple intersections with a much older track and tunnel that I can do some work with.

It's educated-improv hour again at the House of Decimal.

Haifa and I staring at each other, both our yaps open.

I rally: "Okay. Gotta make moves, ladies."

We scamper north now, into one of the wider tunnels that will eventually lead us underneath Grand Central station, me ushering the ladies along, very aware of the ruckus as we kick up water. The dogs seem to be approaching from the east and are getting louder.

Then, fuck if the one in the white caftan comes to a full stop, drops and prostrates herself, starts hiccupping a standard prayer to the good Allah.

"Khalid," says Haifa. "Khalid, for the love of . . . Khalid, get up."

I peel Khalid (kind of a masculine name for that part of

the world, but what do I know?) off the muddy track, her white peignoir now a shit-brown in front. She doesn't resist but certainly doesn't cooperate.

Clear my throat, tease out a soothing rasp: "Your Highness, you're going to have to work with me here."

Khalid fully loses it, starts battering me with ineffectual fists, beseeching God to strike me down. Haifa, to her credit, is trying to pry her off.

But yo. That's fucking enough for this brother. I've had it with this bowing-and-scraping jive. I get shorty in an easy headlock.

The dogs drawing nearer. Time to come raw with these gals.

When Khalid has stopped kicking at me, I speak. "Now, if we're gonna survive this here, I'm gonna have to drop the formalities. Ya heard?"

The girls are silent. Haifa looking up at me like a schoolgirl getting a scolding. Yo, I cannot tell a lie: it's kinda hot—but I gotta put the nix on such thoughts and stick to the program, me saying fast, "This is the realness. Any number of people on this island could have reason to get ahold of you ladies. You wanna get through this thing? Do exactly like I say, exactly when I say it. Otherwise y'all might as well just lie down and die."

Khalid is silent but at least has stopped with the fucking prayer, nobody needs that.

Speed it up, Decimal. I move toward Haifa, who steps backward, stumbling a bit.

"Right, and again—who exactly are you, Mister Mystery?" she says, tough-stuff.

"I'm your black knight in shining armor, come to return you ladies to Narnia." Grabbing her arm.

Haifa allows herself to be guided forth, no longer trying to keep her jeans from getting wet, not looking at me . . . she says quietly, "You're insane. Speaking to us like this. You've no concept." Those dogs closer still. "What are you, you're CIA . . . Are you CIA?"

Laugh like this is a shitty movie, right? "Ha, yo, probably. I'd be last to know, and hey, would I tell you if I was? Be smart. I freelance. And for better or worse, brown sugar, I'm all you got this morning, CIA or NBA or what have you. That's if you wanna see another sunrise off the coast of France. Otherwise y'all are nothing but real exclusive dog food. Ya heard?"

Haifa's mouth agape. "You can't bloody speak that way to me. Do you understand who—"

"Thought you left all that hierarchical shit behind, hon. Now *run*."

Touché, and apparently I'm getting through, cause they pick up the pace, me trying to match them now, closest I can possibly get to jogging with this fucked-up knee I got. Evil water goes *slosh slosh*, and I expect the dogs on us anytime now. Thinking about implants. Tracking devices . . .

Nothing I can do about the thing in my neck. This I've known for years and will not drive myself yet more crazy wondering what the fuck it's all about.

The dogs. In the tunnel with us now for sure.

Khalid continues weeping quietly. Haifa puts her head down and starts to get ahead of me, clearly a runner, going full out in her bare feet and ankle bracelets—

Ankle bracelets.

Khalid moving on her own now, every third step catching the long hem of her ridiculous getup and causing her to have to readjust. I let her go and draw both guns. Slow to a walk, the tunnel feeling tighter . . .

"Lose your jewelry, ladies. Take it off and drop it. The both of you."

Haifa slows, throws a look. "You mad? The dogs—"

"And you, Khalid, it's time you lost the toga, it's just fucking up our flow."

"*Not to display their beauty except to their husbands* . . ." Khalid is quoting the Koran at me in a panicky pitch.

"The dogs," repeats Haifa simply.

"I got this, ditch the rocks and whatnot, dig?"

It's nothing but a hunch, and I may never know, but if I were some state counterintelligence schmo thinking I'm clever, that's what I'd do, short of a subcutaneous implant which I couldn't do shit about as it is.

No, these gals? I'd put some tracking tech in a shorty's jewelry.

Come to a full stop, jerking left, left, and all the way around with my mug toward the way we came. Visibility is a sporadic ten feet, the revolving red light. Raise the guns and wait till I see 'em.

Dog yelps, shrieks and snarls mad amplified like we're descending into yet a lower plane of hell, sound gone totally liquid now, everything could be anywhere. But I was raised ready, they beat it into me. I paid attention. And I breeeathe.

Haifa saying some shit about "heirlooms" but has apparently decided, wisely, that I'm the only game in town, so having shucked her own accessories, she's struggling with her less willing sister, cursing and attempting to disrobe her.

Hey now, I am most certainly not into fucking with anybody's style consciousness, I say drop it how you wanna drop it. And certainly I would be loathe to impinge on a bitch's freedom to worship as she sees fit, but this is an extreme situation.

Tensed for the dogs. Come here, buddies. Come to Dada.

More sweat makes its way out from under the brim of my hat. Feel feverish, achy. Vision splotchy. Itching to grab a pill but I don't wanna break my concentration.

When the NYPD golf cart rolls out of the blackness, I set to firing on it double-handed, thinking it's a bit of an oddity, but hell, nothing surprises me anymore . . . then I'm looking for the pack of frothing dogs to come galloping in, and my next thought is that of course this cart is where the sounds are emanating from, Caribbean Day Parade–style sound system mounted shakily on the roof.

I've squandered some perfectly fine ammunition on an unmanned go-cart. But fuck it, I shoot the thing up anyhow cause it feels good.

When things go quiet they go unnaturally quiet. Like the incurably sick air finally gave it up and died. Swapping out magazines and limping toward the wreck, I dig it's an ad hoc kind of deal, duct tape, a car battery, car stereo . . . sign of the times. Crafty enough, but what the fuck?

What do we have? I note an innocuous-looking camera, think about that stuff for a second.

"Kill your light, princesses." I can't see them, they start to protest, me turning left left left, saying, "I'm for real, pussycats, snuff the light. We're being watched and that's a bet."

They do it.

And it's a good thing too, because the first of what I assume to be a number of bullets goes whistling past my right ear, white-hot wasps. I mean it's that freaking close, y'all, which puts yours truly in a humble, circumspect kind of mindframe. There's a split second that I see a couple lights go out about a hundred feet back down the tunnel, and dig a quick exchange.

Figuring, fuck it, I take a couple wild shots in that direction, *boom boom*, then hit the deck. Punks clownish enough to return fire, as they do, so they gotta know I see those muzzles flare cause I squeeze off another, tighter this time, and reckon I nick somebody cause I register a yelp.

Any further shooting I do, of course, will be spotted as well. So I roll a couple feet through the wet dirt as they shoot up the spot I was just occupying, cause they can't resist either, it's fun to shoot guns, and then we all sit back and let that be that for the moment.

The girls eek and yak, I tell 'em shut their pampered yaps and lie down like the rest of us peasantry. We hush, and I listen good and hard. Sand under my collar. Feel live bodies nearby, maybe as many as four or five, but not more.

Feature this: a stalemate. Figure they were limited to their own lighting and can't turn it on without making themselves an easy target. Since we're all up the same creek, seems like we got a moment or two to take stock.

Sometimes I see myself in hell. Overactive imagination—pipe dreaming or an exclusive sneak peek, I'm not the one to know. Like this: a shitty theme restaurant with a sort of colonial Belgian Congo vibe to it, me bound at the ankles and feet, in a loincloth, rotating via a motorized system on a spit over open flame, fat popping and spitting. Healing over fast to start the cycle again.

What's blacker than total blackness? Having been in a similar setting before, I know there's all kinds of shit to see when encased in this species of dark, and it's whatever your brain reckons you ought to take a long look at. In my case it's a small parade of unsettled, anxious spirits. One or two of whom I murdered myself, either directly or indirectly . . .

Here's Hakim Stanley, a young black American Marine

with his jaw missing courtesy of your narrator. This beautiful young brother. Stanley's the one who will always come back, because what I did to this boy was an affront to the universe. That's one the Devil will charge me full price for, and there's no two ways about it.

Rose Hee, Korean mob queenpin, rises before me in the blood-soaked jumpsuit she died in. Nothing accusing in her gaze, and God knows I loved the crazy girl . . . but motherfucker, I know that one is my fault too.

Then we have DA Daniel Rosenblatt, the sneaky Jew, sad-sacky in his poop-colored bathrobe, skullcap (and by this I'm not talking about a yarmulke . . . I mean I popped his top—the top of his skull) removed courtesy of my trigger finger, he jumps in midsentence, his nasal staccato, *"The things they did to you . . . poking around in your brain . . . shoulda read your file, Decimal. You shoulda read it, you coulda known the truth."*

Shoulda woulda coulda. Shoulda stuck with the engineering and steered clear of the gangs, gone to Howard or Spellman or even Harvard, done some real shit like my late great brother Dos Mac. Coulda been a butterfly. Coulda been born white, with a silver spoon to ward off the vampire hustlers and military recruiters. Who gives a fuck now?

Then, hazy as ever, there's always the apartment in the dream. Within which, under a single sheet, might perhaps lie a female form, and a child. And me, perhaps holding a gun, my heart an unreadable hole. Perhaps raise and point . . . annnnnd the rest is lost to me.

Oh, I know I'm a monster. The question is, am I just garden variety, like everybody else—like I did what I done to keep kicking? Or, despite my Code, despite my System, do I carry a yawning black abscess where my soul should be, burning with fever, flush with infection?

Fever. Things wobble, hazy.

How evil am I? That's the million-dollar question. And that's my forever.

———————————

A hand on my leg, jerk, and I'm back in this miserable world. Musta Freddo'd.

The princess known as Haifa has found me by the light of her flare, saying: "Fucking hell, we've been looking for you for . . . Sir. Sir. They've gone, ages ago. We don't know which direction to go."

Startled, I won't lie. It seems a scant few minutes have passed. I yank the girl to the ground by the lapel of her designer military jacket, she shrieks in protest, me hissing: "Woman, are you crazy, they're gonna—"

She's shaking her head, cuts me off. Khalid hovers and twitches in the background, in sort of a one-piece jumper, face still obscured by fabric; the girl, it seems, had a headpiece on *under* her full-body burqa. Me thinking, *Damn, this is one modest chick. Allah be well pleased here.*

"It's been a bloody half hour. A half hour!" spits Haifa. "We've been frantic. And keep your bloody fucking filthy hands off me, you maniac!"

We both struggle up. I work at the sand in my ear canal, but it's too deep.

Then Haifa hauls off and whacks me in the yapper.

Iron and salt, the girl really clocks me. Blood and sand. Princess spouting: "What is wrong with you? You just disappeared. In this . . . bloody tube-sewer wherever the bloody fuck. You've not the least idea of what we've been through over the last several days, week, whatever it is, you've no idea at all."

NATHAN LARSON ✳ 139

She's near tears, lower lip quivering. I'm straight stunned and at a major loss.

"And this one. And this one here is bloody fucking useless as well, right?" She jerks her chin at her sister. "And you're scarcely fucking better, Mr. CIA. The presumption was," the red light spinning slowly reveals a flash of her lips and healthy teeth, "you were our escort to bloody safety, but at this point—"

Haifa stops cause I put two gloved fingers to her mouth. Light swings around, she looks like a child again. Eyes watering, full of anger and fear, her scar seems raised and engorged.

Then she and I are in darkness again. My chest fills with disproportionate anger. I get up on her fucking ear, wanna communicate who runs this thing.

"Mochachino," I say, "don't want to be smacking me again. Cause I'll bite your pretty hand off, princess or no. Dig?" Snap my filthy chompers, just once, and I swear I feel those grains.

Revolution of the light source and I peep tear tracks down the girls cheekbones. She's definitely scared, piss-her-three-hundred-euro-Swedish-jeans scared.

Shift my hand to her cheek, give her what I hope to be a paternal pat, from which she recoils. Grin, gotta camouflage my confusion. Need to get oriented but I'm dizzy as all hell, trapped in some arty fun house that's no fun at all. The light illuminating the side of the tunnel, Khalid vibrating behind her.

"You were meant to protect us. Please. You said so." Haifa's dark eyes, clearer now.

Duck my head. Honeybunch is dead right. Think, Decimal. What a world-class fuck-up. To buoy myself and reset a little, I bust out the Purell™, rip off my nasty gloves, lather up. In this kinda damp, even the alcohol gel doesn't dry. Pull on a fresh pair of gloves anyway, sticky and squeaky.

Me thinking, *Evade everything and put these ladies somewhere comfortable till we savvy what's doing. I'm solid gold, I got this. I can still pull it out, even operating at half-capacity.*

Out of the tunnels. The tunnels are no fucking good. I work with the streets, work by the System. Discreet exit is imperative. They'll have all known portals covered—

The answer cracks me upside my noggin, how could I have spaced this? Me inadvertently saying: "FDR."

Haifa is quiet for a moment, looking toward her sister, and back to me for clarification. "DR, is that some sort of military acronym, because really . . ."

I'm off, power-gimping what I believe to be uptown. "The thirty-second US president. Dude rocked a wheelchair cause of polio, didn't want the Nazis to get hip to it . . . built a tunnel straight out of the train station up to the . . . Fuck it, just follow me, ladies."

The girls hang back. Sigh. I turn.

"You prefer it down here? I reckon you got another hour's worth of battery on that there lamp, and then it's just y'all. And whoever else is down here in the dark looking for you."

Gets 'em hustling. They've really got no choice. We walk briskly at first, then break into a lopsided jog.

When the doors slide open onto 49th Street, sunlight leaves me momentarily paralyzed, as weak as it is. The girls walk right into me, raring to get out. We collide and I shove them back, as gentle as possible. Already got my Beretta out, hold up a gloved hand.

"Hang tight a moment, gals."

Blinking, lean forward and take a peek, east and west, an easy drizzle now, and not a single human form in sight. The only thing I don't dig is a busted-up city bus about half a block down, partially up on the curb, primarily cause I can't see around it. Tires have been removed. Billboard on the bus's ass, dirty picture of a Mediterranean sky, a plane, and the simple proclamation: EMIRATES.

Listen; nothing but the usual construction buzz and a distant chopper.

Feeling myself, pretty slick as the three of us ease out the gold elevator doors, situated inconspicuously midblock, next to the parking garage for the Waldorf Astoria Hotel. The gals in tow, we duck around the corner into the garage and off the street.

Get my face mask up on automatic. The girls coughing. Not used to sucking the tailpipe. The New York "air." The Stench.

"You'll adjust. Hard to believe, but yo, you'll acclimate. Here . . ." I dig in my pockets, come up with only one clean mask. Khalid is doubled over, shoulders shaking. "Damn. Oh well. Just, ya know. Breathe through the mouth, like I said."

Haifa is holding her shirt up over the lower half of her face. Can't tell if she's crying or if it's just the normal burning shit the atmosphere does to your eyes.

"Absolute nightmare. Breathe through the mouth. Means we're inhaling *this*," she says, muffled, her watery gaze shifting around frantically. "Bloody fucking *nightmare* . . ."

I make a sound like a laugh. "You got that right, angel. And might I be the first to say: Welcome to it."

Haifa glances at me. "Good God, your *face* . . ."

"No, I'm a'ight, that was earlier. That ain't nothing, trust it."

"How," asks Khalid, in a soft voice, genuinely amazed, "how can anyone live here?"

"They can't. *We* can't. But don't sweat yourselves, it kills you real slow." Me thinking we best bizounce, get to higher ground. Wherever that might be. "Listen, girls, I don't know about y'all, but I wanna get somewhere safe, and pronto. Thinking I can get you ladies back to your big-ass boat, and from there . . ." Trail off because Khalid has straightened up.

Takes me a second, but yes, she has a gun in her hand. Pointed this way, jittery.

My gun. I touch my left shoulder holster through my jacket . . . empty.

Sigh. Well, I've still got my other gun. Lift the Beretta, slow.

"Dumpling, I've never shot a lady in a veil. But there's always a first time."

Haifa, for her part, backs away, looking appalled. "Khalid, this is not the intelligent way to—"

"Seriously, sweetheart," I say, chilly chill. "I can put one through your pretty neck faster than you can blink. But I'd rather keep my lady-killer rep to the realm of the romantic."

Haifa laughs. "A lady. Khalid is my brother, sir. Certainly no lady."

Say what? But then I'm checking the hands. The hands don't lie, and Khalid . . .

Realizing the individual I took to be female has in fact been Prince Khalid all along. Me saying, "Well now. Was that you doing all that horror-movie hollering, Your Highness?"

"Harlot," whispers Khalid out of the side of his mouth, words directed at his sister, weapon directed at me. "Whore."

Haifa makes a noise with her throat. "Oh yes, darling. And I daresay Allah takes a dim view of bloody transgressors of all colors, however pious."

"Haifa," says the burqa'd prince, "at least I do not lie with barbarians, display my body like a prostitute."

"Yeah, well, I like to dress nice, have a couple of drinks, enjoy myself. You want to be with other boys, it's all the same in the end, isn't it? Allah despises us both equally."

Family tiff. I stay the fuck out, waiting for an in.

Khalid's got his slits on me, saying: "Not the Allah I know and adore, dear sister."

"Brother, I'm well fucking supportive of your bloody . . . struggle. I'm just pointing out that our imam might not . . . I mean, really, look at our family, look at our own family, look at what they do."

Think fast, Decimal.

Years of this cowboy shit, this frontier living, has given me a bit of a gift, in the sense that I can generally savvy a bitch who is capable of pulling the trigger, and Khalid, even through that hood, is broadcasting willingness in spades.

So I take a calculated risk as Haifa runs her gums. I aim carefully at Khalid's gold open-toed sandal. And I fire.

Only nothing happens. The hammer falls on nothing, with a small click.

A brother can practically hear Khalid's grin flower under the mask, as the magazine from my Beretta is produced. He/she fans his/herself with it.

Me thinking, *Come on, Decimal*. I'm getting played at every turn. A colossal embarrassment to my trade. I deserve to get served.

"Perhaps," Khalid says softly, "this is yours as well?" Dangles that mag.

Haifa's peepers are popping out her head, flipping back and forth, not knowing where to land.

Shrug and pocket my empty pistol. Go sad sack. Say, "Well played, Khalid, shit. Well played. When I'm beat, I'm beat. It's your ball game, Prince Charming. Do your stuff."

The prince inclines his head, all very cultured and polite stuff. "Sister," he says in that quiet voice, "would you be so good as to relieve this *gentleman* of his weapon?"

Haifa swings those eyes, that scar, my way, hesitant . . .

Me trying to keep him off-balance, saying, "So, Khalid, just my curious mind, you dig putting on those silky lady threads, or is it like a deeper scene, like one of those always-knew-I-was-trapped-in-the-wrong—"

"I am not a transvestite, sir," says the prince in that gorgeous voice, "I resent the very suggestion."

"Oh shit, sorry. I just figured with the headwear from the ladies' department—"

"The hijab is a necessity, a disguise, you buffoon," says Khalid.

Haifa pipes up: "He's a poof, so fucking what, huh? Half my friends are shirt-lifters."

Khalid nearly turns to his sister but catches himself and

keeps me on lock. "Now, merely because . . ." he sputters. "I don't like those terms. I don't like your tone. And I'm as much a man as any, sister."

"Khalid, of course you are, my bloody point is that I'm the only one in the family who doesn't give a toss who you sleep with, or where you go, or what—"

"Silence!" snaps Khalid with venom. "Be silent."

Haifa shuts it, me saying, "I'm gonna change the subject. Cool it down."

The prince wiggles the gun. "You shut up too."

But I don't. "How'd they get you here, kids? Cause I got the sense that they didn't just ask you nice."

"Abducted," says Haifa, hugging herself now. Looking at me, looking at her brother.

Khalid nods. "In Paris. A violation." The prince gets choked up a touch. I'm ready to jump on him the moment he wavers but the gun is still in play.

Saying empathetic-like, "Shit, I imagine that was not easy . . . So you're saying, you got snatched. Against your will and all that."

"Correct, right off the street, manhandled and bundled into the back of a van, in the manner of your own CIA."

Haifa is nodding, I look to her. "You get grabbed too, sis?"

The princess exhales. "Like you don't know already, right, love?"

I raise a hand, peace. "I'm just the local guide, sweet stuff. This is learn-as-I-go for me too."

"Well, it was awful. Coming out of Selfridges, rushing to get off filthy *Oxford* Street, not paying enough attention, but no one expects . . ."

Me saying, "This is in London?"

Haifa gives me a repulsed look like I just suggested she, perhaps, was a tranny as well. "Um, yes. I'm sorry, is there another Selfridges on some other Oxford Street I might not be aware of?"

She's trying to bust my chops but I honestly don't have this information handy, so I lift my shoulders. "Fuck if I know, shorty, I'm from the South Bronx. Didn't they have one of those joints in the airport over there, like a chain deal, fancy tea and shit? I did make it as far as the airport in London. But I could tell you all about Frankfurt . . ."

Girl looks confused "The airport . . ." Then she shudders. "Oh God. That's *Harrods*. Worlds apart, Mr. South Bronx. Wasn't that kind of a trendy neighborhood anyway, the Bronx?"

"The South Bronx?" I laugh. "Na. Fuck it, they tried, but na. It's many things but I don't think anybody could accuse that hole of being trendy." This is a weird conversation, it occurs.

"Oh yeah. Of course. I'm thinking of Brooklyn," says the princess. "So right, before I can get to my car I've got a bag over my head and am in a bloody van getting knocked around, headed for Heathrow or Stansted, but I'm quite sure it was Heathrow. They had a police siren and—"

Khalid waves my pistol at my face. "Sister. Perhaps it's wise to leave it at that, disarm this man, and . . ."

The princess turns on her brother. "And what? And what? Oi, genius. Do you know the first thing about how to navigate Manhattan? Especially . . ." She gestures helplessly. "Do you have the least clue as to where we should go? Have you thought that far ahead, darling?"

"This man," replies Khalid, looking back and forth between the two of us, "this, you know, absolute thug, would have shot me, sister. In fact, he did try—"

Clear my throat (sand), trying to work that divide between the siblings. "Splitting hairs here, ya know, I recall me placing myself at your service, and you go jumping up my grill with my own gun. Is what I recall, which ain't exactly courteous."

"Khalid," says Haifa. "Darling, I know it's been ages and there's perhaps a great many . . . unresolved family issues, but I'm asking you . . ." She directs a matte-green fingernail out toward the street. "I mean, it's bloody soldiers and disease and mutant rats and massive piles of rubbish out there, there's nothing left . . ."

"Fact, your sister is right, y'all wouldn't last long. Couple fine-looking gals like yourselves."

If Khalid was wavering, he snaps to. "Sir," his voice quiet but on-the-rocks cold, "I will not stand for insults. I have no patience for such stuff."

I backpedal, damn. Knew a couple dudes like this growing up. You know what, y'all, live and let fucking live. You gotta ask yourself why somebody would put himself through all that social bullshit if he wasn't for rizzle.

But you know the ghetto, and the ghetto hates a faggot. Especially islanders. You gotta be one diamond-tough-assed, patent-leather-skinned faggot to survive the ghetto. Constant deluge of abuse. Beat-downs for shiz. And God forbid you got sent to the joint. You have to own that stuff, you have to put it up in everybody's face and tell 'em to suck a bag of dicks if they don't like it. And you'd better pack a blade, at minimum. Be prepped to cut somebody.

In my estimation, these folk are hard-core soldiers in a hostile land. Figure: cautious flattery is the way of the wise, me saying, "Fine-looking *individuals*. And I mean that sincerely, Khalid, with no offense intended whatsoever, you done had me fooled and then some. Passing as a chick." Switch to the Arabic: "This whole time, I can't get that bit of text from the holy Koran out of my head, and of course I paraphrase, forgive my sloppy recitation: *Say to the believing woman that they shall lower their gaze and guard their modesty, that they shall not display their beauty, that they shall draw their veils around their bosom—*"

"Chapter 24, verse 31, Allah is most merciful," murmurs Khalid. Softening.

Motherfucker, these fundamentalists are easily played, stands to reason. It's all memorization. Snap my fingers, me talking fast, "That's the verse. The very one. Thank you. With great respect. No, Your Highnesses, no." I inch closer to both of them, hands out as if to enfold them both tenderly. "Beyond the fact that I would rather suffer the death of a thousand cuts should you come to harm, my employers would see that I was dealt with if I fail. I am entirely at your service."

Girls trading glances like what gives.

Good stuff. Speed it up, Decimal. Switch back to English: "Get grabbed in New York City? And trust it, they not taking you to the airport for some duty-free at Shahrods." Haifa opens her mouth, closes it. Me continuing, "It gets real but quick out there. People hungry. And if they're not hungry, they're probably the guys who wanna grab you. Ya heard?"

Working her mouth soundlessly again, Haifa looks to her brother. Khalid watching a point over my shoulder, expression vacant. Perhaps deflated.

Reckon: Hell, I got this. The kid is all right. And nobody got hurt.

Then Khalid brings his eyes forward, glinting dark and icy through the slit in the veil. "Down. Kneel."

I don't move. My hands out. Haifa says his name once,

and Khalid silences her with a look. Me saying, "Yo, son, don't—"

Khalid raises his voice a notch: "On your knees." Pulls the hammer back.

Sigh. Did I not try to walk the way of the peaceful warrior?

"Oh, you're not going to really . . ." Haifa is chin-wagging, bemused.

Okay. I drop to a crouch, hang my head like I'm all played out.

Then Khalid fucks up huge, darting over to me willy-nilly like an eager nun, hand extended, reaching for my pocketed pistol.

Haifa more on point than her brother. Gives a warning shriek, but some fools just can't be told.

Wrap my reconstructed hand into a fist—and when the boy gets in range, I punch dude in his royal junk.

Khalid drops everything, clawing at his crotch, and goes down on his shins hard.

Prince making some ugly noises. Fuck knows, I put my back into it. Plus—that was my fake hand, so not exactly a fair matchup.

Can't see his mouth but his eyes tell me homie wasn't wearing a cup.

Scoop up my pistol, and the mag for the Beretta.

Haifa hanging back, looks like she might make a break for it . . . There she goes, sweet thing.

The girl spins, behind her a pile of Port Authority vehicles, and beyond that dusty dark. One can see the elevator shaft, the door stands open, revealing nothing but black. She jogs a couple steps, stops, turns again. She's nowhere.

Her brother incapacitated, me standing between her and the only visible exit.

"See, that was just some totally unnecessary roughness, star," I say, holstering the HK and slapping the mag back in my Beretta. Smile at Haifa. "Y'all should learn some basic self-defense moves. Mind, I do training sessions as well. Jiu-jitsu and shit. But we can talk about that on the flip." Put the Beretta away as well, hold up my hands. Lose gloves, Grab Purell™. Apply. "Enough with the guns. Are we done with the guns?"

Khalid is lying on his side now, breathing ragged.

Haifa embraces herself. Says, "That was bloody *cruel*. He couldn't have possibly hurt you. This is the boy . . . this is the child I once found weeping in our garden, weeping at the beauty of a single Sabi star . . ."

Well, I laugh at that. The husk of a laugh, over-cooked-turkey dry. "Wild-style. Lady, I'm getting the feeling you haven't seen this young man in a while, am I wrong about that? Child done grown up. Plus." Raise my pant leg, indicate the long diver's knife. "Now, that there would have been cruel. Coulda hit him with that."

Khalid moans.

"See, he'll be good to go in a jiff."

Haifa regards her prostrate brother. "Not bloody likely." She emits a long exhale.

I remove his headgear. He groans in protest.

"Hush. I need a face to talk to, masks and shit bug me out."

"Hmm. Yet you seem quite comfortable in your own," says Haifa. All that and observant too.

Christ, the genetics at play with these two . . . Khalid's every bit as beautiful as his sister, sleek and clean, dark hair cut close, slick with product, long face, almond eyes, amazing nose, fantastic skin . . . the only issue is a two-day-stubble kind of beard growth which I suspect bums him out.

He watches me, teeth clenched, looking forlorn.

Whistle. "You kids should be models and whatnot. For real, you know, or like actors. Or actor/models. That's just me talking from the heart."

"Ha," says Haifa, one side of her mouth lifting to create a lopsided smile. "Well, I appreciate the compliment on one hand, and on the other, that's it, isn't it, this is a problem as well, I mean . . . I was once pursuing a career in academia, right, and it's a question of being taken seriously. I mean, it's not on to be making a presentation to a roomful of men just fixated on your tits, is it?"

"Na, I wouldn't think that would feel good at all."

"Never know where you stand, do you? Not that it matters, that's all gone now . . ."

"Plus, the princess thing and shit. Another layer of just . . . what?"

"Nobody in my real life knows about that. I had entirely new papers made up when I left 'home,' the works, right, nobody knows. My first name is as much as I kept. Nobody knows—no one. Or so I had thought. Obviously, I was dead wrong." She shakes her head. "But this is not a subject I'll discuss further, especially with a bloody CIA man. Good God."

I'm looking at her. Wondering how much she knows about her situation here. Figure it's not my place to pry, right? But I do say, "For real, girl. Don't you know the rest of the world is in the business of trying to kill you people? Or at the very least rip you off?" Snap fresh gloves on. "Or if they ain't, they should be."

Haifa bobbing her head. "I am not my family."

"So you say."

"They cast me out. I owe them nothing."

"Huh. What did you do, get caught trying to learn how to read?"

She laughs. Acerbic. "I loved a boy. I loved the wrong boy. And that's all."

"Yeah?"

"And he disappeared. If you understand what I mean."

"Ho shit. Your family don't play. But this, I knew already."

"I wanted to do more with my mind—with my life—than serve the fat pervert they would have me marry. Give him bloody children. No."

At the mention of children I instinctively bust out the Purrell™.

Khalid isn't getting up soon, but he attempts to touch Haifa's foot, saying weakly, "Sister . . . you say far too much to this heathen, please be discreet and cautious . . ."

Haifa picks at her nails. "Oh please, Khalid, what are *you* like? You've got some nerve, trying to lecture me on anything," she says without looking at him.

I pick it up right where we left it: "So you cut out for the UK."

"At fourteen. Why am I telling you this? You reveal nothing of yourself, that's all you get out of me. Who did that to you, your cheek?"

"Took a tumble down our grand bloody ridiculous stairwell. You know, solid marble. *Crack.* Totally my error."

I grunt, shrug, wringing my mitts.

"Oi. What's this ritual you do with your hands?" she asks.

Taken aback, won't lie. Nobody raises this subject. Hear myself saying, "I'm cleaning them, obviously, disinfecting the hands. It's necessary, it's protocol . . . I just touched your brother, he just came off a ship . . . so . . ."

"Yeah? And you were wearing surgical gloves. So I'm not following why . . ."

Me sounding tight and defensive, I continue, "It's not a ritual, damn. Fucked-up word. Make it sound Catholic. Devil worship or some shit. Just trying to keep it clean, it's a filthy fucking scene up in here. You want some Purell™?"

"Do you feel compelled to do it very often?"

A gaggle of choppers come low, down what sounds like the canyon of Park Avenue. It's loud and gives me a moment to recover cause I'm starting to feel a bit short of breath. I don't appreciate being quizzed. I want her to drop it pronto. Plus, we can't skulk around this shit-ass garage forever.

Get my guns out one at a time, checking their magazines, really just something to do with myself. "Ha. Well, sugar cookie, if you're gonna sweat me about every little thing—"

"Don't call me *sugar cookie*, you cunt. I'm not some slag, I'm still a bloody princess in the Royal House of Saud."

I give a half-bow. "Begging your pardon. Your Royal Fly-ness."

Lady can't help but smile. "There, that's more bloody like it. Oi. Remember what we're saying. Your head on a platter. I just need to snap my fingers, and that's it, yeah?"

Clear my throat. Thinking she might be serious, but then the princess winks.

"It's not that I don't like to have the occasional laugh, I do." Girl cracks a grin there. She's all right, Haifa. But then she's right back harping on it, saying, "No, really, with the hands, yeah? Just that I've noticed you've now done this cleansing ritual four times since we've been with you, and that's just the occasions I've seen personally."

Ignoring this. Harder than necessary I slam the mag into my H+K, limp over to Khalid. Squat near his head. I do a little whistle birdcall thing. His peepers track me, but honeybun is pretty much incapacitated. Lay a gloved hand on his chest. Get intimate with the man.

"Hey, son. Real sorry about that just now. Was like a reflex, you know. Get nervous when folks point a gun at me. I'm a vet, man, got these automatic-like reflexes . . ."

Haifa nodding rapidly, like this somehow explains everything. "Ahh, right, and of course you would be former military. Since you're an American, I assume you saw combat somewhere . . ."

Speaking to Khalid, who eyes me woefully: "Your sister the princess seems to dig playing amateur shrink. She drop this on you too? Regarding your love life?"

"Oi. You," says Haifa. "I was this close to completing my postgrad studies in neuroscience up at Oxford. I hold a bachelor's degree in psychology. Bloody useless now, I suppose . . . but I'm not exactly what you might call an amateur, am I?"

"You know what I reckon? Y'all have much more to be concerned about than my freakin modus operandi. Though I'm flattered. And you know you should be concerned about important shit like hand hygiene. Especially when traveling. *Especially* when traveling by sea."

Shudder inwardly. The thought of a luxury liner in the middle of the Atlantic, bacteria, viral mingling, food-borne business . . . cast this off.

"But what y'all need to be thinking about now is where exactly you wanna go from here."

Haifa is looking at her brother. And I'm looking at her. Damn, she is something.

"Anywhere they won't find us, full stop," she says flatly, then turns to me, eyes big.

Me saying, all business: "And yo, what I'm trying to figure out is who the fuck is *they*?"

The choppers are doubling back, up the concrete river.

"They'll be wondering where we've gone off to," she says.

"If by *they* we're talking about everybody, that's a bet."

"But you, mate. I haven't the faintest who you are and
what you're all about. Save a practitioner of extreme hygiene," says the princess. Then: "Can we trust you?"

It's a simple question. Haifa's face is open, guileless. Despite her girl-in-distress status. Me saying, "*Écoute*. These
motherfuckers are shooting at me too. So until I have a little
more information, my two priorities are keeping you kids
standing, and protecting my own shit. Lucky for y'all, I get
the vibe like the two aren't mutually exclusive. "

"But can we *trust* you?"

"What did I just fucking say? And from where I'm leaning, y'all don't have much choice."

A short half-assed stare-down ensues, but the woman
knows she's got no other moves. Blows a lock of hair out of
her eyes, nods.

We get Khalid standing.

A couple of choppers run the length of 49th Street. The
buzzards circling. Time to fucking move. Me saying, "What's
it gonna be, kids? Cause this party? Bout to come to a painful
fucking stop."

Haifa nods. "Take us anywhere. We're tourists. Anywhere but that awful bloody boat."

———————————

S tay left. Stay left.

The Nissan Leaf, as it turns out, is an absolute breeze to hot-wire, the kind of design oversight that makes sense considering the hippies who created it, with visions of wind farms and rooftop farming clouding the realities of the day.

So much the better for a brother in a hurry, like myself.

Ten nineteen a.m. Forty-one minutes remain and I'll be able to enjoy more navigational options. But for the moment it's nothing but lefts.

Which is no problem, screaming eastward out of the garage onto 49th Street in a ragged Port Authority cop car. Rain has picked up again and it slaps the windshield angrily. Figure I'll show 'em what's left of the landmarks. No other destination presents itself.

The royals are comfortably ensconced in the passenger wheel well, under a white plastic tarp bearing the Waldorf Astoria logo.

Boom up and over a welt in the road, my head hitting the ceiling of the car. Trying to find the wipers, I slow up a smidge . . . there. Need to spit, tiny granules scraping my inner cheeks—but try to dry-swallow that spook urge and stay present.

Speed up into the intersection. Park Avenue, gunmen on foot a couple blocks north. Uniforms a mishmash. An army hummer straddles the median of Park, a glance south at the MetLife, its top floor obscured by the overhang. A handful of helicopters make lazy circles.

Nobody clocking us, me with my mask up and welding goggles on, only slightly sweating it. Don't look around too much.

Always working my second Plan A. Don't do Plan Bs, that's a defeatist mode of thinking. Have multiple Plan As and something is bound to pan out, with God's guidance.

The shell that was Macy's looms to our left as we rip past, I think about making a wisecrack about a two-fingered discount on handbags for my royal ducklings, but I doubt if they'd feel me. Plus, the house is all tapped out, of nigh on every little thing.

I'd be one to know. I'm among the many of us who helped empty the joint in the very early days. When it seemed like I'd never run out of sources for a crispy suit and a well-packaged (*sealed*) snack. A PowerBar, a Clif Bar, what have you.

"Macy's," I say.

Fucking lefts. Wanna head uptown but find myself barreling west . . . now the former Rock Center rears up ahead, and I'm busy craning my neck like a fucking tourist, to get a look-see at where they blew up the Rainbow Room, if you can see any damage from the street, so much so that I notice the layers of police barricades too late, calmly note they're just those low metal gates, I'm braking, we go one, two, three, four layers of aluminum tubing in before coming to a stop against a meter-high wall of sandbags.

Put it in reverse, cause I'm not going through that. Haifa and Khalid simultaneously commence hollering, Arabic and English at once; my head is overloaded and I'm unable to make sense of either one.

Looking right, and damn, I just waltzed straight into this one huh? Yonder comes a skinny kid in an NYPD uniform made for a man many times larger than him, limping toward us through the rain, I note idly that he's missing both arms. Correction: he's got one deformed baby arm clutched to his left breast, three fingers clawing a canister of pepper spray or the like.

That's how they do, throw up an impromptu roadblock, jack whomever slides by. Kicking my own ass for sleeping on this.

But is he simple? A lone no-armed cop, we supposed to buy that?

One thing's for sure: this environment is not easy on the human appendage. Witness also Mrs. Marcia's stump, and my kneecap and busted flipper . . .

Confusion creases his young face as I bring the car to a mellow halt and crank down the window, manually. Kid is probably somewhere between fifteen and eighteen years old. He's got a cheap Russian gas mask in his other hand but can't seem to get his act together.

Kid shimmies up to the car, pauses, unsure of my vibe. Mixed race, Asian and other spices, like myself. Working his mouth, he says, "Street closed. Street closed." Two times, then lifts the canister and lets me have it through the driver's-side window.

Which doesn't present a problem as I'm all masked up, plus the rain absorbs a fair bit of it; but I taste the spray, sure enough it's that hot pepper. This stuff is far past its sell-by date, however, and only has the effect of misting up my eyepiece.

Kid looks crushed when I don't have a seizure. I wanna let him down easy. Who's he fucking fooling, a cop with no arms?

Not focusing on the handicapped aspect of things, but I'm reminded of an occasion when I shot a Down's kid a couple years back. Certainly don't want to repeat that kind of karma killer.

"*Esse*," I say, "any pepper spray you find in town is gonna have gone bad awhile back. Shit, you couldn't have known that . . ."

Not defeated yet, kid drops the pepper spray and starts fumbling with his belt, I wonder if he somehow got ahold of another weapon . . . He produces a walkie-talkie, which reminds me I tossed my own out back in the tunnels, didn't I?

Before he gets any further with that, cause I don't want the boy making any calls, I swing the door open hard and catch him in the stomach. He makes a cartoonish "Oof" and staggers back far enough for me to step out, holding my Beretta loosely, safety engaged. His peepers go double wide at the sight of the gun, but Jah bless his heart, he doesn't rabbit. Boy standing his ground, bracing for some shit. I dig his spunk.

Don't want it to vibe like he doesn't present a challenge, so I kinda mock-wrestle a bit with the lad, breathing extra heavy like it's a major exertion, spin him around a couple times, whoopsie daisy, and relieve him of that walkie-talkie. He's batting at me with his shriveled hand, says, "*Maricón*."

Knock him down and put my knee on his chest, attempting to be gentle. Cheek hurting like a motherfucker even from that play-tussle. Child gets to hissing and spitting, biting at me and whatnot.

"Hey," I say.

Youngblood putting up fight, fair enough. I let him do it, glancing up and down the street. Beyond the barricade there's noise and action, but for the moment nobody's in view. Me saying, "Okay, player, you're all right, you're doing good. You had me going with the cop outfit, I bought it for real. *Esse*, you alone out here?"

Kid stops struggling, eyeballs me all fucked up.

"Said: are you alone out here?" I repeat.

Kid hocks one up and cuts loose with a fat globule of spew, which further sullies my goggles.

Not mad at this boy. Quite the opposite. There's a fair number of these rough-living strays, cast off and cut loose, discarded weak links in a chain gang. You can't dig a ditch fast enough, you're not worth much up in these parts. Short-sighted on the part of the companies, perhaps, but it's a big hard world and we're all just rats on a treadmill.

Take junior by the trachea, right hand only, apply pressure. Raw fear spreads across this kid's face, which is only healthy.

Pocket the walkie. "Listen, homie, you know the big library, the one with them stone lions? *Biblioteca*. Behind the big garbage pits . . ."

Kid looks sideways, nods.

"Saying that's my spot. So if you need a place to rest at, say it gets too cold out, you know where to look. They call me Decimal. Holler at me. I can get you some work."

Kid nods again, yap agape.

Release his throat and I'm halfway back in the car. "But yo, if you get stealthy and go trying to creep on me, be advised—I sleep light. Know what I mean? *Cuidado*."

Salute him with my pistol. Slam the car into reverse.

"What the fuck are you up to?" This from Haifa, wanting the score, leaning forward from the backseat. Startling me.

"Girl, get back under that thing, damn."

Bust it up on the curb, blow past this droopy kid, his eyes, reckon he could easily be me. Had things taken a different turn.

The princess and I lock eyes in the rearview, her vibing all *What are you gonna do about it?*

"Melting under there, plastic isn't it?" she says.

Figure it hardly matters who sees a couple of Arab hotties and a brother in a car. People gotta know where we're at. "Your world, ladies." And no doubt it is indeed.

"Where are we going?" Haifa is holding my gaze in the mirror.

Truth is, I don't know yet. Tell the girl to can it and let a man drive.

"Been hearing that most of my bloody fucking life," deadpans the princess.

Blow past the former skate rink at Rock Center, the headless gold statue presiding over a tonnage of smoldering garbage. Ripping beyond the concourse, nearly clip an elderly man, inching a trashed Aeron office chair toward 6th Avenue. Beyond him in a heartbeat, but manage to hear him shrieking, catch a phrase in Russian: ". . . heartless baby-fucking bastards!" He could be talking to or about anyone or everyone. I consider that this man, clearly cut loose from his clan, will probably be dead within a matter of days.

"Rockefeller Center," I say. "Dig, we're sightseeing."

The royal twins absorb these deconstructions in silence.

A ctivity at 50th and 7th Avenue, me wondering what's all that . . . milling cops, fire truck. Oh yeah, Lehman Brothers. Keeps getting burned, that space, a move which is purely symbolic as nothing could possibly remain therein. Not like there's been anything there anyway for years.

Hard right at the former Winter Garden Theater. Right again up Broadway. Nine bleak blocks on and confusion at Columbus Circle. Encounter the largest and most varied assembly of people I have seen on the island since Koreatown was in full swing, before the Chinese cleared 32nd Street entirely.

So many people, and me with not the least clue as to the rumpus.

As I round the traffic circle once more, just to be sure I'm not completely tripping, I take a calculated risk; the joint is heavy with cops and Cyna and varied military goons, and they appear to be preparing to shut off the road . . . silhouettes of workers sitting on Peter Pan and Greyhound buses parked around the obelisk in the center of the roundabout, all apparently waiting for something. Cyna-corp JLTVs parked at odd angles, armed figures coming around toward the larger building to the west.

But none of this is particularly special, and I'm not too concerned about my own ass, because the security types seem entirely focused on the other folks gathered here. Miss Marcia's people? Primarily women and children, amongst them a few scattered males missing limbs. I spy a couple wheelchairs (which must be considered a luxury item at this point) . . . perhaps a hundred and fifty people, forming a human barrier, blocking the entryway into the former Time Warner center.

"Columbus Circle," I say.

"Christ, this looks like bloody Damascus," says Haifa, face pressed to the glass.

Scoff at that. "No ma'am. Ain't no political drama in New York, baby, not no more. They put the smackdown on that stuff years back."

"Then what are we looking at?" asks Khalid quietly. And actually, it's a good fucking question.

The civies are harmless, breakable. They're all compromised in some sense: too small, too female, too wounded. And not a uniform among them, except a few of those now-familiar Parks Department windbreakers scattered here and there.

Small cornrowed black woman in a torn parka and a denim dress got that charisma, has a megaphone to her mouth, though I can't hear her over the approaching helicopters. My peepers wide for Miss Marcia, her little girl . . .

Not understanding what these good people think they're accomplishing. Some sort of paper banner is being unfurled, and I read, DOOMED TO REPEAT, but then the security forces are moving in, somebody opens up a hose and a heavy jet of brown water pummels the assembly, knocking people sideways, and as the Nissan rolls past 7th Avenue I make eye contact with a brown girl, perhaps Colombian or Dominican, maybe twelve or thirteen, no older, who seems to be shouting something, her expression laser-beam focused and not the least bit fearful, just as the butt of an assault rifle is brought down on her skull.

Sharp intake of breath from Haifa who must be watching the same thing.

"Merciful God," says Khalid, and in the rearview I see him cover his mouth.

Well now, I'm not one to sit in judgment, fuck knows—but that type of behavior ain't right. Crowd control and all, you don't take it to the children. No sir.

My ill paw trembles on the wheel. Cause it's so much more than that. My spirit is so fractured. I can only pray that if circumstances were flipped, I would have the moxie to be out there amongst the crowd getting my head caved in too.

But.

We're rounding the circle again, past Broadway southbound, facing the overgrown, fenced-in park for a moment. Military vehicles and, randomly, a horse carcass. Think, *Who the fuck is gonna clean that up?*

I glance up at the Trump Tower, flash on the man I murdered there. Again, the Buddha reminds I can be no moralist.

Step hard on the accelerator, sending us shooting up Broadway.

Reckon I'm beginning to understand. About all this ruckus. This is what happens, eventually. This is what you get, unless you kill everybody. I haven't seen it in a long time, not in this country, but it certainly makes all kinds of sense. Historical patterns, etc.

Color me Switzerland. That is to say: I'm on the fence, but yo, I'm happy to hold onto your money while you sort your shit out. That's the gangster in me talking. I let him steer, he's stronger than my other half. The half that brought that gear up to Miss Marcia. Cursing myself for that. Weakness, weakness on every level.

Get that head right. Dewey Decimal is far too busy

straight grinding. Staying north of the boneyard. He is hardly in the luxurious position to strike a fancy political pose.

This is what I tell myself. Gotta stay mindful, y'all.

Regardless of who or what I am, the System remains, unchanged, unchanging.

"Have you ever actually seen a beheading? Like a real, proper . . ." Haifa drops, like out of motherfucking nowhere.

"Wow, and that would be apropos . . ." I say.

"Martial law. Police state. Have you ever seen a living person get his head cut off?"

I think about that. I don't remember. Probably. "Damn, you know," I say, brushing my little tumor on the back of my neck with a finger, "I don't think I have. Nix that: not a *successful* beheading. I've seen niggas try, flossing like Mex cartel folk. Just make a damn mess. That's some specialized tactics, you gotta know what you're doing, have the right, what. The right tools."

Haifa is quiet.

"Afghanistan, Pakistan, again there were those dudes who would give it a shot. Usually some hayseed yahoos just having a circle-jerk. More like trophy stuff, chest thumping." I peep her in the rearview. "Princesa, you saying you seen some for real executions like that?"

Khalid mumbles, "We were very young."

Gotta be real, it's easy to forget about old Khalid. Wonder if that's always been their dynamic. Just by dint of Haifa's beauty and presence, it must've been tough on her siblings.

"Is that so shocking?" Haifa has her palm pressed to the window. An armored car trundles south, across the median, past a former Pier 1 Imports. "You know where we're from."

"Yeah, well. Y'all people. Got that Middle Ages vibration. With respect. Trust, we do not kick it like that in the United States of America, so you won't see that here."

Of course I'm spitting ironic, but oh Lord does it sounds stupid coming out of my mouth.

No, we don't kick it like that in the USA. Within our own borders. But at the black sites? The Special Access Programs? Our joints in armpit spots like Poland, Romania? The shit is a different story. Talking about some deep, dark-ass *SAW II* type of action.

Haifa lifts her slim eyebrows. Her scar compresses. She says nothing.

"Oh, so you think we're going barbaric here in New York City." Playing the flag-waver, mostly just cause it's fun to be contrary. I know very well we're living like animals.

The princess inclines her head. Khalid says, "Merely making observations, *Inshallah*, your consciousness is perhaps not quite there yet."

Damn, that's one polite gay dude. None of this swish-and-snap attitude.

If I come off insulting to gay dudes, that shit is just ignorant. My man Dos Mac was gay as hell and he was my brother.

I have no further comment. Winking yellow light at the convergence of B'way and 73rd Street. Within a single block I spot multiple sniper positions on upper levels of buildings, several gunmen out in the open on rooftops. I spy evidence of not less than three, four, five former Starbucks outlets. Could be six . . . no, that was an Argo Tea . . . Reaching for a pill. Fumble the bottle, it falls into the wheel well. Fuck. Bend to my right.

Haifa and Khalid shriek in stereo.

Startled, I jerk the wheel, snapping, "Jesus, I'm just

. . ." Haul my peepers back to the road in time to spot the neon-yellow Lamborghini far too late, incongruously I note it appears spotless, with a custom license plate reading, MAKIN$, as the car rockets straight at us, low against the nonexistent traffic the wrong way down Broadway.

oughing up sand and bits of teeth as I come to, on my back like a helpless bug about to get skewered. Once I've regained the ability to speak, I address the Indian dude straddling my chest. Likely I've hit my head real hard but I can still dig his cologne; potent but tasteful. Recently applied . . .

Oh, it's these guys.

Me slurring, "Aren't you motherfuckers a good thirty blocks out of your jurisdiction?"

Dude maybe early forties. Prada eyewear, with tape on one of the hinges. Jeans and expensive boat shoes. Waxed racing-green Burberry jacket worn on top of a salmon sweater, made of what I assume to be cashmere. Uzi.

"The Upper *West* Side is our territory," the man hisses. "The Upper *West* Side. We've got the best schools. Better restaurants . . . We did . . . The museums . . . fuck it. Fuck it!"

"Bala," says one of his three companions, a slightly overweight white guy in blue pinstripe and those miserable neon running shoes with the toes. "Be cool. That's not the first time we've heard this. Right?"

"Yeah, Bala, you're all worked up, bro," says the third. Then looks at Haifa and Khalid, shifting the shotgun he's got trained on them. I can't see them too clearly but they're sitting up, wide-eyed, and appear unhurt. "He's worked up, fired up," he repeats, jerking his head toward the Indian on my chest.

"How is it," asks Bala of the universe, "that people make the assumption that we claim the fucking Upper *East* Side? It makes no sense. It's a piece-of-shit neighborhood. It's just trashy, Rob! It makes us sound like trash. It's not good, just perception-wise. Rob, it's no good."

"Way I hear it," I offer, "it's just 'Midtown.' Like a blanket term. 'Midtown Militia.'"

Bala pokes the Uzi into my chest, mouth contorting. "*Midtown*? Is that supposed to somehow be better that the Upper East Side? What kind of fucking gang would call themselves the Midtown Militia?"

"It's alliterative," me saying around the gun in my yap. "Sounds catchy. Damn, I don't know, star, I didn't make the shit up." These hedge-fund kids. I shoot the twins a look. Yeah, they seem okay, if confused. As they should be. "Thought you all were like an urban legend," I add, noting Bala seems to brighten at that, probably cause *urban legend* sounds gangster, which was my intention.

Everybody wants to be a gangster until they actually have to be one.

Realize I'm drooling out of one side of my mouth. Face aching. Adjusting my mouthpiece, which is all askew, I continue: "We would have never—"

"The thing is," says Rob, who approaches and gently guides Bala off me. "The thing is. We have this, ha, this ongoing back-and-forth with the Port Authority . . ." He comes to a squat, resting his Glock on his knee. His suit is probably Brooks Brothers, woolly and dirty, though he too wears heavy perfume to mask any unseemly odors, a common tactic these days.

Bala is engaged midargument. "Yeah, there was a Shake Shack on fucking East 86th Street, but it was fucking *garbage*, man . . . Put a Shake Shack down and you think your neighborhood is happening."

There's a wall of sound in my ears, my tinnitus being the least of my issues . . . sand on my tongue, my dented noggin, but otherwise I seem okay. Grunt.

"Port Authority . . ."

"Yeah," says Rob. Waves the gun. "Ha. Your vehicle?"

I nod, right. Glance at our humble car in its death throes, steam issuing from its engine, front hood crumpled against what was once a liquor store on the northwest corner of West 74th Street. The Lamborghini parked midstreet at a whimsical angle, winged doors flipped up.

"The thing there is," Rob goes on, "they're just a bunch of thugs, criminals, these Port Authority guys. And they simply refuse to back off. Ha. So we figured you folks were PA. That's why we came at you so hard . . . but hey. It looks like somebody already got to you there. Damn, that's gonna be one hell of a shiner."

"You should see the other girl," I tell him, reflexively tapping my implant, then bringing my hand to my crushed cheekbone . . . could use a painkiller . . .

" . . . was the new *Brooklyn*! Yeah, Port Authority, the guys who are left, that is, a whole bunch of fucking criminals, man!" shouts Bala, needlessly loud. Me thinking, *Cocaine?* Impossible. Man yapping, "Oh yeah. Better watch your valuables around those PA people, man. They're fucking *pirates*. Poachers! Somalis, dude."

Robert gives Bala a hard look, and Bala cans it. A helicopter swoops past, up so high to not really be a concern, but it's enough to wake me up.

"What's with the girls?"

"How you mean?"

"Where'd they come from? I mean. They look . . . clean. Fresh."

"Don't even contemplate it, son," I croak, channeling throat cancer. Guess I sound serious enough that everybody looks to me. I suss the joker holding the girls down, and dig in my heart of hearts that this man could never pull a trigger except at a rifle range, and only then after he's been given explicit permission to do so.

"They look like terrorists, straight up," says Bala. "They look like jihadists or some shit."

"That's kinda racist sounding," says the fat guy.

"Man, I can't be racist. My folks are from India, I'm a full-blooded pure Indian man. So I can't be racist. But these people. This a joke? I don't like this, Rob, man, I don't like it one bit . . ."

Rob raises his hands to silence his friend as I clear my ragged throat once more.

"Gentlemen," I say. Selecting my words here: "We have no argument with y'all. And we have no interest in any, uh . . . any theoretical valuables in your possession—"

Bala is talking before Rob can get to him, straining forward like an angry dog. "What do you know about our stuff, freak? What do you know about it? Lemme tell you something . . ."

"Bala," says Rob, tired, restraining him.

Bala wiggles and kicks, and I'm pulling myself to my feet, drawing both pistols as I do so. Flip the Beretta around so I'm holding the barrel, butt out.

"Gun!" calls the third guy with the shotgun.

Bala makes a confused attempt to bring his Uzi around, but I'm cracking him in the temple with my pistol, following this up with an elbow, quick and hard, into Rob's jaw. Certainly don't want to murder these silly rabbits, so I do it all with as much control as I can muster.

Dude with the rifle is slack-jawed, I'm moving toward him quick with the 9mm trained on his nose.

"Didn't catch your name, star."

"David," he says, pie-eyed.

Desperately wanna Purell™ up.

"David," I repeat. Slobbering again, it's just not on. Try to wipe it on my collar. "Lay it down and we got no further problems, ya heard?"

Clearly David wants to point out the injustice here, since in theory he's got the twins and I don't seem to be allowing him this advantage. Or at least this is what I'd be thinking. He looks at me, at the twins, back to me.

Haifa starts talking. In Arabic.

The militia dudes are awed. Mouths on the pavement.

Haifa saying, "It would be such an irony, wouldn't it, to have come all this bloody way, God willing, only to be raped by some American yuppies in this horrid preppy clothing with their *awful* shoes."

The fancy boys are *floored*. They've never seen or heard this kinda exotica. Haifa's an enchantress. I use it.

"David. For the third time. Drop the weapon."

The pudgy guy shakes it off, says, "Hold on, hold on, the thing is—"

His head explodes. I hear the shot after the fact, which is a fucked-up phenomenon I was once told indicated brain damage. Like, no shit. Damn, I didn't intend to ice this goofball. Haifa and Khalid both shriek.

Then it occurs—it wasn't me. Spin toward Broadway, the men doing the same . . .

Cyna-corp guys leaning out of their SUV, hollering in

tandem. Snuck up on us, like, these silent electric vehicles . . .

"Fucking *nailed* him!" I make out.

Recognize this is a potential point of no return. It's important to breathe and identify these moments, give them respect.

As they shift their attention to me, it's clear that these guys are so rabid that rational communication will not be possible. Multiple gun barrels are being shifted in my direction. My options are swiftly limited.

I raise my left hand, white-flagging the boys in an effort to slow things down, me saying, "Gents. State Department. These two are under the protection of Homeland and are to be treated as diplomatic . . ."

Jaw on in this vein, and with the other hand, dip into my suit jacket pocket and thumb off the pin on Chip's thermite grenade. Produce and lob it under their truck, a soft underhand. Praying it's not a dud.

And with this small movement, I have just gone to war with pretty much every other motherfucker on the island.

"Light 'em up!" yodels one of the cowboys, clearly relishing it all, a half second before the detonation.

War. Which, though distressing, is a condition I'm pretty comfortable with.

B ooyah. First time I've ever pushed a whip like this.

"Christ. Christ. What now?"

I downshift. Haifa is hyperventilating but at least making efforts to hang tough. Khalid, however, concerns me, poor boy, crammed into the small space that passes for a backseat, unresponsive and floppy.

I'm hunched over the wheel of the Aventador, hapless David's shotgun on the dash . . . and I will tell you that my jimmy is hard enough to be steering the vehicle on its own. Distracted only by my cheekbone, which is making itself known.

"I've got . . . I've got fucking blood on my jeans. That man's blood . . . God, the way they just shot him . . . why did that tank thing explode?"

"Haifa," I respond, "this is real. This is happening. I've negotiated jams like this before. Ya heard? We gonna be all right."

Haifa bobs her head. "Okay," she whispers. "Okay."

"Now be a darling," I say, "and feel around in my jacket pocket here. You'll find a bottle of Vicodin."

She does it. "There's two pill bottles here."

"Just read the label. Vicodin. Give me three."

The princess fishes them out. I open my trap. She tosses them in. Dry swallow.

". . . tending to the enemy like your own husband, why not wash his feet . . ." Khalid is mumbling, some shit like that. Haifa lays into him . . .

But I'm all about this car. The Lambo. This bling-bling sex machine has some mad crazy pickup, and after an endless dirge-parade of Leafs and Priuses I am reminded exactly why one might spend a small fortune on a fossil-fuel beast such as this.

Focus, Decimal. Gotta focus. Stay solid.

Bank left onto Columbus, northbound. Angling for the 97th Street Transverse, with not the least clue if the road still exists.

"I'm taking you ladies to have a look at one of our very finest city parks. Seat belts."

See myself in the rearview, face distorted and cracked, eyes crazy, scabs on my forehead. A frothing, twitching zombie. I quickly look away.

I used to be . . .

I used to be a good-looking kid.

Khalid unresponsive. Haifa fumbling with the belt, still talking. "And then this . . . and then this . . . if it gets much worse I'll be bloody—"

"Just so you can start processing now, sis—it's gonna get a lot worse before it gets better. That's just natural law, like gravity."

Clock the multiple helicopters, not overly concerned about them yet as they're a ways off. Scoping the street for something, anything . . . the back of the Natural History Museum flashes past on our left . . . and between 81st and 82nd two words grab my attention. The nucleus of a plan springs forth.

SCHWEITZER LINENS

"Hang on. Stay in the car," I tell the girls.

Haifa says something that I don't catch as I jerk the wheel sideways, jump the curb, and slide to a stop midblock . . . the ridiculous door taking a seeming age to arc up and open . . . piling out with the shotgun in one hand, hustle over and knock a hole in the glass door of the shop.

Apparently, looters have little interest in two-thousand-thread-count Egyptian cotton bedding . . . that is, until now.

A minute later I'm hauling myself back into the Lamborghini, wincing at my broken face, knee, hand, all the points of discomfort in my body beginning to converge . . . toss the two sets of bundled queen-size sheets onto Haifa's lap. Black and white.

"What is all this . . . oh." She gets it.

Reverse back out onto the road and accelerate up Columbus, my gut churning as we hit ninety mph in the count of five. Streetlights no longer even bothering to blink yellow, they just hang there in the wind unlit. No rules.

"Please slow down, my God!" moans Haifa, struggling again with her seat belt . . .

Glancing right toward the park at 86th Street, I notice a snarl of vehicles and metal gates between us and Central Park West. We tear past.

Thinking: *Let it be open.* I swerve easily to avoid a trashed MTA bus making its way south, its windows blacked out save the driver's, a woman in a gas mask who offers us a thumbs-up.

Moment the bus is clear, helicopters start to fall in line behind us, coming in low, which is not unexpected. And here it is.

Dodging an empty halal food cart, I cut east at 96th Street, smacking one of several metal wire garbage cans aside as I do so. Haifa jerks toward me, gets caught by the belt . . . She cradles her neck.

"For fuck's sake, can you give some kind of bloody advance warning?"

Multiple NYPD vehicles, plus I peep the sheer volume of metal in the form of riot gates blocking the mouth into the park . . . plus a low dam of rocks and vegetation. Cars not blocking the entryway but if they move so much as a foot . . . Concerned about the Lamborghini, which is more fiberglass/carbon-filter canoe than solid car, and in this sense not really engineered to do what I'm about to ask it to do.

Helicopters keeping some kinda pace. Situation not looking ideal. But we enjoy one very significant advantage: we're going really motherfucking fast. And I push it harder, the car responding like it's all no big deal. Which calms me like. So I jam it further, dropping a prayer to Satan and all his angels.

Just cause I'm naturally a curious cat, I take a gander at the speedometer as we smash into the barrier at the mouth of the Transverse, and it reads 114 mph. Dirt and rocks cover the windshield momentarily and are just as quickly shucked. Realize that's me shrieking in tandem with the ladies. As we slam through a wood gate, a looming tree clips my rearview mirror neatly off . . . for a period we seem to be off-road, I yank it blindly to the left and we're fishtailing back on the roadway, a good thing too, as the Transverse dips immediately between two stone walls and we peel off onto the northern road.

We hit the first underpass, accelerating. Between the spotty tree cover and the tunnels, I'm hoping and praying we've negated the ghetto-birds, at least. The cops could easily follow us but I'm not planning on being on the main road for too long.

"You kids all right?"

Feeling myself. Making magic. Flow infinitely. Low-hanging branches tickling the roof.

Peep the mirror: Khalid not looking too fresh. Gonna say something encouraging but this thought is cut short . . . gotta rip it hard left to avoid a green-striped cab in the road, scraping the rock wall with my door.

"Where are you bloody *taking* us? Please talk to me," says Haifa.

I glance sideways at her and it occurs to me . . . "Do you know what this is all about, princess? Why you're here in New York?"

She shakes her head. "I told you, I was abducted. Assume money."

Never occurred to me that these kids might not have been filled in as to their . . . pivotal role in all this static.

Sigh. Do I gotta do every little fucking thing?

Want a moment to sanitize but doubt if I can steer with my knees at these speeds . . .

Three or so underpasses on . . . fork nearing 5th Avenue looks completely blocked off, which I don't sweat cause *boom*, and there's the turnoff. Applying the brakes as I cut a sharp left, onto the east road, slowing, no clue as to what I'm gonna find.

Let the motherfucker be passable.

The road ahead is wide and paved, multiple lanes for foot traffic, bikes, and motor vehicles. Weirdly, it appears very much as it did pre–2/14.

Slam on the brakes as I dig that I'm about to emerge from under the tree cover, which isn't much to begin with—and we come to an immediate stop, all of us whipped forward. The belts catch us and we collapse back into our seats.

It's remarkably quiet, save the distinctly nonelectric and unfamiliar sound of a V12 motor idling.

Me saying, "It's like this, kids. You're here to be bred. Like thoroughbred horses. The two of you. You're here to join your family—"

Haifa laughs. I take this opportunity to pop a pill, Purell™ up, and get a fresh mask going.

"That's well sick, that's a well sick fucking joke, mister."

"No joke, Your Highness. At the behest of your family, you and Khalid . . . in order to, you know. Maintain the House and shit."

She laughs again, a laugh that collapses as horror envelops her face. "Maintain the . . . oh my God, you're not joking, are you?"

Say nothing. Haifa starts nodding.

"Sister . . ." says Khalid from the back.

She spins on him and I clock her incisors. "You knew," she hisses in Arabic, eyes shining. "You knew about this, daughter of a donkey?"

Khalid shifts his body. "Sister. Be calm. Muhammad himself married cousins . . ."

"*Ibn himar*, this is very fucking different than . . . Are you trying to use that as a justification for—"

"Sister, I'm saying there are times of extreme crisis when . . . God is great. The Kingdom needs us, our people need . . ."

Haifa is nodding, fumbling with the door handle, which starts to open.

"Do not get out of the car, princess," I say. Shifting my ass what for the goddamn sand . . .

Haifa, still bobbing her head, leans out and retches, trying to push the hair out of her face.

"Princess," I say, reaching out to touch her back. "Haifa."

She half turns, fast, snatches the shotgun off the dash by the barrel, and tries to crack me in the jaw. I duck it pretty easy, grab the stock, and rip it out of her hands, bringing my Beretta around as I do so.

"Shut the fucking door," I tell her. She does it.

"And you, CIA, with your guns. You're a bloody fucking evil monster."

"You're not wrong," I reply, "but lady, I might be the last good thing you got."

"How do you reckon that? You're delivering us to—" She stops, choking on the words.

"Listen to me. I'm not doing anything of the kind."

Haifa stares at me, black eyes, that knot of scar tissue.

"But Haifa. I just need to hear you say it: are you opposed to being impregnated in the manner described?"

"What the fuck? Am I *opposed*?"

"Sir," says Khalid from the back, "if I might. It's not so much your concern—"

"You close your motherfucking yap, *bibi*. I will cut you, savvy? From here on out, you got no say in nothing."

Khalid scoffs, sets to gum-flapping, but I cut him short.

"I'll keep you standing but I don't much like you, son. Keep you alive out of respect for your sister, who I like very much."

Khalid zips it.

"Who says I want him alive?" Haifa chimes in slowly, getting ideas, those peepers flashing.

I check her sideways. "Come on. You're not that kinda girl. This is your kin, a'ight?"

Haifa looks at her hands as if they don't belong at the end of her arms. She nods, shuts her eyes.

"Now spit, princess. It's your body, your call. Wanna do this for your family or do you not?"

"This is a nightmare . . . God no. No. I don't want this. I don't. I don't," says Haifa, a tear making its way over and across her cheekbone.

"Okay. So buckle up."

Khalid starts to say something and I give him the look in the rearview, which is enough to silence him once more.

Haifa orbs on me, glassy moons. "To go against my people is . . . absolute suicide."

"Oh, you concerned about me all of a sudden?"

"I am not sure yet," she says. Then: "My family, you don't know them."

"Uh-huh. And they don't know me neither," I respond. And stomp on the gas.

eading north, the partial tree cover holds pretty much all the way to the impasse. I can hear the helicopters, though I don't see them and I pray they don't see me, but in this I am kidding myself.

Parks Department flatbed with felled trees diagonally across the road, thick forest on either side. We're not getting through that. I kill the engine.

"We leg it from here. Okay, ladies? Out."

Haifa crawls out. I rotate to Khalid, who isn't moving.

"Hey, son, are we gonna have a fucking behavioral problem?"

"God protects me."

"Na, that's where you're . . . Now that's some sad bullshit. God don't protect *anybody*. You think these people won't cut you down like a three-legged dog? I don't give a fuck who you think is with you, you been sold out, kid, ya heard?"

Khalid's a sullen motherfucker. Cocky and spoiled, a miserable combo of bad qualities. "I will not be moved," he says, lower lip jutting out. "My family—"

"Have left you ass-out. You're *alone*. Believe that. Now, am I gonna have to drag your silly sack out of there? Conversation's over, out." Grab the kid's garment, get to hoisting him up and over the seat, him protesting all the while.

"Unhand me this instant!"

Get him clear of the car.

Haifa says, "Keep that bloody fucking bastard away from me or I'll gouge out his eyes. Where do we go?"

I indicate the path north. Shake my pant leg to dislodge the grit in my drawers . . . Refocus. Tell 'em, "Hustle, y'all. Hustle. Stay covered, keep to the side."

Snatch the bedding I hoisted and get stepping, north toward the Conservatory Garden.

Miss Marcia smiles at the Saudis. Gracious.

She looks beat down, and any kind of scary ESP vibe I detected in our first encounter is muted. Muted, but present. She gives me a psychic wink, that's as clear as I can explain it.

"Well, goodness. What beauties. Are you at least going to introduce me?"

"No," I say. The kids have been instructed to keep their lips sealed. "The less you know. All that, ma'am."

She beams at the twins. "Well, isn't this all just so exciting." And to me: "How long do they need shelter?"

"Won't be long. One night, max."

The older lady looks at me now. Bright eyes. Says, "I lost a very good friend today. She was a unique, wonderful woman. Others died as well, many hurt. There's too much death, too much pain. It's reaching a peak of some kind, a crescendo."

"You do it or not, teach? Hang on to the ladies here?"

Marcia turns her head back toward the encampment, then inclines her head. "Yes, yes, of course. My point is only that I don't know if we can protect anyone any longer. I don't know if we can protect ourselves."

I hand Haifa my second gun. Take a long deep drink of her, that scar, that hair, this woman. "If they come before I make it back, just point and squeeze."

Haifa says something but again I miss it, ducking into the tunnel of thorns, swapping out a new pair of gloves.

✳ ✳ ✳

Come barreling out the park at Lenox and 110th. Security there half asleep and I'm moving way too quick in the Lamborghini. Bitches just standing there gawking. Two males. Take 'em down, strip 'em, dress 'em up, and we're out and away easy as American pie.

Choppers dog me all the way down the east side. No shots, but they're straight up my ass.

Which suits me fine. I lift the Cyna-corp helmet partially off my head, pull the recently deceased Faisal's shortwave.

The painkillers hit me all at once and I crack a nasty grin cause everything smoothes out . . . Have a gander at my two new passengers, still out cold.

Dig it. Depress the talk button. Burst of feedback, then in Arabic, "Identify yourself."

"I've got the twins. Bringing them into your consulate, and I'll need some security to hand them over to."

"Identify yourself, please."

"Move your people out there to intercept if you want these kids in one piece. Gate at 47th and 1st Avenue."

I disconnect. They'll get it together. Slap my Cyna-corp headpiece back on.

As I rip down Dag Hammarskjöld Plaza, clock an NYPD/Cyna-corp/UN blue helmet mélange, dudes milling about . . . several vehicles, but the only one that concerns me is the jeep with the mounted machine gun in back. Likely snipers in the area as well.

Bring the bling machine to a hard stop midway across the overpass straddling 1st Avenue. Just gonna let things play out organic like.

Fellas clock me, a cluster of UN and Cyna-corp folks confer. Then a group of seven or eight begin approaching me. Somebody has a megaphone, calling out, "MOVE THE CAR. CAN'T STAND HERE. MOVE THE VEHICLE."

I wait. Feels foul to be back in this uniform, but it is what it is. My suit balled up in the back, all my tools transferred to the Cyna-gear. One thing you can say for these jammies is they got some elegant pockets, and plentiful too . . . so hard a quality to come by in a carbonite paramilitary uniform.

Nudge Darth Vader slumped in the passenger's seat, fully burqa'd in black, cuffed with white plastic. An improv getup in sheets. "Okay, buddy. Wake up now. You too, player." This to the figure in the back, white robe and head covering. Cuffs too. "Your jammies fit me like a love glove, friend. I appreciate the loaner."

Guys shift around, saying some undoubtedly impolite shit that I can't quite make out.

"Sorry? Can y'all breathe through that stuff?"

I'm referring to the gags. Cat in the back starts head-shaking, no no no.

"Yeah you can. Okay, here we go."

Open the doors. Fellas start hollering and many weapons are turned our direction.

"Get out," I say to the black fabric.

Flat out up 1st Avenue, alone now, having deposited the be-sheeted grunts on the corner of 47th Street like a couple of sad ghosts, already mourning my impending divorce from this, the freshest whip I've ever had the pleasure of piloting.

This gray, grim stretch of road has been more or less razed. Though technically Coalition grounds, Samsung had a lease on it for some mysterious project which has yet to see light.

Bounce. The roadway is wet, pocked, and ulcerous . . . any structure less than eight stories high is gone, leaving a patchy, balding expanse occasionally disturbed by massive clutches of cranes, cement mixers, diggers, and other heavy equipment, mostly bearing Korean characters. Frequent NYPD observation towers, like abandoned nests, everything empty, insubstantial.

Wipers not doing much good, getting pelted. Car vibrates lightweight and prone to hydroplane. The flock of choppers has splintered into two groups, probably unclear on who exactly they should be tailing . . . I'm left with three on my bumper, which is still three too many.

My moves are strictly short-term . . . it won't take but a few minutes for the Saudis to suss out that the pair beneath the sheets are in fact shanghaied Cyna-corp soldiers, sloppy motherfuckers who were sleeping on the job uptown and deserved to get sapped, stripped, and grabbed.

Don't slack, y'all. Not in this mess.

This latest feint of mine will hopefully throw yet more confusion into the mix, however slight, and right now what I need is max chaos. Wanna see everybody confused so I can get a moment to read the situation properly.

Scene back there indicates to me that the Saudis and the cops are playing different games, with very different goals . . . suspicion confirmed.

Cyna-corp, at loggerheads with the Saudis?

Recall the soldier's radio in the back of Chip's car, seemingly weeks ago. *"Take out both of them."*

Take out both of them. Chip and me? Or the twins themselves?

Doesn't feature that the Saudis would want their precious royals harmed. So I had reckoned I could strike at least one group off the long list of folks who might be trying to kill me and the ladies.

But now. Not so positive. Think on it: possible splinter group within their own ranks. All these Arab militaries ready to bust a coup at a hat's drop . . .

I can, however, make a safe bet that now Team Saudi are gonna be gunning hardest to run me down. But they gotta have their phasers on stun. Cause right now I'm one of the few who knows where the twins are at. And everybody still wants the twins, right?

Point is—everybody needs me alive. And I like it like that.

96th Street, 106th Street, 110th Street, and I challenge anybody to not get that Bobby Womack track stuck in their craw. Fall for it every time. *Across 110th Street* . . .

Black superhero pushing neon-yellow Lamborghini at 125 mph up 1st Avenue, with a trio of Apaches in hot pursuit. Perhaps a New York City first . . . but in this town you never fucking know, do ya?

I see Haifa's face in all its detail. The girl has soul. You can just tell. I need to get to know her.

I'm angling for the RFK Bridge. Gotta ditch the whip. Slow it down a smidge, and set the cruise control for forty mph. Hard right into the RFK underpass at 125th Street. Go, go. I pop the door, scoping the stack of sandbags . . . fuck, my suit.

At the last second I snatch up my trousers, but that's all there's time for, the window is closing as I roll out the door, come down awkward, but the bags essentially make a comfortable landing pad. It's a move I wouldn't have made without the exoskeleton, believe me.

The hot car carries on, bouncing off the safety walls, onto the Harlem River Drive, over the guardrail like a toy, and into the tainted East River.

Too late, I'm thinking. *There goes another suit . . .*

"**D**ewey Decimal for Senator Clarence Howard."
Leaning fast westbound on 125th in Cyna-corp regalia, eyes on the rooftops and windows.

It got dark in a hurry. Relentless drizzle.

More than 50 percent of the buildings have simply been torn down, leaving me with the impression that I am moving through my own mouth, the wasteland of my dental-scape. The thought makes me wanna pop a pill, which causes me to reach for the Purell™ . . . then I recall I'm encased in this CC exoskeleton.

Consider taking a minute, to strip down and lather up. Consider my situation. Gonna have to wait. The sand locked in here with the rest of me.

"Dewey Decimal for Senator Clarence Howard."

Frequency flipping on the head-com. Switch to the next channel, say it again. And repeat.

Spent a half hour in the old MTA building with the striped city buses, hulking and dark. Once the birds floated off I bounced out the back door. As to the effectiveness of the paltry smoke screen I'm tossing up, I don't have the least clue, but hey, I'm making an effort here.

Harlemworld. Looks like everywhere else now. Gray, gray, gray, and blank.

Keep peeping back at a white Suburban creeping down the wide road, about a block behind me. Don't like that at all. Otherwise traffic is super light—buses and the occasional military transport. The Suburban is having a tough time blending in.

Maintain fucking with the radio, and trying to avoid Cyna-corp's frequency. I got the code for the Saudi kids off of those two chumps I dumped, they flossed tough but at gunpoint they spilled all right.

The code. It's cheesy as fuck, you ready?

The Saudi prince and princess are known collectively as "Gemini." Get it? Like "twins"?

How hood is that? I mean, I reckon it's descriptive enough but it vibes ghetto to me. Sounds like a rapper . . . Shit, it probably was a rapper. Definitely was a rapper. I stopped paying attention back when all my waking energy got diverted into ducking the dirt-nap.

"Dewey Decimal for Senator Clarence Howard."

Doesn't take too long to raise somebody. Didn't expect it to.

A tight, small voice comes back at me: "Mr. Decimal, your ears must be burning. How can I help you?"

"Yeah, gimme the senator, not trying to talk to some flunky. Who the fuck's this?"

"Tim Young. Chief of staff for Senator Howard. We've, ah, met."

The distaste is audible. Oh, sure, I remember this Negro. Snooty Millhouse type.

"'Sup, Tim? You that fancy brother trying to get down with the plantation massas at the Cosmos Club?"

There's a crackle, and Tim comes on again: "Mr. Decimal, you should be aware—"

"Tim, man, you gotta know those crackers might let you in the front door, but you'd best forget about getting in on that private poker game in back. That's a whites-only kinda jam, feel me?"

Pause, another long set of crackles. I casually do a moving turn . . . there's the Suburban, just drifting along. I don't like that. At all.

Tim repeats: "*Yes, Mr. Decimal, you should be aware that listen-ing in we have representatives of the FBI, the NSA, the Arab League, the Saudi Royal Navy, the Saudi ambassador,*" he has to take a breath, "*as well as representatives of Mossad, OPEC, and the Abdulaziz family.*"

Cough into the mouthpiece. "That's a whole lot of bod-ies. Mental picture of all y'all motherfuckers jammed into a shitty little conference room. Coffee and bagels. Hummus and whatnot. Sweaty little carrots—"

"*Yes,*" says Tim, "*I inform you of this for legal reasons.*"

Me thinking, *Why bother?*

And Tim continues, "*There's unanimous concern here, ah . . .*"

Pause. On the other side of the street, beneath a huge set of letters reading, DR. JAYS, clock a set of hazy figures, youthful, headed the opposite direction. They slow up, re-garding me. Gotta keep my eye on them, but I stride forth.

Tim saying, "*. . . deep concern regarding the whereabouts of Prin-cess Haifa Abdulaziz and Prince Khalid Abdulaziz, who arrived in Manhattan this morning on a diplomatic—*"

"Na, man. *You* people sent me down to meet and greet them, I'll remind you. Right, Tim?"

Crackle, then: "*Yes, I can confirm that with my office.*"

"And I don't think it's a state secret that I, personally, set up and ran the whole operation, right, Tim?"

"*That's what we understand.*"

"What you understand? So I'd agree that there's *concern*, right, cause some very highly organized folks attempted to eliminate the royals, their entourage, and myself. If I under-stand things correctly, they were successful in hitting the decoys, and I took basic evasive measures to ensure the roy-als' safety, and my own. There's nothing controversial about that, is there, Tim?"

More crackle. "*I have to inform you that abduction of—*"

"Hold on a motherfucking second. Ain't nobody got *abducted*. Trust that I know when I'm *abducting* a motherfucker cause I've done it plenty before. Na, I pulled those two out until I could recon with your office, which is exactly what I'm doing now. Cousin, I contacted *you!*"

Tim saying again, "*The abduction of foreign nationals, and particularly dignitaries and heads of state, is an international criminal offense which—*"

"Hold up. And I know for positive that *at least* two of y'all on the line right now know exactly what went down this morning, if not *all* y'all."

"*. . . sir, you . . .*" Tim saying, me talking over the boy, "If y'all didn't organize the shit directly, which is, just looking at the facts, huh? Extremely likely . . ."

"*. . . are instructed to surrender yourself to any federal or international agency. And if you do so, providing the location and secure return of the prince and princess, I am to add that the Abdulaziz family will consider waiving the capitol option . . .*"

Fuck this. I flick the radio off. And hasten my gimp. Lope faster. And set out on a lurching run. Glance back over my shoulder.

Stitch-up central. It's an abduction now, is it? Having played the fucking fool more than once, I told y'all I smelled a rig . . . Sadly, this ain't crystal clear till after the fact.

Me. I abducted the twins with wicked intent, thereby endangering the balance of the free world. Making me if not Public Enemy Numero Uno, certainly vaulting my sad ass into the top ten.

Another look backward. Sure, there's the vehicle. I put my head down and move. The Suburban picks up its speed in accordance with my own.

Dewey Decimal, once again, is in the wind.

--- *LLO*, reads the landmark theater's yet-to-be-razed marquee, and I'm amazed it has that much to say.

125th Street. Those storefronts that have not been demo'd are all metal gates and a latticework of two-by-fours.

Nothing remains, really, to indicate that this was once an area with character at all. Though through one of the barricades I see a folk-art illustration of Malcolm X in flight, another black superhero, near a childish rendering of a boat with Marcus Garvey's outsize head poking from the top. Also a faded stencil on the pavement: *9/11 = INSIDE JOB.* Which at this point, though no longer important, looks more and more likely to this brother. There was a period where I would have given deeper thought to this—but that is long past.

Peek east: don't see the Suburban. Though this is no consolation. No choppers either. Only the sound of my respirator, and remote industrial activity to the south.

Cut through the husks of the Hancock Place houses as 125th peels off to the northwest . . . reckoning if I can get down to Morningside, then cut east again through the Jungle via CPW . . . I've had pretty good luck with the parks thus far as temp cover.

Group of kids crouched on the cracked court. A couple stand, there's some chatter, I will them to mind their business, but no, they take interest in yours truly. Rather than step to them I figure I'll just loop back. Though it's a strange moment for this to occur, I realize I used to play ball here . . .

Stay up, Decimal. You're a motherfucking *boss*.

Who are these children? Why would they linger here, with no visible food source, no construction site around which folks tend to congregate? I have the sensation that I'm hallucinating these punks, or am caught in some kinda time-travel jammie . . . but this is not the case.

Decide to back it up and turn it around. Rather than deal with hood children. It's just too depressing, sci-fi shit like I'm about to go back to pop a variation of my younger self.

Spin and realize my supreme fuck-up.

Another grouping of hoodies has floated out of the darkened corners and effectively blocks my double-back. Amongst this crew I see the shadows who have been tailing me on foot down 125th since way east. Me thinking, *C'mon, fuck, the grand irony.*

Having been weaned and shaped by the ghetto, having made an epic escape from its orbit once in my life, would it not be perfect if I were to perish here? Fucking cosmic justice. Plus, what will become of Haifa . . . and the books . . .

"Wheresya clique, hooah?"

Wearily I rotate toward the speaker. "Don't, son, for real . . ." I start, but he's amped up, the kid saying: "Up here by yourself trick-or-treatin like Iron Man out this motherfucker. Whereza X-Men? Weird space suit–wearing motherfucker." Dig the glint, a handgun being withdrawn from a waistband. "Yeah, you best just give ALL your nice shit before we cut you up, Power Ranger."

Sigh. Hand on my weapon, but don't pull it. Open my mouth to set these children straight . . . And the white Suburban is suddenly curbside, driver leaning over the top of the car . . . he whistles once, a sharp ascending tone, and casually hoses off the air with machine-gun fire.

Homie with the niner is looking like he wants to engage, but the other kids scatter pronto, and with that the kid opts out of the hero biz. Though he takes the time to sneer, flexing hard . . . then swivels and follows his people. Loping medium quick, gangster lean, no running, showing us he's nobody's bitch. I dig his stones.

The passenger door flops open.

"Good evening, Mr. White." Buttery, masculine voice out of a woman's throat. Accent: Mideast? Israeli? North African? All I register re: the driver is she's a sizable mannish female in a dishdash mishmash and keffiyeh whatchamacallit.

And I'm thinking, *White?*

Then I recall Chip White's Secret Service badge . . . in my chest pocket.

"Locals come back with bigger guns. Others will find you, and soon," she says, relaxed-like. "All your action so far, clumsy. Amateur. You're fucked without assistance."

I open my mouth, au contraire, white chick cuts in: "This is best option. Get in. I am independent kinda fucking girl."

I can see her big teeth by the light of the dashboard. Israeli, yeah. And hell, I don't know what that means. Me saying, "No thanks, ma'am. I appreciate it, though. Need to stretch my—"

Short burst of bullets on the sidewalk near my feet.

"Nope. Come on, in you go."

Those teeth. Healthy teeth. Not a local.

Lady-man tosses the SS badge across my lap, into the wheel well on my side. Lean over to scoop it up.

"You, Mr. White, are most certainly my contact. So let's proceed, eh?"

Westbound at a clip. I'm going to ride this out and see what shakes loose.

"Ari Only." She releases the short-barreled Colt Commando and offers her hand, dry and a touch scaly. Short, solidly built little woman.

By the interior lights, I dig her close-set eyes scampering back and forth, lizard-like. I read her as all kinds of crazy. Peepers land on my compromised mug.

"Took beating bad, eh?"

Roll my eyes. Does every motherfucker have to make a goddamn comment? "Yeah. Wouldn't give up the nuclear codes. Caught some enhanced shit."

"Ha. My kind of soldier. It's all mental strength, yes, you just . . . Ah, see, they're back!" she says happily, looking up and over the steering wheel.

Ari flips it south off of 125th onto Broadway, I crane my neck and sure enough, there they are, though the choppers have to get fancy to dodge the elevated track that used to service the 1 train.

"Recognize these?" she asks. Sounds amused, but I figure that's just her default state.

Shake my dome. More concerned with the fucking nutcase piloting this machine than the security forces at this very moment. "Nope. Not a model I've seen. Your name rings no bells, hon, what's your angle here?"

Ari ignores my question, bobs her head enthusiastically. "It's all new, new, new. Stuff from the Scandinavians. New weapons, new times, new rules. Out with the old. We must adjust, eh?"

"My vibe is wait and see. I'm old fashioned, don't like change. What's your racket? You Mossad, right?"

Ari laughs pleasantly at that, spits out the window. "Ah,

no. No longer. But I carry on their traditions, you know, the business they're too weak to handle."

The Suburban weaves in and out, avoiding the gaping craters in the road.

"Politicians? These guys? None of this two-state, let's-talk-about-it shit. They cave to Shariastan, eh? Ari Only is on the one true mission."

"Fill me in, Ari, what's your big gig here then?"

She glances sideways at me, eyes flashing, her mouth an ortho's model of how to do it right. Laughs. "Kill haji. Save the fucking world from dogs of Islam. Same as the American soldier, isn't it so?" she chirps, winking at me.

I allow that to coast. Recalibrate my language to commune with a fanatic. "Yeah, sure. Kill 'em all, let Allah sort it out. Now serious, who you with if not Mossad? I don't like not knowing what kinda people I'm talking to, I was told—"

"I'm with you, Chip." With her pronunciation it comes out *Cheep.* "And you're with Ari. Or you're against Ari. To quote a great man, eh? Best American leader, Mr. Bush." She relishes the name, pops the B. My assessment: cray cray.

I let it all one drift, stay tight-grill. This is a postpolitical world here. "How'd you get in the country?"

Ari laughs again. We bump and bounce downtown, despite the expensive suspension.

"Came on the big ship with the Arabush. Got a slot in security detail, been with these animals for a month. Deep-deep cover, you know, very good, all the way."

"You passing for an Arab?"

Ari shrugs modestly, grinning.

"The fuck. You're a straight pale-face. Snowy like Salt Lake, sugar. Plus, you're a *lady.*" *More or less,* I think, but don't spit it cause I'm a gent.

Ari wiggles a finger. "Ah, but you should see me work. My tan, it fades now. They had the tanning beds on the boat. Very convincing as a man, you know?"

Won't argue with that. "Lemme hear your Arabic." I'm playing for time here.

"My comrades! Let's watch both *Sex in the City* films again, God willing. Then a hot tub, salt rub, and some 'foosball.'" She rattles this off, pitch-perfect Arabic. There's no Arabic for "foosball."

I'm impressed and I say so.

Ari twittering on, "Plus, these guys, you know, come on. Dilettantes, eh? They're half asleep, Mr. White."

"You talking about Saudi military?"

"No, no, royal's private security. Very elite, you know. Ha. All they do, these guys? They slap around their hookers, *smack!* Do some coke, talk about jet-ski. TV, lot of romantic comedies, Jennifer Aniston, some action stuff, all American garbage, you know. Respectful. I like romantic comedy too, just not with this Aniston. She has that nose, this I don't like. Not funny anymore like *Friends*. These men, though. You know. Soft as can be, no core, no foundation."

"No doubt. Cut to it, Ari, what's your racket?"

"I'm here for the royal twins, friend."

"Makes you think I know where they're at?"

Ari bunches up her lips. "Let's not fuck this around. Okay? We're meant to be working together, eh?"

Goddamn, I hate being in the dark. Think on it . . . the Secret Service badge . . . play it cool, play it coy, amass intel and act accordingly. "Miss lady, I've got to disinfect. I'm gonna get out some hand sanitizer."

"Sure, sure, it's your pleasure," she says, distracted by the choppers.

As I pull the Purell™, I've successfully worked the C-4 egg out of my sleeve with it. Palm the egg in my bad hand, which is tricky cause I find it difficult to estimate weight over there, and am therefore liable to drop stuff if not paying attention.

Offer some sani to the lady: "Purell™?"

She looks askance. "What is this?"

"Hand sanitizer. You want some?"

"For which?"

"Fucking . . . for *everything*. Shit is filthy here. That steering wheel alone, Jesus. Kills germs, can only help you in every conceivable way."

She looks at it again and contorts her brow, no.

Some people, I don't understand it for a moment. Are they content, comfortable, just ferrying around feces and bacteria and God knows what else, like fucking livestock?

I've got the C-4 in my other hand, working it open, bit clumsy . . . And above all, I stay nice and cool. Raise a shoulder. "Suit yourself. It's a dirty town, s'all I'm saying."

"You know the location of the twins? Give me the location, we head right over?"

"Of course. My thing is just how am I supposed to know *you're* legit? I need assurances, references."

"*References*." Laughs at that. Ari saying, "How about some trust, Mr. White? This too old fashioned? I thought you were the old-fashioned guy."

"My capacity for trust ain't what it used to be, Sheena."

"Ha, of course not. See here. How would I otherwise know about the arrangement our organizations have?"

"Na, girl, I gotta have more than that."

Ari shifts in her seat. "Okay, make it simple for you. Just give me location, I take it from there. You sit it out, Mr. White. No problem."

Consider this one. Consider the available plays. Consider how I feel about handing a young lady like Haifa over to this bruiser, and that's no, no, and no way, no how. Khalid, on the other hand, I could be persuaded . . .

Ari carries on, "They have no *humanity*, Cheep. This is the moment to put an end to tyranny, real tyranny. History, eh?"

"Hey, I don't give a shit about the larger issues, doll. But I let you do this on your own, what's my slice?"

Ari giggles, tsks. "Listen, man, this is courtesy visit. Okay? I do what I want. I give you options, you throw them back in the face, not polite."

"And I ask again what I got to gain, giving up bitches to any motherfucker who rolls up."

"So crass with language. Well, time is . . . fleeting, okay? Your *slice*: you get to go home today. And not in a bag, okay?"

Renew my grip on my pistol hanging at my left side. With my other hand I'm breaking off a small bit of the C-4, balling it up.

"You gonna come and threaten me now? I'll make it home any which way, pumpkin. Asking you what I get for serving up some scalp, and you with no voucher. Dig, this is my world up here, peaches, you're just driving around in it, talking your Zionist mess—"

Wham. The SUV jerks and bounces up the curb, cutting hard to the right, as Ari leans across and opens the door, through which I tumble. Oopsie daisy.

Boom. I didn't notice her smacking me but I've been hit in the head. The Israeli looms, leering, gat pressed to my gut.

Reach up and hold the barrel with one hand. Somewhere else I find the wherewithal to click off the safety on the pistol pinned behind my back.

Ari saying, "See, I find this money cunt with or without

you, Mr. White. You're not capable of slowing me down. Inferior training. But I had thought, eh, perhaps it's a good thing. We can be working together, okay."

She spiels personable, but "inferior training"? It's an ill way to kick off a potential working relationship.

I'm easing a marble-sized bit of C-4 putty into the mouth of her weapon, saying, "Like, partner up."

Ari shrugs. Rictus smile. One thing she's not good at. "Why not?"

Me saying, "Well, miss, that's downright neighborly of you."

She nods. "Our countries, is special relationship like bond. So?"

"Na, I do better riding solo. It's just a thing with me. 'Sides. Y'all fundamentalists give me a rash."

The Israeli clucks her tongue. "Ach. Pity."

"Ari. I just stopped up this heater with some C-4. FYI, darling."

She studies my blasted face for a spell, flat and unreadable. The smile is gone.

I continue, "Pull the trigger and you got yourself a hot old mess. Fair warning, big girl."

Her eye twitches. She doesn't buy it.

"Straight up, Ari, no bluff. Best way forward, just let me up and let's shake on it, start fresh. Checkmate. No shame, angel, let's just back it up."

Ari shifts. Fuck me. Do I not try, people?

As she pulls the trigger I'm getting my gat out, get it up, crack her kneecap hard with the butt. Her weapon blows up. Gun shrapnel seasons my exoskeleton and I thank Jah for pricey military tech. Prepare for further, more intense explosions . . . gotta hustle.

Lose my awkward grasp on my chrome as she shuffles sideways. While she's going down, that's me scrambling to get up, scooping up my gun, careening ugly toward the edge of the park and the black density of the undergrowth. Working some Purell™ out of my bag.

"Cheep!" Ari is calling. Elated. "Impressed with this resolve! My friend! Me, I can be more convinced than ever. Our collaboration will bear much fruit!"

Fucking loons I gotta deal with. I crash into the woods gracelessly, twigs and dead leaves raking my helmet.

Smoke coming off the garden is pretty easy to scope from the North Woods, all the way across the park, even without the choppers, solid ebony smoke dark against the ever-present golden smog. My heart is in my gut, desperate, flopping like a beached fish.

Smoke.

Haifa. Haifa, I'm coming.

I ditch caution and break into my best approximation of a run, a stumble, a lumber, mumbling, "No . . . no . . . no . . ." like it wasn't completely inevitable, like I could have somehow altered this outcome in the slightest.

Legging it down the old East Drive, rounding the bend near the old skating rink, brown with algae and dead moss. The sand making its way into my nostrils now, coming up my sinuses, working its way to the brain.

Cause clearly something is fucking up my brain. Might as well be sand.

Chopper with a Parks Department leaf on its side cuts loose, spits a long rope of fire out of its dorsal.

Push it, Decimal. Knowing it's way past too late. Knowing I'm only witnessing the cleanup effort, knowing the work is done. Still I push it, all the time with this useless "no, no, no . . ." The weight of my "weightless" space suit, the weight of my equipment, my less-than-fully-functional legs . . .

The first wave hits me hard as I leave the paved road to cut straight through the brush, sulfur, burning wood, and the far more sinister touch of something meaty-organic. It's not an odor you mistake if you've experienced it once, and I can't help but dry-retch into the mouthpiece, trying to control my innards cause I don't want to be breathing my own puke . . . stumbling over a protruding root . . .

No. It's just not possible that they would do it like this. Mass arrest, yes. Beating, yes, that would be par for the course. But this . . .

And yet I said it myself, didn't I? "*Vietnam ugly.*" And that's just what this is.

Catch a heavy branch on my face mask, *smack*, and again I dance sideways, regain my legs, and push forward. I've lost sight of the smoke and the choppers what for the tree cover. At this point, horribly enough, I've only got to follow the smell.

Inexplicable silence, except for my own torn panting. My nose catches onto something new, recalling a public pool . . .

Chlorine. And it might be psychosomatic but my cheeks are immediately streaked with tears, despite the filter in my helmet.

Fucking chlorine? And I must be downwind of it. Gotta cut south.

Sweat. Cause even in this moment I feel the aura of a Freeze. Please, no.

And without warning I'm in a clearing, closer than I thought I was. I clock it all in extreme detail.

It's quite simple, really. The tent 100 percent encased in flame, burning unnatural blue with accelerants. A connect-the-dots halo of bodies surrounding it like moons in every direction. Here and there, trails of fire and the occasional small dark form at the center. These details indicating the manner in which they dispatched those who tried to make a break for it.

Cyna-corp insects strolling around, poking at things.

This is profoundly on me. How I could have thought any protection . . . Somebody dropped a dime. Or simply observed us crawl in here. God forgive me.

Squat near a sad clump of brush, dial the 'com till I'm on the Cyna-corp frequency.

"*. . . air support pulling out, over.*"

"*Copy that.*"

Not a lot of folks made it out of the tent. The rest died within. Smoldering forms here and there, unrecognizable as anything, really, so reduced, they could be dogs. Or children.

Did I cause this to be?

A scuba suit puts a bullet in something, and it stops moving. They're combing the grounds. They're eliminating everybody. They're not discriminating.

Miss Marcia, the White Witch.

Haifa. The twins.

Did I . . . is it on me, this too? The killer in me drops science: If you go to that place, Decimal, you're finished. Finito. There is no direction but forward.

Forward. Grasping. Go, Decimal. *Fucking think.* Stay frosty.

Plenty Cyna-corp here. Relative disorder, the vast bonfire a distraction.

Approach the tent. Figure it this way: if there was any suspicion that the Saudis were on the premises, this would not have gone down in this manner.

Unless the Saudis were identified. Removed beforehand.

Watch a group of soldiers, masking up, smoking and laughing, just looking at the fire. Assuming everybody knows I jumped those two soldiers and stole a suit, I get on the 'com anyway. Suicide play. Knowing my signal will ID me right away.

"Yeah, control, can I get a twenty on Gemini?"

The intervening silence seems unbearably long. I'm about to duck back into the woods and simply say fuck it, then: "*You've been off-com, Thompson. Just hold your position, please.*"

"My signal is intermittent, think I got it fixed here. You got that twenty?" Such a Hail Mary. This won't work.

Another tense pause. I'm just positive I'm gonna get caught out. My eyes darting here and there. A soldier comes around the side of the tent, doesn't even look at me.

"*Gemini en route, over.*" Another voice. Amazing. Huge snafu on their part. They just confirmed the twins are alive.

Dispatch cuts in with a sharp, "*Radio silence, please. Thompson, just stay put a moment.*"

Gemini en route. They're alive, they're being transported . . . where? Knowing it won't work, me pushing it, saying, "Gemini en route to which facility? Trying to recon, assuming I'm still on security detail, over."

Fuck, I've gone too far and I done gambled wrong. I can hear the gears whirring on the other end. Fumbling with the latches on my neck, lose the helmet pronto, dispatcher saying, "Two-fourteen. All boots converge on . . ."

Two-fourteen: rogue unit, i.e., me.

Jerk the headpiece off and hurl the thing straight through the wall of the tent, into the gut of the flames. Commence wobbling toward some cover, nothing too fast, naked without the head covering, scoping the group of soldiers to my right. They don't look my direction. I'm already weeping copiously, undeniably from the chlorinated air, but I reckon: I got this. Thinking, *Alive, she's alive.*

Solid gold. Ripping off my uniform, nude in the bushes.

Pulling my pants out of my bag, my suit pants, I struggle into them. I *got* this. *Haifa, I'm on my way . . .*

That's what I'm thinking, as my legs are unceremoniously knocked sideway. Come down hard, eating dirt and charcoal. Vicious hands are on me, dragging my carcass into the shrubbery, where I'm flipped over like a toasted cheese. Massive figure straddles my chest. Fuck.

All-too-familiar voice rasping eager and triumphant, "Nobody but me, bitch. Nobody but me gets to eat your evil fucking heart."

B linding spotlight in my face.
Table, empty metal folding chair.
My hands are restrained. Sand partially obstructs my throat. Rest my eyes a moment, open them again and a big dude in a Cyna-corp outfit is seated across from me. Scratchy peels off his helmet. All these years and I've never seen his face, till now. Besides being white, he looks nothing like I'd assumed.

Dude flips a pack of cigarettes on the table, exhales. Blue eyes, receding reddish-brown hair cut Marine short. Older than I reckoned. Didn't figure on a gingersnap. Forehead shiny with sweat.

Almost completely disfiguring eczema and traces of a harelip set off a small jolt of compassion, but the vibe is gone as quick as it came. It's like I can't control it, this empathy thing, extremely disturbing.

Cause this dude is officially a tremendous problem.

The tattoo rat-a-tat of rain against a metal gate, somewhere beyond all this. Grit on my tongue, I try to conjure up some spit without success. Gullet bone dry, me rasping, "Scratch, I got no active beef with you. Personally, dog. But you keep giving me all kinds of reasons to fuck you up."

This is amusing to Scratch, which he indicates by raising his brows and flashing his incisors. "Goddamn, Decimal. You best take a look at yourself. You're done, kid, it's already over. Better start figuring that out."

Trying to get a sense of the room we occupy, if we're alone. Eyes still acclimating.

"You were stone crazy over there in the Suck. I'll give you that. Crazy and good with a unit. Thought you had mucho heart, Decimal. Otherwise we would've never given you responsibilities."

"Crazy where?" But I know where. I see the rippled sand, the metal huts, the Hummers. The desert on fire.

"The fuck," spits Scratch. "The sandbox, man. Whaddya think? Don't bullshit me with the amnesia bit, that nonsense is old. And way too convenient."

Yeah. Convenient. It suits me to continue not recalling stuff. "Shit's not a 'bit,' pal. Sorry to disappoint. I'm just as God made me."

"News flash: *Nobody believes you.* And nobody gives a flying fuck about you neither, so there's that too. You're not worth the goddamn tattoo on your back, you get that, Decimal? Nobody, but nobody, is gonna stand up with you, kid. So knock off the fucking around."

"I live in the present, dog. That's just my real." My teeth are akimbo again. I try to work them back into place with my tattered lips . . .

"Don't get it, Decimal. You talk like ghetto trash. You dress up like a clown. It's like an act. You don't even make sense. Either you're just fucking damaged goods or you actually know more than the rest of us, which I highly fucking doubt. I just don't get you, Decimal. And *you don't get it.* It's like this." Leans in. "Me? Deluccia? We would have never, ever handed you that mission pack if we didn't think you had the stones to execute." Man spits on me. "You're a disgrace. You disgraced us. You disgraced *the nation.* You're a motherfucking traitor, and a coward."

Clear my throat. "Yo, Scratch, I'd be getting all worked up if I knew what the fuck you were talking about."

He gapes at me as if for the first time. "The library, cock-sucker. You were supposed to take it down? Hello? And you fucked all of us. Why do I gotta sit here and tell you this like I'm talking about some other nigger?"

Tilt my head. Yeah. That tracks. The explosives in the subbasement. It tracks.

"Na. Not me, Scratch. This a gag? That's my joint. That's home. You got told wrong, heard?" But it tracks. I see the sand again, and I taste it at the back of my tongue. Burning oil.

Scratch wags his noggin. "Deluccia was a father to both of us and you know that's true."

I shrug.

"Like I say, it's a fucking shame. And you're not enough Marine to get up and cop to it."

I shrug again. I'm shaken though. "What you know about me, son?"

"Plenty. More than enough."

Let that fall off my shoulder. "Where we at, Scratch?"

"My office. You're a privileged man. This is where I go for some R and R, just kicking back."

As my vision adjusts I make out a row of cartoony head-stones, rubber Angry Bird and Fifty Shades masks, plastic rats . . . "A fucking Halloween shop? You gotta be playing."

"You're gonna see," he responds simply. I work my gums. My piece back in place, more or less.

"Na, you know what? They got magic shit here, joke stuff like rubber puke and whoopee cushions . . . suits you. Cause you yourself, you're a big fucking joke, Scratch."

He grins. Flips the light around and directs it at the wall to our left. The other direction.

At first—I reckon we got some more masks and spooky

gear, but nobody would mass manufacture something as boring as a nondescript Chinese-guy mask . . . nobody would make a torso of some moderately overweight white male or a . . . or a . . .

Then I really *see it.*

Heads. Fingers. Hands. Unidentifiable bits.

Some have been molested almost past recognition, others look strangely unruffled. A female peers out at us as if lacquered, lips pulling into a faint leer. Too many, too much to register. There's the hides, dried out. Tattoos blurred, numbers and symbols. Moles.

Then there's all the wigs . . . That's what finally turns my stomach. Funny what will do it. It's the scalps. There's just so many. It seems impossible.

Clear my throat. Proceed with caution.

Feels like duct tape on my wrists. I get to working on it. Systematically working my hands in a knitting motion. I'm not going out like this, not here. My fake paddle can absorb a lot of pain, so I'm letting that one do most of the work . . .

"Okay, man," I say, attempting to keep my voice steady, breezy. "I got it. I get it."

Scratch spins the light back into position. I try and fail to stare him down, but my eyes itch and I have to blink. Sand clogging my nostrils. I drop my chin, open my mouth, breathe.

"Just so you take your situation seriously," he whispers.

I don't want to give him the satisfaction. Breathing into my gut, "So I can dig. You got hobbies."

He laughs. "Sure. Why not?"

Shake my head. "No reason. It doesn't matter a fucking bit. No rules. Fuck it. Do what you want. That's my attitude. Whatever it is . . . any kinda stuff." I'm talking too much but I can't stop, saying, "I don't judge, man. I don't judge nobody. No rules, kid."

A long stretch of silence, Scratch looking at me, bobbing his head in slow motion. I try and fail to swallow. Working on my hands . . .

"No rules," he echoes, and produces a pistol, lays it on the table next to the cigarettes. Then he produces a machete, and adds it to the equation.

"Can I ask, though, is it like a thing where you start with squirrels and whatnot, or is that just kind of a media—"

"All right. Brass tacks," the big man cuts me off.

I nod. "Yup. Let's do this." Quick, maybe too quick. Work those wrists. Don't vibe rattled.

Scratch continues, "Where are the twins, Decimal? Where are the royals? You tell me fast, you don't die slow."

Hold up. Let me think. Let me think.

He doesn't know. Means what? I need time to sort this. My implant trembles. I wanna cleanse. My right hand has more mobility . . . I keep working at it, like I'm knitting a pair of socks. Say, "Who's that?"

The man rubs at the machete with a fingernail, not breaking eye contact.

I say, "Them Saudi kids?"

"Decimal. This is your last and final chance to spare yourself . . . unimaginable agony. And to redeem yourself, if only very slightly, as an American." He leans in, the sweat still coming. I'll be goddamned if he's nervous. What does this mean? Divisions within the Corp? A fall-out with the Coalition? Ten to one he's acting on his own steam. Scratch repeats, "Where's the twins, Dewey?"

Reeling with the implications here. My voice warbles a touch, "What up, Scratch, you out of the loop, son? Outside looking in? Cause damn, I thought you were a righteous boss."

Unruffled, Scratch says it again: "Where. Are. The. Twins."

"Barking up the wrong pole, Cap'n Crunch."

He blinks at me for a moment. Moves his eyebrows and sighs, like he's got a major chore ahead of him.

Come on, Decimal. Worrying my hands. Working at 'em.

The big man saying, "I'm gonna chop you into sad little ribbons, you diseased, traitorous fuck. There's no downside to that from my perspective."

"Sounds like a real effort, Scratch. Why bother, man? Just put a fucking cap in me and call it macaroni."

Scratch takes a deep, slow inhale. "You got no fucking idea what's really going down, do you, Decimal?"

Go for bravado. "Your dead mama going down on my dick. That's about all I know for sure."

He waves that aside. "You're getting played for a punk, Decimal. Don't you know that? Think you're fucking smart."

"How you figure that, professor?"

"You think you get put in charge of a major motherfucking operation like this business with the Saudis? A head case like you? The degree to which you continue to majorly fuck shit up?"

I'm listening cause I reckon I know where this is headed, and as I hope I've made plain, this was my suspicion all along.

Big Scratch saying, "A cake-eater like Howard. This fake motherfucker *needs* you to fall on your ass. That should be abundantly clear."

"Clear as New York water. Why Howard gonna want me to fuck up if I'm his agent, just reflects bad on the man." Can't help but fish a bit.

"Decimal, you're so lost, it's depressing. I'll talk slow."
Scratch's face stretches into disturbing extremes as he par-
odies speaking to a small child. "*His* side: *wants* the twins to
die. You get it? His people are *with* the Saudi military. Saudi
military is conducting a *coup*. SO! They get *stupid*." And here
he indicates me. "To fuck it all up *for* them. Do you read me?
It's all a big game they're running."

Run my tongue across my teeth, at a slight loss. "And
what, you figure you're gonna step in and sort it all out for
everybody, Scratch?"

"Yeah, cause I'm with the *right* people, it's simple. The
other side."

"Doesn't sound simple from where I'm sitting, big boss."

Scratch shakes his head impatiently. "Listen good. You
fuck. Bigger picture. We've had our differences, I grant you."
He looks at his blade, then back to me. "I give you Jimmy,
he iced your partner. That's all right. He was a scumbag, no
loss. A real serious prick, Jimmy."

"White of you."

"He knew you were coming anyhow. Been waiting for
you. Wouldn't *shut up* about it. Said to him: *You scared of that
skinny motherfucker, Jimmy?* Couldn't shake it. Never mind."
Now he shifts gears: "Decimal, you dumb fuck. Get it
straight. Coalition assholes are split right down the middle.
Apparently you fail to register this. Let me try again. We've
been watching this fall apart over there for a good while.
Saudi military *finally* running a coup against these fucking
pasha sand-nigger kings, and they got us looped in."

"I don't worry politics, scout." Unconvincing as hell.

"Well, maybe start worrying about something, maybe
you should pay some attention, huh? Especially when they're
playing you. They worked it all out, see? Got any number of

bodies after you. Our crew, Howard's crew, some cuckoo Mossad bitch we're monitoring, every Saudi military on the island."

"And yet, magic. I'm still standing, son," I say, calm and cool on the outside.

"No sir. Hardly. Look at you, man. Falling apart piece by piece. No, you're gonna come out of this deader than fuck, burnt like bacon, with ID that calls you out as a Mr. White, Secret Service. Mr. White. The final joke. On your black ass."

Huh. I absorb this. Massaging my paws behind me . . . man in a semirant now.

"Always knew you were a crazy son of a bitch—but never took you for a complete stooge, Decimal. That's what you are, a fucking *patsy*. Now *that's* an embarrassment."

Come on, Dewey. Come on. Looser and looser. Keep him talking. "What's your percentage, Scratch, why you give a shit?"

"I'm on the winning side, Decimal. I want to do the right thing. Protect those twins. Howard wants to see them dead, and my people are not going to let that happen."

"You're like the greatest American hero and whatnot." This tape. Working, working at it. Do it methodical.

"Think it's funny? Okay, that's all right, that's how you want to be."

"Don't think anything's funny, Scratch. I just can't imagine how you can expect me to swallow your rap. How you expect me to do that? Shit is not credible, and plus. Every time I run into you, you kick my ass and come with all kinda threats."

"Well, let's put it like this. What are your options? So your options are not great, Decimal. Let's look at it." He extends a dirty thumb. I flinch, and am pleased he doesn't seem to have noticed.

Rotating my hands, back and forth, back and forth. Come on.

"You tell me where the twins are. You save the day, you save a couple lives, you maintain the union, and you preserve the nation, then you go back to your library, bravo." He extends his index finger. "Option B: you don't tell me where the twins are. Best case, I kill you. Worst case, I kill you, and Howard's boys get their hands on the twins. Kill them too." Scratch makes a pistol with his stubby fingers, jams it into my forehead. "Boom. You read me?" He's sweating. This is his big play.

"I read you scared, Scratch."

"I fear nothing. Least of all a little piece of pork like you, Decimal."

"How about this: I tell you where you'll find the twins, you kill me anyhoo just cause why wouldn't you?"

Scratch can't help but grin huge at that. "Anything's possible these days, Decimal. Anything's possible. That's the risk you run cause you fucked up this much so far. All I'm saying is here's your chance to put events back on track, do the proper thing by your country."

I think about this. I consider this a good while, shaking my head slow like I'm concentrating on the issue. Fuck, I *am* concentrating, twisting against this fucking duct tape. Come on Dewey.

Then I say, "Got a big problem, Scratch. Cause I can't tell you where the twins are. Last time I saw 'em they were up at that squatter's camp, which your crew saw fit to burn to the ground. So for all I know, pal—you already went and done 'em. It'd be a damn shame, hell of a thing . . ." It's truth, plain as yogurt. Hangs there for a bit. Scratch blinks at me.

Right hand pretty close to getting clear of the tape. Feel like puking, my stomach churning butter.

Finally the man says, "Bullshit." Stands and places a boot on my chest, kicking me backward.

Midair I'm trying to jerk my mitts so the chair hits the tape. I almost succeed, landing on my lame right hand, which comes free, praise Jah—roll sideways so as to conceal this from Scratch.

Man comes around and squats, dragging the machete across the concrete, creating a tremendous screech, like some prehistoric bird. "I'm gonna truly enjoy this. Maybe as much as back when I did your lady and kid."

Hold it.

I'm genuinely winded. Guppy-gulp like I'm trying to catch air.

South Bronx housing project in winter . . .

"My wife . . . my kid . . ." I wheeze.

"Price you pay to fuck up a grand op like the Occurrence, Decimal. Was a *pleasure*. And I should have done you back when. Like I say, you've been wandering around dead and you don't even know."

"Please . . ." I exhale. My guns are gone. I'm stripped to the waist, only my trousers and my scrawny rib cage.

But he missed one thing, old Scratch. Getting sloppy. He missed my knife.

Scratch saying, "Faking like, *I don't remember*. Please. That's some coward's bullshit."

Going for the knife, slow.

"Want to know what your wife said before I cut her throat?"

Freeze. I'm no longer openly struggling. Open my maw, shut it. Slowly lifting my leg up behind me to get at the blade on my ankle.

"Shit, you must remember, old man. You were there. You let us in the door. Nobody else had a key, Decimal. Or don't you recall?"

My key is in the lock . . .

Freeze. Freddo.

"Well here's a refresher. I'll tell you what she said. Nothing. Cause she was busy choking on my cock. She put up a decent fight, though, I'll give that to her."

Freddo. Somewhere remote I'm waiting patiently for it to pass so I can make my move.

"Unlike you. Faggot. Bye bye, Dewey. This is for Nick—"

Midst of his dedication, I slam my knife handle deep in his abdomen. His brow raises, this time less in amusement than surprise.

"Ah. Goddamn, Decimal," the man says, quite calmly, as if conceding a hand of cards. "Where the hell did that come from? That's my fuck-up there. Goddamnit . . ."

And in the midst of my Freeze, I know only that he must die, and thoroughly, though I couldn't tell you exactly why.

And I know it's gotta be dramatic.

So. Get both hands around the dagger, drag the thing upward toward his heart, he recoils, and timber, over he goes.

I gain some leverage, put my weight on my knees, and steady myself. Grip the handle, pushing the knife down again, then left and right. Gut him like a trout. All this I observe at a remove.

Scratch looks shocked, dismayed. More resolved than angry. A blood bubble pops out the man's nose . . . I'm on top of him. With an effort I work the knife loose from his sternum. I wanna cut him more, I wanna break him down into the smallest possible particles, I wanna take a bite out of his face. Yet as the adrenaline drains, I'm exhausted, winded.

Blinking at me. He's done talking.

But I'm not, now I'm leaning over his corpse, getting up in his right ear. I'm shaking, giddy with rage, trembling, my muscles barely behaving.

I need to do it, and my purpose comes back in a painful rush. Say this, in a ragged whisper: "When you land in hell, son? Stay the fuck away from my wife."

elly flop out the door onto 4th Avenue, into the rain, my battered body in full revolt.

Disassociation. That's the word. I watch from the opposite corner, the thrashings of an unnaturally thin man.

On my back. From whence I came, I dig the window that's not boarded up:

HALLOWEEN ADVENTURE

GAGS

MAGIC

So I put myself just south of Union Square.

Unable to spit, I roll on my side so as to avoid choking. I've found a center of calm, which is where my spirit takes a seat to observe. The drizzle pitter-patters in my ear.

In other local news, my corporeal self appears to be having a seizure, a for-real seizure. My ankle sheath is hanging loose, and I have the wherewithal to shove the leather in my craw lest I chew off my tongue.

This body, rejecting that which it knows to be true like a failed skin graft.

Failed, yes. Because I failed everyone. Failed my crew, my brothers, abandoned my post in the midst of the grand op of February 14.

Failed my wife and child, and let the wolves take them.

Failed those I love, again and again, and allowed them to perish while I stood by and did nothing.

Failed civilians and allowed them to die, opening the door for the wolves yet again.

Failed my employers, whatever their unknowable intentions are or were, whether for ill or its opposite; I am a shitty earner, I am unreliable, and I have failed them.

Failed my city, in being party to its destruction.

Failed my System, neglecting the beauty of its architecture.

All that stops. I won't fail Haifa. I will not.

The lump on my neck seems to be fully sentient, pulsating.

Pulses about four seconds apart. And I know without doubt, and without logic, that this machine is attempting to squelch everything my deeper consciousness is disgorging. Information that has now been released into the stream of my direct awareness, impossible not to re-bury. The machine throbs angrily. From a distance I recognize it as the source of my seizure.

As I convulse, I'm laughing through the rain and the cowhide, because I've finally beat this fucking monster. With Scratch as the trigger, and all the attendant irony. I'm laughing, because I've been right all along about this living implant, its level of control over my movements now graphically obvious.

I'm laughing, my fake front teeth sliding down the side of my face . . . even as the convulsions intensify, and multiply, an obscene puppet, my head smacking the pavement wetly, my flippers flapping of their own accord, until with a nearly audible thump the mains on my apprehension are cut, and I disappear.

T hen there's the dream, as familiar as sleep itself, almost comforting in its frequency.

American housing project in winter. My perspective is from the parking lot, which is sparsely occupied.

Sweep through a sad play area. Toddler-size Rocawear sneaker, always one shoe, these city mysteries. Chicken bones, discarded malt liquor bottles, crushed packs of Salems. Proceed.

I have the two men with me, two men from the unit. Scratch catches the exterior door with a gloved hand. Another dude, Ace, whom I know less.

In the stainless steel elevator, we breath each other's air, slightly winded as if one is coming out of the cold. Nothing is said.

Exit the elevator into the hallway. Key in hand.

Check my pistol and disengage the safety. Listen at the door. Within I can feel the female and the child, feel their fear.

Let the boys in. Need to reassure my family. After all, I'm just having some buddies over. My wife always said: "How come I never getta meet your friends?"

Alls I'm doing is making that happen.

———————

Beep.

I wait, listening, awake now. The discomfort in my neck has blossomed out across my skull, and a full migraine sits up and says howdy-do.

Beep. Blip.

Again the not-unpleasant tapping of rain on a window pane.

Okay. Before I attempt to open my eyes, I run a status check. My limbs are apparently still attached, though I make no attempt to move them. I seem to be unrestrained.

Half of my gut sinks. Better I had died. Simpler. Cleaner.

But my other half? Says, *Fuck it. Get to work. Wreck motherfuckers.*

Crack an eyeball. As I'd gathered, I'm in a medical facility of some kind. Scope it: hooked to an IV, EKG, the standard bleeps and boops.

Déjà-fuckin-vu.

IV drip-drop, clear liquid. Nude underneath a thin cotton gown.

"Major."

I start, having not noticed the man seated to my right. "Sergeant major," I manage. "Give me a second."

Guy inclines his head. Squints at a folder, brow knotted. "Hmm. Wasn't aware . . . no, just major. According to this."

My head. Takes a moment to focus, tunnel vision . . .

Brylcreem is the vibe. Glasses, white military uniform, couple of gold bars. Navy? No. Maybe early sixties, a healthy early sixties, clean shaven. Looks like he popped out of the Eisenhower era. I can smell his cheap aftershave. Old Spice, same as my dad, may he roast in the lowest levels of Hades.

"Who the fuck are you, fancy man? You got that Clark Kent kinda thing working. "

Regards me like one might peep a misbehaving car engine. "So you have absolutely no recollection." He looks to a white-coated blur, who seems to be making notes at a distance.

"I recollect waking up just now in 1965 with some retro government dude hanging over me, yeah. Unless you brought me my disability check, you can fuck right off."

The man crosses one leg over the other. He has a certain elegance, though I knee-jerk hate him.

"Forthright as ever. The funny thing is, major, we've never been out of contact, so to speak." A dry smile.

"Sergeant major. Uh-huh. I ask once more: who the fuck are you?"

Again the glance to the lurker in the background.

"Hey," I say.

"Yes. Well, I'm Dr. Kavan, with the National Institutes of Health. Formerly. Public Health Service. I served as your liaison, first at Walter Reed and then at the NIH. This would have been—"

"I don't know you, man."

And again the smile, the glance. "Well. We're aware of the memory loss, so it's not surprising—"

"I mean like I've never seen you in my life, doc. On my fucking honor."

The man flips open a briefcase. "Be that as it may, I know you. And . . . here we are. I've got some paperwork that requires a signature," he says, placing a document on the edge of my bed.

"Paperwork?"

He nods, clicks and sets down a black G.I. ballpoint. Even the pen looks out of time.

"Paperw . . . ? You people are shameless, man. This is pertaining to what, exactly?"

"Pertaining to the return of government property. And liability, any damages associated with—"

"Get the fuck out of here. Just get the fuck out, ya heard?"

Kavan flinches. Tosses a furtive look at the white coat. Leans forward. "Major, I am not unsympathetic to your . . . confusion here. You've had a very complex, protracted ordeal. I'm not able to discuss certain aspects of the . . . well, your situation, but I'm authorized to make clear anything relevant to the execution of this form."

Glance at the papers, my head tom-tomming, photosensitive. Blink, the words swim and slowly drift into place . . . read it partial: NATIONAL INSTITUTE OF BIO-MEDICAL ENGINEERING—NONDISCLOSURE AGREEMENT.

"I read this more like a gag order, Kavan, or whoever you are."

He tugs on his ear, shifts toward the figure near the exit. "Can you give us a moment? It's perfectly all right, we just need a moment . . . Thank you." As the figure withdraws, Kavan shifts back to me.

I'm thinking about ways I might kill him, but I don't seem to be able to move.

"You're immobilized. Temporarily." He gives a reassuring look. "For your own safety, really."

My neck clenches immediately. "Where's my fucking drugs?"

Kavan gives me an indecipherable look, then leans back

and locates a bottle of my pills, this and a paper cup. "These pills, I should say . . . well. Here."

I'm a baby bird. He pops one in my mouth, follows that up with some water, which helps a bit with the sand . . . the man saying, "After your deployment, you agreed to a clinical trial. I don't suppose . . ."

I blank him. But yeah, I know where this is headed.

"No, fine. We developed the program for diplomatic purposes, primarily for language aptitude. But as these things go, its potential military applications overwhelmed everything else."

Say nothing. I watch his eyes behind his spectacles, reckon I'd gouge 'em out with my thumbs given the chance.

He indicates the back of his neck with a folder. "I'm referring of course to the subcutaneous biotech unit. You were equipped with this in order to provide various enhancements, and behavioral assistance, guidance."

"As in remote control. Just tell it like it is."

Kavan shakes his head, pinches the bridge of his nose. "No. It doesn't function in exactly that way. No. But . . ." The doctor watches the hallway for a bit. An MP passes. Kavan turns to me with lowered voice and raised intensity. "This conversation . . . this conversation is not happening. It's a tremendous risk for me . . ." He trails off.

Look askance at the guy for a spell, the intensity of his mug. I nod.

"It was determined," he goes on, "that elements within the government were intent on engaging in domestic terrorist activity."

"Oh, you don't say. I'm assuming that'd include what happened here in town."

"I won't confirm that, nor will I deny it. One of the

military-contracting groups involved was an association with whom you were already a ranking officer."

I've heard enough. My head . . . "You can just hold it right there, hoss."

"The tech was functioning perfectly with respect to language comprehension, motor skills, etc. There were side effects—"

"Kavan, I'm not fucking playing, I'm not trying to hear this." But no, I can't move.

"It's important you know. Actually, part of the contract. Consider this your debrief. As I say, the mechanism was in place and fully functional, until we engaged the basal ganglia—"

"Stop." I'm starting to overbreathe.

And the man keeps rolling it out: "Suffice to say, there was an unforeseen outcome. Some disengagement. The results couldn't have been predicted. Rather than continue with your . . . tasks, you withdrew, and the larger event took place regardless. In retrospect . . ."

Sand has all but filled my nasal passages. I'm struggling to pull air. Kavan seems to be thinking aloud, talking to himself. I'm just another object in the room.

". . . the problem wasn't the mechanism, but has something to do with overloading brain function. In other words, material and information you were not receiving directly from the unit was lost."

"Lost."

The doctor seems to become aware of me once more. "I want it to be clear that I am sympathetic—"

"Yeah, you've said that twice now, I feel the love flow so deep and wide . . ."

He's rifling through his briefcase again. "You were not

coerced in any way to take part in this project. I have your agreement here, if you'd like you can review—"

"No, thank you. Please."

"So as I was saying, when it came time to engage higher functions of your unit, there was significant failure of the device. I'm afraid it had adverse effects on your system, which is of course regrettable. I will say just as a matter of legality, you were made aware of the risks in advance."

"The risks . . ."

Kavan appears agitated. "I am being this specific only because I feel some responsibility. Your memory loss notwithstanding, you and I spent a considerable amount of time together."

I blink at him, can't really come up with a response.

He sighs. "As far as we can ascertain, the malfunction occurred as you were in midoperation, at the public library—"

"The library." I'm just echoing him, almost dreamy.

"Yes, apparently this was one of your paramilitary group's many targets throughout the area. And if what followed is any indication, you appear to have created an intimate attachment to this particular place, which I would associate with the unit error."

"What do you mean, *unit?* You mean me, or the thing in my neck? Or you reckon there's no difference?"

Kavan chuckles, but his eyes float to the exit. "This is all speculative, as I would have to . . . get in there and have a look to come up with more concrete answers."

"Get in there . . ."

Kavan taps the form he's placed at my bedside. "The government is at this point recalling its property."

"And I don't follow you."

"To be more specific, we want the implant back."

I look at the paper. Huh. "You stuck the thing in, and now you're gonna pull it out. Just like that. Is that it?"

Kavan nods. "Baldly put, but yes."

"What if I don't sign this fucking thing here?"

Kavan smiles sadly. "As you wish. It would be cleaner, but . . . as you wish."

"Player, please. What are you gonna do with that there paper, should I sign the shit?"

He seems to think about this, then laughs. "You're quite right. I would put the documents in my briefcase and take them with me, but honestly, there's no one to give them to. The department that handled such things . . . well, I never took you for a fool, major."

"So what's the point?"

"Habit. I'm a stickler. The procedure happens regardless."

"A'ight, so there it is. You gonna patch it up, replace the shit?" I'm slurring heavily, which don't bode well.

He shakes his head. "This particular experiment has run its course. Frankly, I can't offer you any more insight."

"Run its course . . ."

Kavan seems agitated. "Don't you understand, sir, our intention was to halt this tragedy here? As I've said. We were aware of your group's activity, and so we did what we could to . . . well, in your case, we were successful to a degree, correct? Your mission was interrupted. In some small way, we saved—"

"Whole lot of other shit in my brain got *interrupted*, as you say—"

"Listen here. I am out of this business. Shortly after our work together, I moved into genomic obstetrics, another field altogether. Now, if you'd just sign, we're nearly out of time . . ."

Genomic obstetrics. As I try to translate that, the room is expanding, periphery dimming yet more. "Fuck you, Kavan. Fuck all y'all. Wreck my head and toss me out."

"Major. I'm sorry to say, to use your terminology, your 'head' was not particularly solvent, this was well before we even made contact. We extended your lifespan by a good margin, to speak frankly. Listen, there's much more . . ." Kavan glances at the doorway, his image leaving trails of color. "The situation has evolved. And the group I work for now, they . . ."

I'm fading, still focused on my anger. Hear myself say, "Well then, I should thank you, 'sat what you're telling me? Don't do me no favors next time. Fuck all y'all."

He looks distressed. "Listen to me. I understand your feelings. But right now, there are pressing matters, very fluid. There are things you must know, divisions now within . . ."

And all at once I make a connection. *Genomic obstetrics . . .* "Where's the Saudis? Where's the girl?"

Others have entered the room and a flurry of shit commences.

". . . there's so much more." I think Kavan says it, though it's barely a whisper. "Let's get him prepped," he now speaks clearly, a thousand miles off.

Then tight on the man, I can see his pores, there's his glasses, the Old Spice. "We used to be close, you and me. Believe it or not."

"Where's the girl?" I'm saying . . . but I drift elsewhere . . . I want to tell him to go fuck himself, yet again, this preternatural stranger, and I want him to hear me—

My tongue doesn't cooperate in time to beat the swift spiral to black.

A wake.

In the midst of it I'm suddenly cognizant of my body, of pressure at the nape of my neck, a firm tug. And then another.

I'm facing the waxy floor, suspended about a meter in the air . . . my mug stuffed through a hole in the table like I'm at a spa. The paper lining surrounding my lips drenched with spit. Speckles of iodine, brown blood embossing the tiles below me. If I look left I can see a pair of feet in green surgical shoe covers.

The suggestion of presences, machines, emitting sounds, murmurs, all of it untranslatable, and I realize with a vertigo-inducing smack that I cannot comprehend language. Any language. All of it lost to me.

There is a final bit of pressure and something is disengaged from the top of my spine, and with it comes a shockingly intense sense of loss, despair. But I find I can speak, saying, "I'm awake. I'm awake."

Although as soon as it's out there, it's no longer true.

A wake.

A blurry female figure is seated on a high metal stool nearby. Lab coat over brownish-green scrubs, white chick. Skinny, eyeglasses.

Pulling focus. More than a passing resemblance to a young Rita Hayworth.

I gotta be dead. All right then, I'll roll with it.

The room has taken on qualities of the 1940s. My vision goes black-and-white, though I know her hair to be a deep, delicious red . . . like Rita Hayworth, in: "Gilda," I croak.

She starts. She's got a slightly lazy eye, honey saying, "I'm sorry?" Some kind of accent . . . can't place it.

"Rita?" Having a tough time focusing.

Blanks me. She clicks her ballpoint pen.

"Were you *expecting* a Rita, or a Brenda?" She says it slowly, making a note on a legal pad.

"Gilda. Na, you know, the redhead thing, I'm referencing a freakin *classic* . . . never mind. I'ma call you Gilda, though."

"Is that your wife's name?"

This gives me a hefty jolt. Now I'm awake. "What the fuck do you know about my wife?"

There's a pause. I hear helicopters.

"Well, we've just been discussing your wife for the last ten, fifteen minutes. "

"Bullshit," I say, scanning the area around her head. "Straight. Up. Bull. Shit. My wife's been . . . been gone for . . . na, miss, I don't have a wife, full stop."

Glenda gives a long sideways look, then sighs.

"Where's Kavan?"

I am ignored. She returns to her papers. "So I see the prosthetic metacarpal in the hand . . . the patella in the leg . . . and we went ahead and shored up the cheekbone fracture, as it was looking like it could involve the eye."

Bob my skull. "Huh, yeah. All that. Thanks are in order then, right?"

"Otherwise . . ."

I smack my gums. "Where's my teeth at."

Girl glances with distaste at a table near my bedside. There's my gold mouthpiece bling-a-ding-ding, looking very much out of place.

"Can I put 'em in?"

She nods, looking vaguely nauseous. I do it. Then: indicates a bottle of pills with a pen. My pills. "These, uh . . ."

Blink. She blinks back. Moves paper around in a big file. "This is the only medication you're on, currently?"

"Yeah. Which hospital—"

"You're perfectly safe."

"Sure I am, sugar knees, but which hospital—"

"How long have you been taking these, the pills, exclusively?"

I swallow. This here is a bunch of nonsense. "Exclusive like how? Where's Kavan?"

She ignores this. "As opposed to other medication."

Say what? Shrug. "Fuck, I don't know. What other medication you talking about? Been taking those guys upward of two years, more probably. If that's my real chart, you'll know why."

Tight smile. "Who wrote the initial prescription?"

Getting defensive cause I truly do not recall. I indicate

the fat file she balances on her knee. "Gotta be scribbled in there somewhere, right? Probably one of you people. You folks like to write shit down. Gotta tell you now, I've got more pressing business to—"

"I ask because these are the generic placebo we used to distribute in clinical trials prior to—"

"Please. Those are my fucking *pills*, hon. I'd be—"

"Sir, these are generic placebo."

"Just come with it, you're saying what, now?"

Exhales and touches her glasses. "These particular pills wouldn't be any more helpful than aspirin. For managing the HIV virus. I assume you know . . ."

Oh, I get it, she's confused. Phew. Bitch had me nervous. Say, "No, sugar, wrong number. Next room over or something. Y'all must've gotten the charts mixed up here. My shit is a congenital heart thing, not—"

"Sir . . ."

"Listen to me talking, now." Jab a finger at the bottle. "This here is *heart* medication, I've been on these mother-fuckers nonstop for an age, and trust me, I go through all types of fiery freaking hoops to make pos I got a supply flow."

She's scratching at that yellow pad.

"Hey, I know when something is working, cause on those occasions when I couldn't keep with my dosage schedule for whatever reason, it got unpleasant in a hurry. Get the shakes, go all woozy and shit. Think I know my own body." That bullshit proclamation hovers in the air, stinking.

She's still making notes. Exhales again and raises her index finger to readjust her glasses.

Sense an awful tightening in my gut. I repeat, to her, to the room, to myself, "That there is my heart medication."

Again, the words just kind of hang there uncomfortably, and I wanna swat them away, cause fact is, I'm not . . .

"Okay," she says eventually. Looks at her watch. "I'm simply basing this on the information I have in front of me. That's all I'm doing."

"That's right, and you have been misinformed. It's not a problem."

"Your chart . . ."

Make a face. "We both know that could be anybody's fucking paper. Where'd that shit come from anyhow? I need to speak to Kavan, this is some—"

Talking over me, saying, "Your Walter Reed chart indicates you testing positive for hep C and HIV in, let me look here . . . as early as fourteen years back. Testing positive again in May of that year. And again in . . ."

I'm laughing cause this is some who's-on-first kinda routine. Tip my chin at the blue folder. "Doc. I'm not new to this machine, you see what I'm saying? Somebody told you wrong. I'm not that guy. Let's get Kavan in here, he'll tell you—"

"So I'm going to be putting you *back* on your Nortriptyline, and provided we just keep you monitored, I think there's a good chance that we can reverse . . ."

I'm working at the tape over my IV on my left hand. Don't like what's being said.

"No, see. Done with this here."

"Sir, I'm not discharging you."

Get that pesky tape free. "No, that's right, *I'm* discharging me, know what I'm saying?" Rip out the IV, clasp my palm over the slight blood flow. Looking around the joint for my shit. *Done* with this. Everybody trying to fuck with my mind . . .

"All right," she says. "Calling security. Okay?"

Swing my legs over the side, Dr. Gilda backing up. My "papers" go tumbling and she makes an instinctive grab for them, which is where she fucks up, cause I'm easily across the floor, twisting her elbow up and over, whoops, and the doctor is kneeling on the linoleum, the girl trying to keep it reasonable, lowering her voice, back to me, talking to the door, saying, "It's not a death sentence, you know that . . . but . . . sir, you're hurting me . . . continue to leave your condition untreated, over a number of years there's a cumulative—"

With my free hand I pull a rubber tourniquet over her head.

"Sir? Don't do this," she says, but she's not struggling particularly. Eyes on my bleeding hand.

Snatch a roll of gauze and jam it in her mouth, lock it in there with the big rubber band.

"I apologize, doctor. Be out your way momentarily." Shaking. Shaky. Because . . .

Flip her, tape up her hands and feet. Roll her back to face me, saying: "Me, I don't shoot the messenger, and I reckon that's all you are. Where is my shit?"

She rotates her eyes to my leakage once more, then whips her gaze around to a cabinet.

Throw this open. My pants, unceremoniously crumpled into a ball. That's it, that's all. Pull 'em out, cursing, start stepping into them. Do up the fly, jam my hand into the pockets, hold on . . . A slip of paper . . . Unfold it, have a look, my vision wonky: *Procedure/Abdulaziz royals successful. In recovery at the Mercer Hotel. Understand what purpose they serve and act accordingly. God bless the true Union.*

Illegible signature. Could only be the doctor, right?

Processing. Too much action afoot here. It's either an idiot's trap or . . .

Genomic obstetrics. Kavan. Haifa.

I turn to the lady doctor, shoving the note back into my pants, arms out in a what-the-fuck gesture. "Where is the *rest of my shit?*"

The gal rolls her orbs some more, flips them down as if to indicate the tape covering her mouth.

"Lemme recast that. I came in with a whole mess of—" Stop cause it occurs I'd lost all of my gear in my tête-à-tête with Scratch.

She's shaking her head.

Sigh.

I toss the room, Gilda watching me ruefully. Come up with:

- four bottles of an *off-brand* hand sanitizer
- a box of surgical gloves
- handful of procedure masks
- two scalpels (I hesitate for a scant moment, then grab them)
- A white penlight with the GlaxoSmithKline logo

All to the good, but this leaves me gunless, hatless, shirtless . . . lacking rations, lacking all my sources of comfort, I'm barefoot in baggy suit-pants and a hospital gown.

My chest flutters like a moth. Grab my molested pill bottle off the metal table, along with a half dozen alcohol swabs. Take a gander at the white girl on the floor as I'm wiping down the bottle. She's gone and lost her glasses in our quick tussle just now. See 'em on the floor nearby, flimsy tortoiseshell plastic . . . get a new set of gloves and, sweeping up the eyewear, gently slide it over her ears. Pat her under the chin with my bloody hand, leaving a smudge there.

Blinking at me. That wall eye.

"You can tell your supervisor I wasn't cooperative, honey bun," I say. "You wouldn't be lying." Feeling pretty proud of myself as I get primed to bounce.

At which point the lights go out, and I hear the groan, the sub-bassy dip of the entire building losing power.

Shit.

Then the gunfire begins.

There's about ten minutes of consistent shooting, automatic and semiautomatic fire. I can't quite determine how many actors might be involved, and neither can I get a read on its location . . . the action seems to be moving between floors.

Dig up a flashlight, swing it back and forth along the far wall. There's a window, sealed and painted over. My pulse is hot in my neck as I grab the bubble-eyed girl again, put the light in her face along with a scalpel.

"Now don't be shy. We might be in here a spell. Listen to my voice, all right, boo?"

Lady jiggles her head.

"I'm gonna loosen this here. Scream and I cut your throat, no problem."

Another head wag. I loosen the gag.

"Question. What. Hospital. Are. We. In. Quick."

"It's a private military—"

"What'd they used to call it?"

"Beth Israel, I think? I'm from Ottawa."

"Fuck's that got to do with anything?"

"We're on 16th Street and 1st Avenue."

"Good girl. How high up are we?"

"Seventh . . . no, eighth floor."

Goddamnit. And what's more: outside the door, heavy

footfalls. I hear some radio static. I slip the gag back on her. She's trembling.

Goddamnit.

Drag her back behind some heavy equipment. The sounds recede slightly. Pull her gag off again.

"Out the door here, which direction are the stairs?"

Her peepers scurry to and fro.

"It's okay, sweetheart, just keep—"

A prolonged exchange of gunfire, this time extremely close.

Considering my exit options, grim as they are. If the info in her file is correct . . . if I'm sick, I might do just as well to throw open the door and fall out into bullet traffic.

Throw the penlight over to the window. I could knock it out, lift myself through, a quick drop to the street . . .

I finger the scalpel. One clean deep cut from the middle of my arm to the center of my wrists would sever the max number of arteries. It would be a swift bleed-out, and a hasty curtain call for one Dewey Decimal.

Then I get real with myself.

Hold the credits. Cause I ain't going out like that. As tempting as it may be. Bitches, I can only be me.

I ball hard. I rip all the spots. And I won't be faded.

Am I terminally ill? Am I days, weeks, months from death?

It vibes true. My body says yes, yes. At last we can address this thing.

I'm on my knees now, getting prepped to retch. Breathing.

The girl is calling to me but I can't hear her over the gunplay and my own inhalation.

Yeah. The pills.

Snippets here and there: a glint in the DA's peepers. The fucking joke was on me all along. Feeding me candy.

Bite my hand. Bite it hard. Draw blood.

There's tears too. I wipe at them, leaving a smudgy trail, I imagine . . . then I put my knuckles to my cheek and do a little face-painting.

War paint. Eye black on a quarterback.

Hand to Allah: the sole reason the thought of my death disturbs me is the simple fact that *I am not done here.*

But I am so tired. Would that I could lay down and sleep . . .

The gunfire slows, then stops completely. I listen and count to twenty. No, I am not finished. I will grind forth till the ugly motherfucking finale, trailing my tainted blood behind me like a slug.

Pity? I don't need it. I don't want it, especially from myself.

Grind forth.

Turn to the redhead, repeat: "What direction? The stairs?"

"Right, down the hall and around the corner. Should be in the middle of the hallway. I've never used them and can't speak to their condition."

Start to pull her gag back into place.

"Sir . . ."

I pause.

"If you get back on the Nortriptyline, you've got a very strong chance. I can point you toward some stock."

I smile, put the gag back over her mouth. She blinks at me from behind her glasses.

Replace my procedure mask. Press my lips to her forehead. Withdraw. Say, "Ottawa must be a nice town."

S tairwells, relentless with these tragic stairwells. Almost without exception they're both wet and absolutely devoid of any illumination.

Pull my penlight, deciding better to risk it than bust my head up. Shoulder the weapons I scavenged off a dead soldier . . . machine gun and pistol fitted with silencer. Pull the dead man's gas mask over my face.

Stairwells. In a blacked-out town. There's the Death Star, there's the private sites with generators, but for the most part it's a dark chocolate–covered licorice town without electric light.

Speaking of dark chocolate, this is where Hakim Stanley will inevitably seek my skinny ass out.

Right about now, while I'm waiting for my ghosts, I reckon it's time to run it all down. Cause nothing's making sense. And in these instances, a wise man once told me: start with what you know.

All right, the bullet points, which I run down as I descend:

- The goodly Senator Howard calls on me to weed out squatters. Squatters potentially extremely disruptive to his operation . . . why? Knowing they'd find in me a sympathetic soul? Knowing perhaps I would help them? It doesn't compute.
- Even more inexplicable: said senator entrusts me, of all fucking people, to essentially assure the continued life of the New World. In handing me the

Saudi twins, he more of less gave the doomsday machine to a man prone to seizure, amnesia, and paranoid episodes (yes, I have this much insight . . . and with horror I realize my insight sharpens with every passing moment). It was a recipe for complete disaster, which is exactly what has come of it.

- Rogue elements in the Mossad and the Secret Service, tasked with taking the twins out.
- Mysterious Dr. Kavan, materializes to hip me to the pedigree of my implant . . . and now I see his attempts to fill me in vis-à-vis loggerheaded governmental factions caught in a struggle for control, the implication being the outcome w/r/t the twins was key . . . all this jibing with Scratch's ramblings.
- Factions and fissures abound: within Cyna-corp. Within the clans. It's like civil war upon civil war.

This chaos, this confusion, is the only, and truly the *one and only*, reason I am still on my grind and have thus far evaded the dirtnap. I don't doubt that for a heartbeat.

So the odds are about as even as they get. Despite being trapped, outgunned, and overrun, stuck in a dark stairwell—I'm still on the scene, and despite it all, my rap is strong. Or at the very least: I ain't dead yet.

Before I can finish myself off with the masturbatory reach-around, I freeze midstep.

Hold tight. A door below me is slammed open, and a bouquet of lasers is thrown up in my direction. Hold it. Boots scuffling.

Count the dots, they're moving around, reckon it's between nine and twelve dudes.

A muted, guttural exchange. And for the first time in memory, I can't understand a word, not for lack of clarity—but because I lack comprehension of the language.

Though I understand it to be Russian, or some Slavic dialect. Just from the movies.

The gravity of this loss . . . I am devalued. And it's irreparable. Feature this: me mourning the removal of the implant that's compromised and molested my most intimate workings . . .

Sit my ass down and hold tight, though, cause, yo . . . in my old age I'm less inclined to take on groups in a gun battle. Starting to prefer things one-on-one. Less running around.

Guys downstairs hashing it out.

Touch the back of my neck . . . gauze, tape, still a bit numb. Lean over, wincing. Raise my head and Hakim's seated next to me. My heart almost vaults out my mouth, but I recover . . . in a fucked-up kind of way I'm getting used to these visitations.

Hakim is still a nice-looking youth, even without his jaw. He's got that freshness one would describe as "corn-fed" or "wholesome" if describing a white person. Being black, terms like "well-spoken" and "promising" would be employed, as if he were such an anomaly, overcoming his environment against great odds, as if all black people come from an environment that needs to be overcome.

It's just the way we talk about shit, isn't it?

Anyways, the fact that I killed this young man is apparently going to continue to haunt me forever and always, even without the implant.

"Hakim. Youngblood. Do I gotta apologize for shooting you every time we hang out?"

Hakim dips his chinless head. "Na."

"A'ight. How you doing then?"

"I'm okay. . . sir," he slurs, and salutes. Polite but with a minimum of eye contact.

He carries with him his own radiance, so I don't need a light source to see the exposed muscles of his throat and tongue. His trachea. The detail is impeccable, certainly for a hallucination.

"You gonna keep creeping up on a brother, Private Stanley?" I ask, keeping it quiet.

Hakim shrugs. His exposed anatomy is fascinating. "Not up to me, sir." Like he's talking through a mouthful of honey.

"How's that?" Crazy that we're having an actual conversation.

"You keep showing up, sir."

I don't understand that and wait for something further. Finally I say, "Yeah, I reckon I do, huh."

Stanley makes a sound like I used to make as a kid when I got to the bottom of my McDonald's shake, something I'd do to annoy my moms. A ferocious throttle.

"Apologies for that, sir," he says. Motherfucker is too polite. Then, "Lotta folks here waiting on you, sir."

My lips go cold. "Where's *here*, son?"

Hakim shakes his head. "It's nowhere, sir. Just wanted to let you know a lotta folks here talking about what they're gonna do when you arrive, sir. And word is you're real close by. Sir."

"What the fuck is that—"

A short laugh from one of the boys downstairs, who's quickly shushed.

And Hakim is gone.

I'm alone in the dark. I'm chilled. And I don't mean

chilled out. I mean ice-down-the-Y-fronts kinda chilled.
Cause that place Hakim spoke on . . . feel like I'm hurtling
toward it, spinning, twisting, picking up speed.

Movement. Soldiers definitely headed in my direction,
half-assedly attempting to be quiet.

Fucking stairwells, I'm telling you right now. No good
shit has ever happened in a fucking stairwell.

I stand, gripping my guns. Time is nigh to move, Decimal.

Try to generate a mental picture of the building I'm in,
having only ever seen it from the outside . . . rounded tower
of windows facing east and south, north of this additions to
which the tower is connected . . . Without a sense of where
I am within the structure, either I'm going to exit onto 1st
Avenue, or 16th Street.

Both would suck, but the avenue would very likely prove
fatal.

Here they come, gear a-clatter, jangle jangle.

Only one way to go, really.

N atural light, even light as compromised as this, stuns me as I collapse onto the roof, not due to intensity, more due to my disbelief that this kind of light can still be found. I had expected night, heaviest night. Was depending on it, unwisely, to serve as cover. And shit—gotta get straight with the System, very much tied to the clock.

Now I'm ass-out, facedown on some wet roofing tile, chopped raw like steak tartar. Soft rain tickles my back, works at my wounds.

Sliver cuts . . . microbes just need a point of entry . . .

Get up, Decimal. Get up.

I dig hubbub as the Russians clock the daylight.

Move, Decimal.

As if I needed further motivation, at least two helicopters are audible, becoming louder by the moment.

What finally gets me into cat-cow position is the thought of the books.

Section 320. Political science.

I'm nowhere near completion of this category. Crazy-making business. But, but . . . what motivates me to haul my body off the ground is a pretty simple, cornball conceit.

Standing now, I commence hobbling toward the northern end of the roof. If I don't complete my work, and if the as-yet-unorganized piles are left to rot—no one will ever know we were once a well-intentioned experiment. This nation. No one will be aware that we were ever anything but a despised techno-corpocracy, that for all our failures we had at one point some reasonable concepts to add to the mix of human history. All that will be left will be . . .

Plus: the twins. If they've survived this, and I can get to them—I'll be holding a pretty nice hand, and might be able to affect some real-world shit . . .

At the edge now. Across an expanse of empty is a former apartment complex. The distance is about ten feet. Easy enough.

The Russians have joined me on the roof. Nice paramilitary kit, six guys. If they know who I am, if I am a shoot-on-sight kinda target, they would have done shot my ass already. Instead they're approaching with care, the cat running point calling out to me, his voice lost to the din of the helicopters. Two choppers making the scene. I assess the rooftops . . .

Now. If you grew up male in an American inner-city setting, when it came to sports—you balled, period. And unless you were a big motherfucker destined to play center, to be a proper hooper, you had to learn how to jump.

Which is what I do now.

Throw the rifle across my shoulders. While backing up to get a running start, the Russians get wise and try to rush me, but I'm airborne, and it's beautiful, baby, so glorious, this sensation amplified because I suspect it's probably the last time I'll experience this sort of physical freedom.

Lofty talk.

Gets real raw double-time as I bounce off the guardrail of a balcony, having missed the roof completely, I'm scrabbling for purchase, slippery, saying *fuck fuck fuck*, gripping the top rail, not contemplating the drop, I've got my bare foot between the bars on the concrete, dragging myself painfully up and over the railing.

Roll off my stomach, onto the pistol, which gouges my

naked back . . . .pulling the machine gun front, and I'm up and pawing at the glass sliding door leading into the apartment . . .

I get it open just as one of the birds comes level with me, thinking, *Dive, dive,* which was a solid call, cause I'm immediately covered in glass, first from the doors through which I just entered, then from the large plasma television that is atomized by the chopper's guns. Wood, foam, bits of fabric are kicked up, and it occurs to me that I should shield my eyes.

Work myself sideways and back from the balcony, belly crawl, most painful thing at the moment being the rug burn. Fragments of the apartment tickle my back.

Gunfire ceases, I stay low and try to dig my surroundings peripherally. I'm facing a salmon-colored couch. Just visible is a Keith Haring print, an artist I've truly never appreciated (*Crack Is Wack*: go the fuck back downtown or do something real).

The rotary blades keeping the furniture stuffing aloft.

Spy the top of a door on the far wall. Hoping to fuck I'm not headed into a closet, I stagger up, staying low around the couch, jerk the handle, and Allah is great, I'm in a hallway—and now it's a question of which crew can get downstairs first . . .

Shirts or skins.

Yet another fucking stairwell.

Thirteen flights. For good luck.

W ell well now. I'm crouched in the foyer of the apartment complex next to a mummified Pekingese complete with leash and doggy sweater, forever baring its little shark teeth. My labored breath loud in my ears.

Dig it. Past the double doors.

White Suburban across 1st Avenue. Beyond this, the haunted forest that was once called Stuyvesant Town.

I gotta smile—cause clearly nobody's talking to each other anymore. Factions within factions. It's pretty much a free-for-all, as far as I can ascertain.

Goddamn. Watch gone. Err safe, assume it's before eleven a.m. . . .

The chopper remains, sounds like roof-level, and thus far no foot traffic. Though undoubtedly I have only moments to make any kind of move.

Lotta white Suburbans in this town. But smart money says . . .

Fuck it, I'm up and pushing through the doors, aiming for the vehicle. Immediately there's commotion to my right under the old Beth Israel overhang, the Russians shouting this and that, I pick up the pace. . . in the middle of the avenue now and they cut loose with some "warning" shots that go way, way wide.

Nope, they're not gonna take me out.

I don't stop my hustle, but rotate (left) with the MP7 and spray the area a couple meters above their heads, the boys ducking for some cover as chunks of plaster and plastic drop on them, then I've got a hand on the back door, throw it open, and vault into the rear of the Suburban.

Ari has a small dart protruding from her neck, slumped over the steering wheel. Huh. Some Tintin shit.

Okay, so either she's dead or . . . I jerk the thing out, working it sideways.

This wakes the sleeping Israeli in a damn hurry. Lady's confusedly reaching for her gun on the dash, but I jam the Glock in her ear and she locks up, me saying, "Drive, Ari."

Sloppy gal, sleeping on the j.o.b.

She commences speaking, which is obscured by a downpour of bullets tearing through the roof of the vehicle, pulverizing the passenger's seat, propelling Ari into action.

Chopper.

The Israeli slams the gearbox into drive and we jerk forward, me hollering, "Left, left, into the buildings!"

Car bounces off a traffic pole, up and over the low concrete divider, jerks left and into false night.

Ari flicks on the headlights, revealing overgrown hedges and trees, the bases of massive darkened buildings, a village of sleeping giants.

"They let me live," she says, forlorn.

"Who's that?"

"They came at me. Why am I alive?" Ari is tremendously saddened by all this, seemingly more that she didn't have the honor of being slain than anything else.

All I can say is: "Fuck if I know. Everybody trying to whack everybody else, it seems."

"They spoke Russian or one of these languages . . . your people, eh?"

Shake my head. "Not *my* people. I got no more people. Now get ready to stop—"

"So, Mr. White, you're one seriously crazy kind of guy. You bounce right back, huh?"

"I do my damndest, baby."

When we get to the first curve, at least a city block deep into the huge housing complex, I tap her shoulder with the barrel of the Glock. "Stop. Kill the car."

She does it, opens her yap.

"Shut the fuck up," I hiss. Listening hard.

Chopper buzzing, far overhead. No way can it get to us through this overgrowth, between the buildings . . . We're good. For the very, very short term. I exhale, feeling profoundly ill. Abruptly dizzy, head lolling . . . Ari observing me in the rearview. She bares her gums.

Bitch is fast, I'll say that for her, as it seems I'm no longer holding my gun. Which I contemplate for the quarter-second it takes her to smash me in the mouth with it.

Reeling, but I manage to catch her hand. Twist. My gold grill dug partially into my mouth proper.

Again I savvy those healthy teeth.

"Wasn't expecting to see you come back out of there, Mr. White. Thought you were dead going in. Figured I'd bet on you, though, and now here you are . . ."

Me nodding. I twist further and Ari gasps, leaning awkwardly into the backseat.

Hawk out some blood.

"No more fucking around. You wanna grab the twins, I know where they're at. We got very little time."

Ari winces. "I know exactly where they are too. Back at the hospital. They've—"

"Been relocated."

"How could you possibly know this?"

"New information and I do believe it's good. But we have to move *right now*."

Ari regards me, then nods. "Okay." Then adds pleasantly: "Oh, I have new information too. If you're wrong? I get to kill you. This is new!"

Me thinking: *Yeah. And if I'm right about the twins, you'll kill me all the same.* No doubt. Say, "Great to be working together, Ari."

Locating another vehicle to get us out of there unrecognized is far easier than convincing a skeptical dyke ex-Mossad operative mission priority number one is, in fact, getting me a new outfit. And not some bullshit either. Something tight. Talking about *priorities*, ya heard?

Take a left. Another left. Left again. Me calling it, Ari not asking.

We hit the former site of the Paul Smith store at Greene and Houston . . . my argument being hell, it's right on the fucking way, and what's more, I can't do much without a shirt and shoes. No shirt, no shoes—no service, right?

It's Chinese territory now, of course . . . but trust, those people have no need for British designer clothing. My only hope is that they haven't yet demo'd the block . . . but no, there it is. The Chinese taking their time with their rebuild . . .

Oh, I've been here before. I scarcely need a light down in the storeroom. In fact, I'm quite sure I'm the primary looter on the scene, and most probably their best (posthumous) customer.

"Gimme ten minutes. Twelve minutes," I say to Ari. She's talking but I slam the door in her face, come around the car (left), flip open the hood, and disable the battery. This vehicle will not be moving. If a patrol comes, so be it.

Bingo.

Within fifteen, I step out the joint in a light-gray broken twill three-piece, crisp white shirt, black/dark-green striped silk tie, black felt trilby hat, and a slightly large pair of black high-shine brogues. Got a three-pack of handkerchiefs, one of which I'm employing to soak up the blood still leaking from my eternally split lip.

Top this off with a charcoal double-breasted wool coat and I am good to motherfucking go. Dubious. I lather up with the generic sanitizer.

Ari has no comment but is shaking her head in disbelief.

Fucking people don't understand the importance of shining out and coming correct with the freshness.

Given good luck, this will be my last suit. Stock is pretty scant down there.

My last suit. This elicits a small shiver.

Wordlessly, I point the Housing Authority cop car in the direction of Mercer and Prince streets, adjusting my large gun so the new coat partially conceals it, speed forth . . .

I'm coming, princess.

A t the hotel we go ahead and shoot our way in, old-school cowboy style.

Roll up pon dem gangster, me hanging out the window with the light assault rifle, primed for a mess of boots . . . Ridiculously, there's only a handful of uniforms, Saudis and a couple Cyna-corp, and they are just not ready for us, so it's with relative speed that they go down as we converge on them, heaters blazing.

Half of them are flat on the sidewalk before we're even out of the car. It's too easy to be any good. But fuck it, I'm having fun. Feel like I'm flying, and I channel that leap from roof to balcony . . .

Ari's enjoying herself as well, a faint smile, happily rolling one of those tea-tree oil toothpicks between her well-kept teeth.

Through the upturned lobby, emptied of anything useful. Several wooden cases of wine sit untouched near the door, the French lettering gibberish to me now. Building's dead quiet. The utter ease with which we float on in solidifies my suspicion that this mission is a major head fuck. But what can I do, if not push forward . . .

Listen. I pause, lifting two fingers to halt Ari . . . listen. Yeah, there it is . . . music. Tinny.

Around the corner. Sure.

Signal to Ari. Who for all I know could put a bullet in my ass at any moment. At this point, who cares?

Laser sight on my rifle enough to see by. We flip around

the wall (left) Seal style, me with head fully in the game. This is my element.

Cyna-corper parked near the elevators. Some sorry shit. Bugman has his headphones cranked so goddamn loud he missed out on our not-so-subtle entrance. His head wobbles to the metal within.

On top of him in a heartbeat, prying off that headgear, which pops off with a hiss of oxygen—Slayer or whatever it is fills the hallway. I kick his helmet away, put my gun in his face.

"Hush, child," I say to him.

He's probably midtwenties, indeterminate race, unshaven, and terrified.

"Fuckin . . ." he whispers. "I got kids. I got kids."

"That's good. You'll get to tell them the scary story of how Daddy almost died—if you're straight with us. Otherwise . . ." I put a round into the tiling next to his head, a little eruption of glass. "Ya heard me now?"

He nods, nods.

"Solid. Where are the twins, son?"

"210 and 312. The guy, the male, is in 210—"

Kick him in the face. He sputters. I kick him again.

Kneel and make sure he's breathing.

Which is stupid. Cause in a heartbeat Ari's got her gun up on me. Naturally. Cause the girl doesn't need Dewey Decimal anymore.

I turn and rise with my pistol in her gut.

This is us, then, squaring off. Ari and I. Both of us grinning.

"Respect, Ari. You crazy like I and I. Cap me if you gotta. I could give a fuck."

"You've got option to run. *Maybe* might not shoot you in the back," she says playfully.

"No, I truly could give a fuck. I got the AIDS. I'm a dead man." There, I said it. I said it *out loud*. I repeat myself, almost in disbelief: "I've got advanced AIDS. I'm dying. Do you hear me? I'm dying anyway."

Ari's smile falters then drops off her face entirely. The toothpick sags.

"So I'm fresh out of patience here. Can you dig? Let's get these kids, cause I wanna go lie down."

Ari's doing the math. I don't think she's gonna let me walk, once the twins are secured. But till then, it's in her interest to have me doing the work.

"I'm sorry to hear this, White," she says, lowering her weapon.

I snort, turn toward the fire exit, toward Haifa. "The fuck you are."

The body of Prince Khalid is suspended from the sprinkler piping in the middle of his suite, having strung himself up with a bedsheet.

"Damn," I mumble. Thinking for all the world the kid looks like a Klansman, white on white on white, the headgear.

Strange fruit. Flipped.

Feel kinda bad but I'm finding it tricky to get emotional here.

"This is the male?" mumbles Ari through her toothpick.

"Yeah," I say. Don't wanna enter the room, though, lest there be cameras. Plus Khalid, as one does, has shat himself, and this I can detect from the doorway. "Wonder if they made him jizz in a beaker or what. Turkey baster and shit."

Ari shrugs, chewing that stick. Must be a nerves thing with her, the toothpick. "You're a disgusting man," she says.

"It's a disgusting fucking world. I'm just the narrator, cheesecake." But my stomach is in my mouth, thinking . . . *Haifa*.

In the doorway, a neatly folded note, in English script: *To my family*. Kneel and flip it open. Shit's in floral Arabic, meaningless to me now, somehow menacing and needlessly complicated looking. Is this how all non-Arabic speakers see these characters? Once again, I feel a sharp loss.

Crush it one-handed, and chuck it at the leather trash bin near the desk. *Swish*. Three points from behind the line.

Upstairs in a jiffy, we locate room 312 dead easy, unguarded and ajar as downstairs. Are these people joking? Again my stitch-up meter is pinned red. And my heart rests on the back of my tongue. My tummy's in knots. To see Haifa again. I'm a teenager.

Coax the door open, me bracing for any kinda trickery . . . yet all is quiet, spa-like. Spot is plush, some high-thread-count shit. In the center of the room, a king-size bed, Duxiana kinda outfit, a body under the comforter.

Me and Ari parked in the doorway, breathing, weapons in hand. Me thinking: *Fuck. There she is.* "Cameras," I say to the Israeli out of the corner of my mouth.

Lady's humming a little tune through that toothpick, minor-y, with some Arabic inflection. "Huh," she says quietly, peeking into the room. "You think so?"

"Oh yeah, hon."

"Can you ID that cunt?"

I wince at that. Would never use the word myself. Would I? Reckon, how dare you? But say, "Not from here."

"Huh," she repeats. Swapping a fresh mag.

"Fuck it, cameras. Let 'em watch. End of the line, yeah?"

She smacks the cartridge into place, raises the gun, and saunters straight at the prone princess.

I pop the Israeli in the back of the head, two shots, *thwip thwip*. Pair of clean hits at the base of her skull. Ari tumbles forward, the blood Rorschach splatter a complex fan across the off-white duvet.

She wouldn't have let anybody live. It was a solid call. Shame, cause the gal was kind of a good time. But no way was she so much as touching Haifa. No fucking way.

Toss back the cover, Haifa fetal in a black lacy night-gown, steeling myself. Nauseous.

"Princess," I hiss. Nudge her hard with my knee.

Slack-mouthed, the girl is out. Assuming drugged to the gills. Ear to her nose. She's breathing. God is great. My throat eases up.

I admire her teeth . . . like Ari, the mark of a tourist. I admire her face. It's a miraculous face. I will see this woman to a safe space if it kills me. That alone would assign this wretched life meaning.

However. Out of habit I take a moment to raid the warm minibar. Why not? A couple bottles of water, a Kit Kat. I leave the alcohol.

Back to the princess. Pretty lady. Roll her gently off the bed, swap out Ari's body.

One bullet's exit path direct through her socket, and the other eye regards me askance. Tuck the big girl in—g'night, baby.

Not very convincing. Too much fucking blood. Plus, it'd be tough to imagine Ari passing for female. But might buy me a half second, and that could make all the difference. Plus, they're probably clocking me on video right about now. Like it matters.

I heft and shoulder the slack Haifa, one-two. More difficult than it sounds.

Corridor empty for the moment. A fire alarm is going off on another, higher floor, could be unrelated. Straight across the hall, the stairs.

Ease that door open with my foot, and we descend into dark.

Left out the main entrance onto Mercer Street, the bodies of the sentries resting quietly, as yet undisturbed. All is tranquility.

Expecting an ambush. Can't be this easy.

"HIV," I say again, aloud. "AIDS. Acquired Immunodeficiency Syndrome." I'm dying. Weirdly, this helps. There's something in my throat, though, and now I have the sense to know it's not sand.

No more of that.

They've lied to me before. Yes. They have not been entirely straight with a brother. Maybe this too . . . but I don't think so.

Ouch. I have to set Haifa down. I'm shaky as fuck and even a gal as petite as this seems too much.

Fuck. I gotta do this.

"Dead man!" I call down Mercer Street. Silence is the response.

Dead man or not, I've been sloppy with the System, and it's now my intention, especially now, after all of this, for the sake of my body, for the sake of balance, to follow System protocol to the letter. The Mercer clock still ticking, reads 9:35.

Haul her back up, wincing. I just gotta do it.

Left onto Houston. Abercrombie and Fitch mural on the single remaining wall of a decimated twenty-odd-story building, the model's abs . . .

I gotta ease the girl off me again. Legs shaking, my shoulder in excruciating pain from the exertion. Look back to the hotel. Look to Haifa. Slack, out deep. I drag her into a doorway, prop her up . . .

In two minutes I'm back with a porter's luggage cart from the hotel. I slip on my newly acquired gas mask. Light-headed. This'll work. I got this, y'all . . . solid gold.

Left, left, left. Left on MacDougal. Duck under a tattered canopy, clock a low-flying group of choppers. Proceed north. Breath loud in my gas mask. *Thump thump*, some gigantor sound system pumping four-on-the-floor to the west.

We rattle over uneven ground. I push from behind, trying to scan ahead for any big dips. Watch Haifa unconscious jiggle and twerk, and even in this she manages to read classy. But the girl is *out*.

Skimming the concrete area once occupied by Washington Square Park, I pull a left onto Washington Place with the intention of heading up 6th Avenue. A mash-up of amplified Russian language dubstep (a genre I cannot bear in any language) and the sounds of heavy industry, the noise collision grows clearer ahead . . . Sure enough, as I get halfway down the block I can dig massive bulldozers doing their thing.

I can't help it, I gotta see what gives.

Close enough now. Despite the din, the cart makes a crazy rattle.

The entirety of 6th Avenue has been broken up and scooped out, for reasons unknown. Peep deeper: lit by floodlights, I can see the exposed subway tracks, either for the A/C/E or the F train. Partial view of the tile that must have at one point been the West 4th Street station . . .

It all looks pretty motherfucking pointless. The crew

is clearly Ukrainians and Russians as the garbage-y music would indicate, and I've got no desire to get with that group anytime soon.

Plus this is Russian turf, north of West 3rd. Gotta move. Take a second and sanitize, scoping the scene.

Another left and a jog across the street, quick now before anybody makes me, then another left back toward the former park. Rerouting.

Cause news flash: there are no black Russians. Not a one, barring the cocktail.

Left back at the park border, beat cheeks up to 8th Street, one wheel on the cart starts to go wonky . . . shit. Crunk west and do a full spin, cheating a bit now, so I'm pointed at Fifth. Have to stop periodically to readjust Haifa's outfit for modesty's sake . . .

Another gaggle of choppers gives me pause . . . then it's on to the relative exposure of 5th Avenue. Start to stepping once again, and with a jerk the princess sits up and nearly tumbles off the cart.

"Bloody fucking . . ."

Ease her gently to the concrete, she's on her hands and knees panting, me saying, "Haifa . . ."

The princess rotates her torso and commences smacking me, her face smeared with rage, wiped clean of makeup.

Manhandle the lady up and back into a recessed doorway. I note the gold house number 11, still intact, the facade untouched.

"Haifa. Your Highness—"

She takes a final weak swipe at my mug, and I lift my gas mask.

"It's Decimal. Your escort. It's me. Look here. It's me." Grab her chin, bring that face front. Takes her a moment.

Me saying, "I apologize, I lost you. I lost you—"

She spits something in Arabic. My heart sinks, because—agonizingly—it sounds like nothing at all.

"I can't understand that. I can't understand that anymore," I tell her.

"What do you mean?"

"Let's just stick with English."

"Fuuuucking hell . . . Where's Khalid?"

"Haifa . . ."

"Where is he, you bloody bastard!" She struggles out of my grasp and sinks to her knees.

I kneel next to her, withdraw my hand sanitizer.

Cheeks flushed, wild. She's still wobbly, half-drugged.

"Haifa. Have some Purell™. Well, it's not actually Purell™ . . . It's been a—"

She slaps at the bottle of sanitizer, and then her hands jump to her mouth. "Fuck me. Please tell me he's okay. Khalid. He's okay."

Consider this, decide I'm gonna talk straight with the lady. "Khalid didn't make it. Won't sugarcoat it. Took his own life. So at least this was a choice. Haifa, I'm so sorry."

The princess puts her palms in her eye sockets. "No. No. Why should I believe a bloody fucking word you say?"

"I don't know what else you'd wanna do, I'm your best bet now. It comes to this. And we've gotta keep moving if we're gonna stay—"

"You were to protect us, mate, and you made a bloody botch-up of the whole—" She stops, removes her palms, slowly, horror freezing her face. "*Elif air ab* . . . Do not tell me . . . they successfully . . ."

I don't say anything. It's all there in my face. And hers, imploring.

NATHAN LARSON ✳ 265

". . . the Prophet. Please. Tell me this is not happening."

My silence is just slightly too long, then I manage, "Your Highness, I need you to breathe—"

Haifa vomits, it's extremely sudden, and I find myself at pains to get the fuck out of the radius of the spray while simultaneously attempting to provide comfort. Maybe it's a reaction to the appearance of fresh vomit on the scene, but in my throat there's so much grit I get panicky, my trachea seemingly obstructed . . .

"Gotta get you some water," I wheeze. Fuck, me too.

She is on her hands and knees now, spitting, hair in her face, the *boom-boom* of the loudspeakers down the block. Whispering something. I move in.

". . . not natural. It's not right. It's bloody . . ."

"We have to keep moving, Your Highness. You gotta find a way to get up and move forward. I understand it's a nightmare. I got railroaded here too. One thing at a time, you know? And right now we gotta bounce."

The princess doesn't look up. Goes down on her forearms, hair in her puke. "I want to die. This monstrous . . . this unnatural . . . I want it dead . . ." She keeps talking. More helicopters rip by overhead.

"Let's stay in the moment. I'm hearing you. You gotta stand up and walk. Gotta be mobile." Fumbling through my bag. Thank Allah I raided the minibar. "Here," I say, getting the cap off a warm bottle of Evian. "Drink."

Only a matter of time before we encounter a clique on foot. Only a matter of minutes.

"Drink it," I say again, with greater emphasis.

Haifa is startled out of her fugue. She takes the bottle wordlessly.

"You're dehydrated as fuck, drink it."

"Where are we?" she mumbles, bringing the bottle to her lips.

"In trouble. Downtown. Haifa. Please stand."

She's nodding. I take her arm and we get her upright.

"I'm well fucked, Mr. Decimal. It doesn't matter anymore, I'm so very well fucked. Curse my fucking family, a thousand cocks upon them. Better I die."

Start steering her toward Fifth. "That's enough of this nonsense. Okay? You don't know how this is gonna play out." I'm babbling, out of my depth, scanning the rooftops, trying to put my eyes everywhere. "Babies don't always survive, and that's just nature. Especially in this environment. It's early on. See what I mean? All kinds of factors."

She shakes her head. Says dreamily, "No. No. This is real. I feel it, and it's strong. It wants to live."

My eyes on the buildings, the upper floors. Always thinking about snipers, cameras . . . "You can't possibly know that," I say. Pregnant chicks always talk crazy smack. "Haifa, you can't know that, you're in shock, girl . . ."

She smiles. It's a tight, thin movement. "I feel it. It's a fighter, and it bloody well intends to make it."

I wanna tell her that she can't know this. It's not even a real thing yet. It's just a bunch of protein, a cell-clot, hours old, if it took at all . . .

I open my craw just as a stretch limousine comes around the corner.

Pull my handgun and come to a crouch.

The problem with everything at this point is that no new development, nothing whatsoever, can be good. Only different degrees of bad.

A placard in the front window reads, WHO. This throws me . . . then I think, World Health Organization, and relax, though I'm not sure why . . . Limo comes to a stop nearby. Glass smoked over. Electric window slides down.

"Major," greets Dr. Kavan, "unbecoming of an officer. Your discharge wasn't sanctioned. Came to follow up, and whoops. No patient. You're gone."

I stand, saying, "Yeah, well, I had business elsewhere. 'Sides, some big Russians kinda hustled me out."

The door opens. "Please. We're headed out of town, but we've got just enough time to drop you off wherever you choose. It's the least I can do. We can speak a little."

I look to Haifa, who is making big eyes. I nod, it's okay. Take her arm and duck in.

Dr. Kavan is seated, wearing his uniform. Boxes marked MRE—US ARMY—30 UNITS fill the seat next to him and the floor.

"Getting ready to bunk down, doctor? Stockpilin'? News flash, the apocalypse already hit."

Kavan gives this a stiff smile, indicates Haifa. "I see you got my note. That was a gamble, but . . ." he half bows. "Your Highness."

"Who is this?" asks Haifa.

"An old coworker," I say. "Apparently."

"Where are we headed?" asks Kavan.

I think about this. I think about this pretty hard. "The Main Branch of the library. Forty-Second and Fifth."

The doctor gives me an unreadable smile.

North on 5th Avenue at a clip.

I'm moving in circles, with one leg stapled to the ground.

Gray, gray, white, gray. A construction site. Another construction site. They're popping up overnight, rising from the core of the planet. Tremendous structures with tremendous history, once so alive, have been carved out and stuffed with alien material, stuffed with emptiness.

And the warnings:

STAFF ENTRANCE ONLY
KEEP OUT
SECURITY WILL USE LETHAL FORCE

Afresh, afresh, I dig it all afresh.

Maybe it's that with the loss of language comprehension, I have more space in my head to mull shit over. Maybe I'm just in a broody kinda mood.

Cause what do I see: it's not my city. The space through which I move. I've been rendered blind by nostalgia. Allowed to see only what once was. In the empty lots, phantom shapes to which I ascribe meaning.

But there is no meaning left here. It's not a city at all.

Wait, Decimal. That's not entirely true. There is the *precursor* to meaning. There is the precursor to whatever "meaning" one might ascribe those Chinese industrial villages we used to hear so much about. The energy that filled the air

surrounding the construction of such not-quite-places.
This is what has replaced my home. My home, spiritually, has been systematically removed. Taste its absence in my throat where a grain or two of sand lingers.

Why did I not see it in quite this way before? Because hope springs eternal. The mind is cruel. The city has split the scene, and with it, anything you might call God.

Entire streets cordoned off. Those signs in English that I spot share a theme:

DO NOT ENTER

PRIVATE PROPERTY

TRESSPASERS WILL BE SHOT

Foot traffic at zero. No more civilians. It happened quickly.

I dig Cyrillic, Mandarin, Arabic lettering on the sides of trucks, on fences. And I can interpret none of it.

"Must be disconcerting," says Kavan, sucking me back to my present. In a van headed uptown.

"Not knowing anymore," he continues.

Some psychic shit. Maybe I was moving my mouth. I turn away from the window. Though he could be talking about anything.

Haifa is there and I realize she's gripping my numb robotic hand.

Decimal, she's looking to you, like a little kid. *Guide me now.* You gotta handle this. Try to vibe reassuring, but that's a much larger project. For the moment I say, "Why didn't you have the decency to tell me I was sick, Kavan? I'm a big grown-up man."

"Tell you about what, officer?"

"My illness. Why the fuck wouldn't you mention this? What, it ain't relevant? Aren't you a cocksucking health professional?"

Kavan pinches his nose. "Major. Am I supposed to keep careful track of what you do and do not remember about your own life? Is that my *purpose*? I am not your personal secretary. I am not your biographer. Plus, I have no idea what you're referring to by *illness*."

"My *illness*, you motherfucker."

"The only illness I'm aware of . . . and mind you, I haven't run any blood tests or anything of that nature, that's simply not possible anymore—the only illness I'm aware of is your mental illness. Which, I think, in removing the implant, we have gone a long way toward alleviating."

My jaw is slack. I valiantly attempt to snap to. "Your nurse . . . your, ah, coworker. The redhead? Glasses?"

"Who might that be?" says Kavan, look genuinely confused.

Jesus. Just when I thought I had a solid grasp on this noise. "The girl . . ."

Kavan sighs. Offers me a weary, practiced smile, which I am sure many many others have seen as well, designed to remind me that I am most decidedly the *patient*. "It's not uncommon. To hallucinate, or to hear voices, et cetera, after such a traumatic alteration, and they can seem extremely real . . ."

But I'm not hearing him. "We spoke. We spoke for a long time. She had files. She had files on me." Sounding crazy . . . sounding unstable. I shut it.

Kavan regards me, seems to be watching my mouth. Waiting.

Hold up . . . having difficulty organizing my thoughts. I mentioned the red-haired white girl? Wanna chase this butterfly down, but it's gone. I change course. "What's your fucking objective then, Kavan? You come back and dig me up, just to what? Head-fuck me? Throw me off my game? What are you after?"

"Oh, I don't think you can help me with what I'm really after," says the man dismissively.

"Try me. We've gone this far. Try me."

"I am after, what. *Democracy*." He follows this up with a gut-busty bark, which is shockingly loud in the confines of the limousine.

Haifa looks on incredulously. Flipping between the doctor and me like a tennis match.

"Democracy," he repeats, with more than a little sarcasm.

"Yeah, sure," I say. Is he insane?

"You know, that quaint little concept we clung to. Or, in your case, made great and noble sacrifices for."

Is he fucking trifling? He wanna rile me up?

"Kavan, I'm not a goddamn fool. Got my eyes wide open and shit. I do what I do and did what I did cause it's a *job*. The military . . . might as well have been working at a . . . Best Buy, the shit is all the same to me. I'm an agnostic, you know what I'm saying?" The doctor is nodding along. I carry on, wondering where this is coming from: "None of these terms mean a fucking thing. It's all just control and survival, man, that's it."

Kavan nods impatiently, and shifts gears. "Fine, major. Now, this is perhaps the last chance we'll get to speak. I don't want to get into semantics. We're faced with huge challenges here, and we've got to address them."

"You got a *for instance*? Cause from where I'm sitting, we already done fucked it all up. Look. Outside. Here. At. This. There. Is. Nothing. Left." I jab the window with each word. We're passing a massive expanse of emptiness, stretching an entire city block, 26th through 28th streets. I can see straight though to Broadway.

"This is what my former colleagues would call movement forward, Decimal. Part and parcel to what I would discuss with you now."

I wait. Trying to remember . . . trying to remember what was there, in that block . . . because once I forget . . .

"Seeing as our post-op debrief was somehow cut short, major," says Kavan, "there's still more to say."

"Yeah, we're discussing," I manage. Whipping past Koreatown, which is in the process of gradually being painted over, by my reckoning. Less protrusions. But then I'm apparently not the most trustworthy lookout.

"As I mentioned prior to your most recent operation, major. And I'll speak frankly, if you excuse me, Your Highness."

Haifa stares at the man. "I've no idea what you're on about as it is," she says. Then to me, quietly: "What illness?"

But Kavan is talking: "It's just as well you not know, ma'am. Major, this is a . . . deeply strange period in our history as a nation."

"Huh. You think?"

"And as I mentioned, major, I'm not telling you anything you don't know, but I want to be as clear as possible."

I do my utmost to refocus on this man, possibly one of the most important figures in my life, of whom I have absolutely no recall.

Kavan touches his forehead, then continues: "Factions . . . factions within the government that have always existed were allowed the space to actively assault each other, thanks to the disruptive events here and elsewhere. At the moment, one such splinter group is dominant, of course, this being your current employer, major."

"Yeah. But that's basic Darwin, ain't it?" Can't keep the acid out of my voice.

"For years," Kavan is saying woodenly, "we operated alongside the very people we knew to be working actively to short-circuit our society. For years we strove to find methods to thwart them. We knew that the only way to accomplish this was from within. We had to be extremely careful. We had to use every possible tool—"

"Tools like me, " I cut in.

He regards my mouth, then lifts his eyes to mine. "If you must, yes, we used everything and everyone available. For the larger good."

Overwhelming urge to slaughter, maim, kill.

Grip Haifa's hand, for my sake as much as hers.

She says again, with greater vigor: "What illness?" But I ignore her.

Kavan tilts his chin. "What I'm telling you now: we find ourselves at a crossroads. My group has not prevailed. We're defeated. We're exposed. Our only option is to retreat and regroup."

"Some brave motherfuckers."

"Bravery, it's not about bravery. Do you not see that should we completely disappear, that's the end of the story? There is nothing, I mean nothing, preventing them from achieving their goals at this point. Except . . ."

Buncha crap. "Yeah, except?"

"There is an opportunity here." He indicates us, generally.

"We're listening."

"Whether you appreciate it or not yourself, major, and Your Royal Highness . . . the both of you are critical to how this thing plays out."

Kavan's peepers flit over Haifa's midriff.

I nod. I get it. I know where this is headed.

"So I'm here to tell you: there's still time."

"To do what, exactly?" says Haifa.

Kavan exhales. "I am leaving New York City, and the both of you should join me."

Can't help but scoff at this folly, saying, "Exactly how you gonna get out, you reckon?"

Kavan looks at me for a moment, then speaks again: "278."

"The Verrazano? You fucking crazy? Nobody gets through there. Don't care what kinda badge you got."

"Remember, I'm government. Legitimately."

"Trying to say I'm not legit?"

"That's not what I meant. Have you ever tried to leave via that road yourself?"

"No, but you're gonna have to take a fucking boat around Fresh Kills."

Kavan raises his eyebrows, this being entirely obvious. He would have planned accordingly.

"Okay, it's your world. And then where you plan on going?" I ask.

"A secure location."

"No such motherfucking thing, doc. Not anymore."

He wags his head. "But this is all completely beside the point. If you join us, the child—"

"Join you? You're not gonna get anywhere."

"You're wrong about that. This is not an impulsive move on my part. We've been anticipating this situation. If you join us, we've got a shot, we've got some leverage."

"More tools," I say.

Haifa glances at me, at Kavan, the princess saying, "Can someone please not speak in bloody code so I can partici-pate in this conversation—"

"They'll run you down, Kavan, no sweat. I don't like your odds."

"We have a very effective plan in place."

"I don't like your odds," I repeat. "You're a bad bet. They're gonna reach out and touch you, easy. They're good with that. You're not a soldier, are you?" Kavan blinks. I grin broad, wolfish. This boy is nervous. Lean forward. "They'll be coming after you, huh. Oh yes, they will."

Kavan bobs his well-groomed do. I dig that I get to him.

"You're gonna see how it feels, Kavan. Real character builder."

Kavan sighs. "Yes. Well. Technically, I face only court-martial. Which as you're well aware . . . at this juncture means a firing squad."

"Yeah. On the spot, like." I nod, still grinning.

Kavan's eyes slip to the princess, then back to me quickly. "And honestly? As a physician . . . well, as a moral animal, I feel quite some responsibility. To both of you. For my role here. So yet another reason to present this offer to you."

I look at Haifa. Something eclipses her face. "Are you the . . . ? Did you . . . ?"

Kavan doesn't look at her.

"Yeah, he is. Yes, he did," I say. Think about my gun. Anger collects in my throat like tears, like sand, surprising in its intensity and mass.

Haifa covers her face and lowers her head.

Kavan is wearing a tight expression. "That's as much as I'll say. Now, I've extended myself to the degree that I'm willing. Regardless of how you feel about me, the situation is what it is."

The vehicle is coming to a stop. We're here. We're home.

"You have a minute. Think it through," says Kavan.

"So we come with you. Then what?"

Kavan shrugs. "We improvise. We start over. Like we've always done." He smiles tightly at Haifa.

The princess glances my way again.

"Start over with what, you reckon?" I am credulous.

Kavan merely shifts his shoulder.

Christ. Decisions.

Look outside at the library. The low-lying yellow cloud cover obscures its roof. The building appears bruised.

My chest, my heart flood with a sharp sorrow that eclipses any anger.

Consider killing this man. It would be extremely simple. *Pop:* Kavan. *Wham:* the driver.

Accomplishing nothing.

Decisions that ain't really decisions.

Finally, I remove my hat, and shift toward him. "Kavan. I guess this is your loopy version of an apology. For playing the Nazi scientist. Well, hey. Water under the bridge, man."

He cracks his maw, shuts it.

"Na, that's enough out of you. Just following orders. I've used that stale-ass line myself. Historically it's been useful, huh. Dig it. You've done your thing, you wanna have it all kinds of ways, and now you're jetting."

The doctor meets my stare unblinkingly.

"Correct me if I mischaracterize," I say, then open the door. Take Haifa's upper arm.

"I just wonder," says Kavan, his voice hollow. We pause, half in and half out. "After all you've been put through, and after all you've accomplished . . . if you can still differentiate between right and wrong."

"Oh, I don't think that's a problem," I respond, not looking at him. "Come on, Your Highness."

"Between true sacrifice and love of country, and treason disguised as such. Do you follow, major?"

"Yeah, I fucking follow."

We're still halfway out, and Kavan speaks again: "Oh, and major?" He hands me a plastic bag, print on the front, MEDICAL WASTE, the biohazard logo. It contains something metallic, smaller than an old Brit pound coin, but with the same relative thickness and color. Vibes like a hairy watch battery. "For posterity. It's entirely disabled, so we'd only throw it out."

Hesitate. Then take the bag warily.

Dr. Kavan sits, his impeccable whites sullied slightly, a swath of reddish brown on one pant leg. The man salutes me. "Thank you for your patriotism, son. Godspeed."

The doctor holds the salute, which I do not return, and the limousine door is closed on him with a solid thunk.

Up the marble stairs. Through wet corridors. I steer the princess. We do not speak.

The hidden door in the Map Room. The long descent into the vast chamber, deep beneath my home.

I need to show it to her.

Dual Louis Vuitton steamer trunks—grimy, the fungus and watermarks evidence of their years in the dank sub-basement of the library, though the big boxes are structurally sound.

I've wrestled the tops open, the generous array of explosives exposed. C-4, various RDX compositions, blocks of TNT. Knew there was a reason I kept this shit hanging around.

Haifa and I look on in respectful silence for a spell. She breaks it with: "Is it true, then. You're very ill?"

I'm feeling the weight of tens of thousands of books, as yet unsorted. This work needs completion. A successor . . . I never got around to it.

"Is it true?" Haifa repeats quietly.

Back to the moment. Am I sick?

I nod. "Yeah. Yes, I am." So many bodies.

Though my ability to envision a three-dimensional diorama of the city is all but gone, I can still read a map. Quite a dense dot matrix is created, when I pinpoint the bodies.

On Church Street, between Ann and Liberty, the white man wedged into a support column of the tallest building in the world.

Midblock on 4th Avenue, between 12th and 11th streets.

In a silent hotel suite, in a designer bed, on Mercer Street between Prince and Houston.

Deep in Chinatown, at 165 Hester Street.

In a disused wine cellar, beneath the Chelsea Market on 9th Avenue and 15th Street.

In an old café in Brooklyn, on Manhattan Avenue near Huron.

On a dirt incline at the mouth of Central Park, near 68th Street and Central Park West.

In a ugly high-rise on Columbus Circle, in a two-bedroom apartment.

In a half-flooded traffic tunnel on Park Avenue between 32nd and 41st streets.

In the Conservatory Garden, in great numbers, under a burnt tent.

At the northern entrance to Grand Central Terminal.

In the Bronx, in a housing project known as the Gun Hill Houses.

Too many to acknowledge, too many to name.

Does it matter how many? Does it matter how they got where they are?

Does it matter who and what they were?

And where will they put me?

A distant helicopter brings me around. Realize what's happening. Haifa sleeps in my arms.

I'm mourning my implant. Had no idea what it was protecting me from.

This fear. This sadness, that accompanies seeing things as they truly are.

We're lying under a table in the Rose Reading Room. I don't

know what time it is. And I don't care. I am no longer beholden to any System. Haifa's breathing has changed and I believe she's awake.

"Hey," I say.

"Hey yourself," says Haifa.

"You know how this ends."

A long period passes. I must have nodded off cause I start as Haifa says, "Yeah, I know how this ends."

Look at her face, free of paint. Blink. It's too dark. I can see shapes.

Remove my gloves. With my real hand, I trace her scar, raised, ridged. Must've been some big staples.

"Where'd you get this, Your Highness?"

It's light enough to see Haifa's slight smile, though I can't make out her eyes.

She shakes her head. "It doesn't really matter, does it?"

I think about that. "No," I finally say. "I reckon it doesn't."

"Hey," I say. It must be later. I surmise I've slept too.

"What?" she whispers back. "Keep your voice down."

I nod. "There's another scenario," I whisper. Surprised to see we're now sprawled near the door leading to the subbasement.

"What's that, major?" she whispers back.

"Dig it. You and me . . . somewhere else. North or south, find some land. Fuck Kavan and his crew. Do it ourselves. Raise that child. Grow food. Live how people live if they're not . . . here."

I can't see her face in the darkness.

Eventually she kisses my cheek. "I think we both know that can't happen," she says.

Yeah, I think. But it sure sounded nice.

Nobody on the senatorial staff is going to believe that I stowed the princess amongst squatting anarchists for her own safety, then went on a shooting rampage across the entire borough, again with her security in mind. Not for one moment.

Nobody will believe that I snatched the princess from the Mercer Hotel, leaving in her place the corpse of another woman, for the sake of the princess's health.

And yet this is more or less what I tell Tim when I radio over to let them know that I'm coming in from the cold with the princess in tow.

And: that she will only allow herself to be released into the custody of her own family, in the presence of as many of the remaining world players as possible.

"I'ma explain everything, my-nigga-my-mellow," I tell Tim, laying on the dated ghetto-speak, aware the racial epitaph grates more than I can imagine. "Big misunderstanding, big drama. Shit's straight up and down now. I'ma stroll over soon, heard? So we good?"

"We're good," replies Tim tonelessly.

I sign off, toss the radio aside. Turn and regard my library.

"This is it, yo," I say under my breath, unconsciously flipping the top on some actual Purell™ from my stash. "Any secrets to reveal," I say to the vast space, the hundreds of thousands of volumes, "now would be the time."

But there is only silence, the hum of the generator. I recap the Purell™: my hands are clean enough.

More and more apparent that I am nothing more than part of the problem.

I have enabled and enforced an agenda that, in an unaltered state, I might have rallied against. The question then would be: can I divorce Howard? A question to which I already know the answer . . .

The heavy stillness of the library broken by approaching footfalls.

Here's Haifa, in improvised traditional wear fashioned from curtains out of the Map Room, complete with full head covering, though her hair hangs loose for the moment. Those eyes, those eyes. She has lined them with a Sharpie.

I've shaved and groomed. Got my suit as clean as possible. Reckon I look as sharp as I'm ever gonna.

Pop a sugar pill, just out of habit, something to suck on. Not out of need. I set the Purell™ down. This I don't need either.

Now that we're headed out—it seems so intimate. And momentous. Like prom night. But like way more momentous than that. I can't conjure an analogy.

Our eyes graze each other for a moment, shift away. I cannot see her expression, of course, but I imagine she's blushing. In a heady rush, I am overcome by the genius of the head covering.

I get it, y'all. I'm done hating on the full cover-up concept. I *get* it. Makes everything just that few degrees hotter.

I proffer an arm. "It's a nice evening. I figured we'd walk."

Haifa lifts her eyes to meet mine. She adjusts her head cover. Then, ever so gently, raises my face-wear, checking the rubber straps to make sure nothing's tangled. The princess smoothes it into place across my busted lips and nose.

Holds her hands to my face for a moment. Then steps away, toward the exit, toward the stairs.

Be sure to secure you own mask before assisting others.

As we near the Ark, the lights are just coming on, prismatic through the glistening poison clouds. It's crazy gorgeous.

"Under different circumstances," I say, feeling light-headed, "I'd ask if you wanted to grab some dinner."

Haifa laughs. Looks at her feet. "Cheeky . . ."

My knee seizes up and I slip. Haifa catches me easily.

Thing is, I'm mad clutch down the stretch. Good in a corner. Even if I gotta crawl across the finish, I'm all clutch.

But as I feel Haifa's musculature . . . strikes me: she's so much stronger than me.

"Good God. Can you walk?" asks the girl.

Drag my bones back up. Leaning on the lady. She doesn't seem to mind. "Yeah, yeah. Dinner." I resume. "Shit. Someplace. Someplace real pricey. I never went, but there used to be a joint at the top of the Time Warner . . . Par, par, per . . ."

Haifa squeezes my arm. "Per Se. I never went there either, but it was supposed to be nice, wasn't it? I always enjoyed that hotel there . . . what, the Mandarin Oriental. The spa, bloody amazing. The view from there . . ."

"Way outta my league. But yeah, it woulda been sweet . . ." I trail off.

Haifa lifts her peepers to me. "Yes. That would have been lovely."

"But here we are."

She looks away, back at the ground. At this point we fall silent because there remains nothing to be said.

The Ark, the Death Star, the Tower of Power looming.

I lose my footing once more on our quick journey, and again she's there to intercept.

We're met by faceless soldiers. Everybody exchanges head-wags, awkward. I'm patted down, swaying. Clean. Soldier approaches Haifa.

"If you disgrace me with your touch, I will have you eviscerated," she says calmly, and catches my elbow.

Soldier blinks. Fair enough. Backs off.

Haifa stabilizes me. Apparently I keep falling down, nearly.

Stay clutch, Decimal. I'm so clutch.

Radio crackle.

"Coming up. Coming up," mumbles the dude on my right.

Herded into that ungodly lift, for which I no longer feel apprehension. Concerned they'd kill us before we got upstairs, but that's looking less likely.

And now, that Wild West bell dings dusty at the 101st floor. Haifa grips my sleeve, hard this time.

Into the Star Chamber.

Incredibly they're all there, but I barely see them, the shot-callers and string-pullers, the Secret Chiefs, the Illuminati, the world government, Arab garb, congressional blue suits and ties, open-necked shirts, casual wear, and you might take some sort of distant comfort in the variety of skin tones represented—although almost 100 percent male, there's a level of rainbow diversity that I might wax lengthy upon.

They're all here. Seems they take this situation seriously.

But I'm looking for Howard's mug in this crowd.

I guide Haifa forward, or rather we guide each other.

Locate Howard in the crowd, scowly and conk-o-licious.

Give him a loving smile. His eyes narrow, but only slightly. He looks drawn, sickly . . . and extremely suspicious.

Tim is to his right. Howard starts to speak to him, stops.

In the final analysis—the only clan in town were the landlords. Money trumps all.

A post–2/14 Monopoly board pops into my mind's eye, fully formed and deliciously three-dimensional.

I could continue. That would be if I gave a fuck. But the truth is, I just don't. If ever, certainly not anymore. I'm coming apart, y'all. This body is packing it in, regardless. Closing up shop. Fire sale.

All this ridiculous thrashing, this struggle, this over-whelming compulsion to stay standing.

Someone begins speaking in Arabic.

Haifa takes my hand and everything fades gracefully, slows to a held breath. I make an effort to register the de-tails. She draws me toward her. Embraces this body. Her hair is pine, lavender, and burnt plastic. I exhale, which seems to take hours. This is all according to plan.

Haifa's giggly. "Does this make me look fat?" she starts, and I hush her with a squeeze to her upper arm.

Soldiers moving forward. Those high-end thugs who have observed the low life long enough to know when a sit-uation's hinky commence heading for the exits.

But it's too late for them too.

I push off her head covering, cradle the back of Haifa's neck in my human palm.

With my Frankenstein paw, I grip the rip cord on her suicide vest, the trigger that will ignite enough C-4 to clear this and any adjacent floors.

These are the tools with which I was entrusted to level my library.

"Are you sure?" I say into her hair.

She nods and whispers, "God is great," hot on my ear.

Last thing I observe as I pull the cord is that the sand is gone entirely, and my throat is clear, relaxed, open.

So as everything ends, I have only gratitude.

Which is far more than I ever deserved.